BY THE BOOK

Also by Laura Jensen Walker

Dreaming in Black and White

Dreaming in Technicolor

Reconstructing Natalie
(Women of Faith Novel of the Year, 2006)

Miss Invisible

Daring Chloe

Turning the Paige

A GETAWAY GIRLS NOVEL

Becca
BY THE BOOK

Book Three

Laura Jensen Walker

ZONDERVAN®

ZONDERVAN.com/
AUTHORTRACKER
follow your favorite authors

We want to hear from you. Please send your comments about this book to us in care of zreview@zondervan.com. Thank you.

ZONDERVAN

Becca by the Book
Copyright © 2009 by Laura Jensen Walker

Requests for information should be addressed to:
Zondervan, *Grand Rapids, Michigan* 49530

Library of Congress Cataloging-in-Publication Data

Walker, Laura Jensen.
     Becca by the book : a Getaway Girls novel : book three / Laura Jensen Walker.
       p.   cm. — (Getaway girls ; bk. 3)
     ISBN 978-0-310-27697-5 (pbk.)
     1. Book clubs (Discussion groups) — Fiction. I. Title.
PS3623.A3595B43 2010
813'.6 — dc22   2009041415

Published in association with the literary agency of Alive Communications, Inc., 7680 Goddard Street, Suite 200, Colorado Springs, CO 80920. www.alivecommunications.com.

Interior design by Christine Orejuela-Winkelman
Interior illustration by Ruth Pettis

Printed in the United States of America

---

09 10 11 12 13 14 15 • 22 21 20 19 18 17 16 15 14 13 12 11 10 9 8 7 6 5 4 3 2 1

For Sheri, so much more than a sister-in-law.

And to Jennie and Kari, with love and gratitude for welcoming me into your family.

Snorts and all.

And for Alexandria Skye Damron, who filled our lives with so much joy.

Jesus loves you, this we know ... but we love you too and we miss you, sweet Princess Lexi, more than words can say ...

The soul should always stand ajar to welcome the ecstatic experience.

Emily Dickinson

I fled Him, down the nights and down the days;
  I fled Him, down the arches of the years;
I fled Him, down the labyrinthine ways
  Of my own mind; and in the midst of tears
I hid from him …

The Hound of Heaven

Becca

BY THE BOOK

I have lifted my plane from the Nairobi airport for perhaps a thousand flights and I have never felt her wheels glide from the earth into the air without knowing the uncertainty and the exhilaration of first-born adventure.

West with the Night

Oh. My. God. What a rush.

I couldn't believe I was skydiving. At last. This totally rocked! As the wind whipped my face and I plummeted toward the ground, Lynrd Skynrd's *Freebird* filled my head.

Me, Becca Daniels, sharing airspace with eagles. How cool is that?

Cool. And cold. My skin tingled and my cheeks flattened into my skull from the force of the wind and the tight goofy glasses they made me wear. But who cares? I was free-falling.

I could stay up here forever. Away from dreary, mundane earthly pursuits like going to work, paying bills, and schlepping to the Laundromat. How boring is that? Talk about tedious. At least I don't have a happy hubster, 2.5 kids, and a house in the suburbs.

Thank God for that.

I've never understood the appeal of that particular American dream. Being tied down to one guy, a mortgage, and a couple of rug rats?

Not for this chick. I've got better things to do.

Like traveling.

Exploring.

And skydiving.

It doesn't get much better than this.

I felt a tap on my shoulder and Zach, my instructor who was strapped against my back for our tandem jump, let me know it was time to pull my chute. I reached down by my hip and pulled the cord. The harness jerked my body and we came to an abrupt halt.

Only it wasn't really a halt. Just an immediate slowing down — a huge change from when we were hurtling toward the ground mere seconds ago. Now instead of speeding downward, we were gently floating. Zach gave me the handles which controlled our descent, and I led us into a spin. And then another.

Rock my world. Definitely the best adventure ever.

"So what'd you think?" Zach asked after we landed and he unbuckled the harness that strapped us together.

"Loved it! Can we do it again?"

"A woman after my own heart." He favored me with a sexy, gap-toothed smile.

I never did like guys who were too perfect. The slight space — the width of a thin stick of gum — between his front teeth just made him all the more appealing.

"Another hundred and fifty bucks and we're back up there," Zach said.

That wasn't as appealing. I'd hoped he might offer to take me up again. For free.

In my dreams.

I heard a squeal behind me. As I turned, the squeal turned into a roar as Jenna, my adventure buddy in crime, rushed toward me. With a giant bear hug, she tackled me, knocking me to the ground.

Jenna's usually a high-five girl, but your basic high five was totally inadequate for the moment. "So, was that sweet or what?" she asked.

"Oh, wow." I untangled my arms and legs, the adrenaline still pumping. "It rocked! I want to go again."

My roommate Kailyn joined us from the safety of the sidelines, shaking her head. "I can't believe you really did it."

"And I can't believe you didn't," I said. "Oh wait, yes I can. You wouldn't want to break a nail."

Kailyn, with her flawless blonde hair, killer body, and designer flip-flops, is the girliest girl roomie I've ever had. Ever. And I've had plenty of roomies over the years. Of them all though, Chloe was the best.

Even though she was a church chick.

Too bad she had to dump me to go find herself in Paris. Not that I blamed her. I'd dump my grandmother for the chance to live in Paris for three months. Or Rome. Peru. Beijing ... anywhere overseas. The more exotic, the better.

Kailyn, my roommate of financial necessity, thinks I'm crazy for wanting to live in China. Or anywhere exotic, for that matter. "Don't they eat cats and dogs in those places?"

She's another church chick. One of those perky ones.

Do Christian girls take lessons in perkiness or what? Maybe it's one of the Ten Commandments: Thou shalt always be perky.

Whatever.

Sometimes, though, it's like fingers on chalkboard. Especially in the morning. Kailyn's one of those disgusting morning people. She bounds out of bed at seven a.m., all bright-eyed and squirrel-tailed, humming and dancing around like some Disney princess with a halo of happy bluebirds twittering around her head.

Good thing I'm a pacifist. Otherwise, I'd blast those stinkin' bluebirds to kingdom come.

Our first Sunday under the same roof, she sang in the shower while she shampooed her perky blonde hair, rummaged through her closet for her perkiest outfit to wear to church, nuked two perky cinnamon rolls, and then rapped on my door, singing out in her perky blonde voice, "Rise and shine, sleepyhead, breakfast is ready. Want to go to church with me?"

I lifted my Seven Dwarves Grumpy head from beneath my pillow and yelled something I know she's never heard in Sunday school.

But we're good now.

Kailyn knows not to wake me before nine on the weekends, that I'm more a fruit and granola girl, and not to even attempt to make conversation before I've had coffee.

She also knows better than to ask me to go to church. Not my thing. Too many rules and regs. And glitz. Some of those churches, especially those big ones, really creep me out. Too much Splenda razzle-dazzle.

Like Mister Rogers on crack.

Dancing girls, bright, shiny choirs, and men with Italian leather on their feet and more product in their hair than I've used my entire life. And don't even get me started on the Stepford women in their ice-cream-colored suits, plastic smiles, and matching pumps.

My ratty Birkenstocks would definitely be out of place.

And what's up with all the committees, meetings, and

campaigns? Is it a church or a corporation? Then there are all those holier-than-thou types putting on a show on Sunday like they're all that, and then turning around on Monday and snorting coke or hitting on the hot barista at the coffeehouse when their wives aren't around.

Don't get me wrong. I don't have anything against Jesus. Jesus was cool.

He took care of the poor, hung out with the lepers, and treated women well — unlike most of the men of his time. Really, if you think about it, Jesus was a feminist. But to some people, that f-word is a dirty word. And applying it to Jesus? Heresy.

Another reason I'm not into church. Everyone gets so uptight if you take Jesus out of their churchy box.

And that whole women and submission thing? Not in this universe. I so can't believe women buy into that in this day and age. Hello. Is this the fifties or the new millennium?

Seriously.

As Kailyn drove back to our duplex, chattering all the way about some *amazing* close out sale at her favorite shoe store, I tuned out and relived every high-flying second of my morning skydive.

While we were watching the informational video at the parachute center that said they weren't legally responsible if you died on your jump, one guy in the group turned white and booked it.

Wuss.

Hey, if it's your time, it's your time. Why not go out with a major rush?

Once home, I log onto my laptop to scope out my Visa statement. Last I checked, I was close to maxing out my card. It didn't help that my last job turned out to be a bust. Marketing, my foot. I didn't get a degree in English to be a sign waver.

Like Teddy Roosevelt said, "A man who has never gone to school may steal from a freight car, but if he has a university education, he may steal the whole railroad."

I didn't want the whole railroad, but I did want a job with a little more meaning.

My friends told me I should never have left Dunkeld's Bookstore, but I'd been there over three years—a record for me—and gotten bored of the same-old, same-old. Yeah, it was great to be surrounded by books all day long, but at the end of the day, it was still retail.

Unfortunately, in the two months since I'd quit, all I'd been able to find was a telemarketing job—where I got tired of people yelling and hanging up on me—a part-time barista job where I spent most of my paycheck on lattes, and this last marketing job where I spent an entire day waving a *30% OFF ALL FURNITURE!* sign on a street corner.

Really meaningful, that.

I needed something exciting to get me out of my unemployed funk. And as I checked my credit card statement, I found it.

The next day, I was up in the air again with Zach. Free-falling in that wild blue yonder on a clear, crisp April morning. And it was just as cool as the first time.

Until the landing.

2

Seabiscuit surged forward, coming down heavily on his left foreleg. Woolf heard a sharp *crack*. Seabiscuit took an awkward, skipping step. His head pitched downward ...

Seabiscuit

Leave it to me to break my ankle in two places — the tibia and fibula. Tibia and Fibula. Sounds like bustling fairies from some Disney princess film. Either that or the latest hip-hop duo.

But I had no one to blame but myself. I didn't raise both my knees the way Zach had told me to, so my left leg was in the wrong position as we approached the ground. And when we landed, I heard this sickening snap.

The pain was so bad I passed out. When I came to, I was in the hospital and the doctor was telling me I'd need surgery.

Another new experience. But somehow I didn't think it would be as fun as skydiving.

A few hours later The Getaway Girls clustered around my hospital bed with flowers, balloons, and assorted goodies, concern etching their faces. They took care not to bump my splinted leg that the nurse had propped on pillows.

"How are you feeling?" Paige asked as she set a huge bouquet of wildflowers down next to my bed.

"Like I've been run over by a freaking truck."

"You poor thing," Annette clucked, patting my hand. "I told y'all skydiving was dangerous."

Pushing fifty-two, Annette's the oldest member of our book club, and the only one who's served in the Air Force. As such, she'd tried to talk us out of our skydiving adventure, insisting that the pilots she knew said the only way you'd catch them jumping out of a perfectly good airplane was if the plane were going down.

"Yeah, what were you *thinking*?" Kailyn demanded as she plopped a stuffed polar bear on my bedside table. She knows I have a thing for polar bears.

"I was thinking how I wanted to feel that rush again. That freedom."

"Well, I hope you enjoyed it," Tess said, "because you're not going to be free again for a few months."

"A few *months*? But we're supposed to go horseback riding next month after we read *Seabiscuit*."

"No horseback riding for you, young lady," Annette said.

"Maybe we could just rent the movie instead of going riding," Paige suggested. Paige is our resident movie buff. She knows more movie trivia than anyone I've ever met, and is always quoting from movies—especially the old ones.

Me? I'm a book-quote girl. English major and all that. "Last night I dreamt of Manderley again." "All happy families are alike. Each unhappy family is unhappy in its own way."

Unlike most of the group, I don't come from a happy, Mom-and-apple-pie family. My stoner dad left when I was six, and I spent the next decade-plus with my alky mother and her menagerie of husbands moving from one trailer park or cheap apartment to another. By the time I was a senior in high school, I'd lived in thirteen states. My biological mother—I didn't think of her as Mom, since she lacked the maternal gene—missed my high school graduation. She was in jail.

Again.

For being drunk and disorderly. And when husband number four, Dirk the jerk, tried to give me his own special graduation present, I kneed him, slugged him, and left.

I haven't looked back since.

Anyhow, my family is my friends—my book group friends, the Getaway Girls. And they're an eclectic bunch.

Annette and Tess are the oldest, in their early fifties. Tess is a little more hip than Annette though, with her cool red glasses and willingness to try new things. Annette's a little more old-school. She and Tess are both married, although Tess is still a newlywed of sorts—not quite married a year.

Chloe, my artsy former roommate who, at twenty-eight, is only two years and some change older than me, is even more of a newlywed. Sickeningly so. She and Ryan just got back from their honeymoon a couple weeks ago. They're still in that sticky-icky sweet phase, all gooey for each other. Too gooey for me. I get a sugar high just from being near them.

Get a room already.

Paige is the next oldest member of our group, at thirty-six. But we don't see Paige all that much these days. She's crazy busy with work, going back to school to get her degree, and being a foster mom. And of course, dating Marc, Annie's boss.

I can tell that Paige will be the next one to bite the marriage dust. We should rename our group the Ball-and-Chain Girls instead of the Getaway Girls.

Even Kailyn's gaga over a guy. Although, when isn't she?

Her current crush is the actor who plays her love interest in her latest community theater production.

Thank God for Jenna and Annie. Neither of them is even remotely close to a serious relationship, much less the dreaded M word. Jenna's too busy competing in triathlons and climbing up the supervisory ladder at work, and Annie's focused on school and way too young to get tied down.

At twenty, Annie's the youngest Getaway Girl and our newest member. She has short red hair with spiky platinum tips, a pierced eyebrow, and two small tattoos. And she always wears these great slogan T-shirts. Today her black tee says *When God made me, he was just showing off.*

"Nice shirt," I said.

"I can get you one if you like."

"Maybe later." I didn't want to hurt Annie's feelings, but I didn't want to walk around with God plastered all over my chest. It was bad enough that I was going to have a cast plastered on my leg.

"It's going to be tricky driving my car with this cast," I said. "Especially shifting."

"Um, did you not hear what the doctor said earlier?" Kailyn asked.

"Kind of."

"She was still in a haze from the pain meds, I don't think it penetrated," Tess said, looking at me over her glasses. "The doctor said you'll stay off that foot for several weeks, with no driving for at least a month—maybe two."

"You've got to be kidding. How does he expect me to get around and look for a job?"

Good thing I kept up that insurance policy from Dunkeld's after I quit, or I'd be in some serious financial hurt right now. More than normal, which isn't saying much.

"It's called friends," Chloe said. "We'll take you wherever

you need to go. And you don't need to be looking for a job right now either. The only place you're going when you leave this hospital is home."

"That's right. You're not to even leave the house for four or five weeks," Paige said.

"I'll go stir-crazy. What am I supposed to do all day long?"

"Rest and heal," Annette said. "And let your friends look after you."

"Thanks, but I can take care of myself. Always have."

"Trust me, Miss Independent," Tess said. "I broke my leg years ago skiing and you're going to need some help, so shut up and don't be ungracious. We just need to make up a plan." She pulled out her Crackberry and the rest followed suit with assorted Blackberries, iPhones, and PDAs. All except Annette, who balked at technology and still carried a leather day planner.

There was a flurry of conversation and activity as they compared calendars and figured out who would do what when, with each one entering it into their respective planners.

All except Jenna

Tess looked at Jenna over her red-rectangled glasses. "What's your schedule like? Which nights of the week are best for you?"

"Actually" — she sent me an apologetic glance — "I'm afraid none."

"Did your schedule get changed?" Paige asked. "I thought you usually worked days."

"I do. Usually. But ... well, actually, I have some news."

"You've met someone!" Kailyn's eyes sparkled.

"No." Jenna lifted an eyebrow at my roommate. "Everything doesn't revolve around romance, you know."

"That's what *I'm* sayin'," I chimed in. Jenna and I were always on the same page while Kailyn went straight to the happily-ever-after ending. "So, what's your news? Did you get that promotion at work? Are they making you manager of the gym at last?"

"I did get a manager position—"

"Congratulations! About time. I'm glad they finally recognize your worth. So will we get a discount now when we come to work out? Although"—I glanced at my splint—"I guess I won't be working out anytime soon."

"Ya got that right," Kailyn said. "The only working out you'll be doing is hand-to-mouth as you shovel in all that delicious food Mama's going to make you."

"I'll turn into a blimp! No offense, Annette." I avoided looking at her middle-aged spread. "You're a great cook, but if I eat too many fried foods, I'll swell up like a balloon."

"I do know how to cook things without fryin' them."

"That's right," Tess interjected. "Besides, we're taking turns cooking, so you'll get a wide variety. I'm sure Jenna will make some of her healthy vegetarian dishes."

"I'm afraid I can't," Jenna said. "Thing is ... I was promoted to manager, but not in Sacramento. I'll be managing a new gym and spa we're opening in Napa."

"Napa? But that's nearly two hours away," Kailyn said. "That's going to be an awfully long commute."

"I won't be commuting." Jenna took a deep breath. "That's the other part of my news ... I'm moving. To Napa."

"What?" I screeched. "You're kidding! When?"

"Two weeks. That's when my new job starts."

"But don't you have to give thirty days' notice on your apartment?" Paige asked.

"Uh huh, but the company's going to pick up my rent for the first month, so I don't have to pay double rent."

"Score," Annie said. "Where do I go to sign up?"

"You're not leaving the flower shop." Paige sent her a mock

stern look. "Marc would be lost without you. We all would. That goes for you too, Jenna," she said. "I'm happy for you, but the Getaway Girls just won't be the same without you."

"Yeah. Who's going to suggest all those dark and twisty mysteries?" Kailyn asked.

"And classic horror, like *Dracula*?" Tess said.

"No worries." Annie grinned. "I'll be happy to take over the dark and twisty mantle. Horror too. I'm thinkin' maybe a little Stephen King."

Annette paled. And I laughed.

"Yeah, good luck with that," Jenna said, chuckling. "I've been trying for years." She slid me a conspiratorial grin, which quickly morphed into a frown of regret. "I feel really bad that I can't help you, Bec. But for the next couple weeks, I'll be going back and forth to Napa, helping get the new gym ready to open, and I have to pack and—"

"Don't worry." I waved it off. "I know how long and hard you've worked to get this promotion. You just do what you need to do. But once my leg heals and I'm back on my feet again, I'm coming to Napa to get one of those full spa treatments. The works. Courtesy of the manager, of course."

"You got it," Jenna said.

"Can the rest of us get in on that too?" Kailyn asked. "Or do we have to break a leg to qualify?"

3

From that time on, the world was hers for the reading. She would never be lonely again, never miss the lack of intimate friends. Books became her friends and there was one for every mood.

A Tree Grows in Brooklyn

I missed Jenna. She was my athletic partner in crime. None of the other girls even came close. I loved 'em, but other than Tess and Annie, they were pretty much all indoor adventure types.

Of course, so was I right now.

I scowled at the hated cast propped up on a pillow on the coffee table. No running, hiking, climbing, bicycling ... none of my usual outdoor activities. Nothing at all. A sigh slipped out. At least I got a cool cast out of the deal—a lime green one that started just below my knee and went beneath my foot.

Only my toes were visible. My chipped, blue-polished toes.

Thank God for books. Without them, my enforced convalescence would have been even worse agony. In the four weeks since I'd been off my feet, I'd devoured *Seabiscuit, A Tree Grows in Brooklyn, Rebecca,* and the remainder of our book club selections for the year.

Growing up and moving all the time with my birth mom and her latest flavor-of-the-month husband, books were the only constant in my life. They never failed me. But a girl — even a book-loving one — can only read so much.

After finishing off all our Getaway Girl selections, a couple biographies, and the latest David Sedaris, I started flipping through radio stations. I discovered that a lot of those radio shows have contests where you can win cool things — like DVDs, movie passes, even trips. I programmed their numbers into my cell and began hitting redial so I could be the seventh caller, or whatever number they assigned that day.

Pretty soon, I was winning things left and right. The dinner for two at a romantic restaurant I gave to Chloe and Ryan; passes to the latest Jane Austen movie to our resident Janeites Tess and Annette; and theater tickets to Kailyn and Drew, her latest actor crush.

But the Jason Castro CD I kept for myself. The dreadlocked dude from Texas with the laid-back style and beautiful eyes was my favorite Idol contestant. I wouldn't go so far as to say I loved him, but I would admit to a serious crush.

The one thing I didn't love, or even understand, was hate radio.

Some people call it talk radio, but the few times I've heard it when flipping through stations, the guy was all mean and yelling and calling everyone names who weren't exactly like him, or believed exactly the same way he did.

On a Christian radio station, no less.

I thought Christians were supposed to be all about love? I sure didn't feel an ounce of love coming over the airwaves. And Kailyn and Annette wonder why I don't want to go to church with them …

The worst was a couple years ago when I had to have a root canal. I'd found this dentist through Dial-a-Dentist and his rates were better than most, so I decided to give him a chance. Big mistake. Even on my best day, I don't like going to the dentist. I tense up just when my teeth are being cleaned. Something about all those metal tools messing around inside my mouth. So not one of my favorite things. Add in a root canal and the tense factor goes off the charts.

So I'm lying there with my mouth wide open, my fingers digging into the vinyl armrest as his latexed hand does its dental thing inside my mouth, sticking me with a needle—"a little sting here"—and shooting me full of Novocaine.

More than a little sting.

The tears leak down the sides of my face and into my ears, and that's when the torture really begins. The mellow music that had been playing overhead is suddenly replaced by the angry, belligerent tones of the popular hate-radio host blasting African-Americans, Latinos, gays, Jews, moms who work, and everyone else who doesn't fit into his we're right, they're wrong, and we know it worldview. As Mr. Hate eviscerates each minority, or as he calls them, *fringe* group and jokes that his .38 special would be the answer, my Dial-a-Sadist-Dentist is beaming and nodding in agreement while he drills deeper inside my mouth.

And there's nothing I can do.

I can't speak or even flinch, not with that Makita in my mouth. I feel as if I've been transported back to the Deep South in the sixties. Or Nazi Germany. Maybe I'm just hallucinating from the gas he gave me ...

"Becca? Are you sleeping?" There was a buzzing in my head and my roommate's voice hovered above me.

I opened my eyes to find Kailyn, Annette, Tess, Chloe, and

Annie looking down at me on the couch. "Sorry. I must have dozed off. What are you guys doing here?"

"It's book club night, remember?" Chloe said. "We're having dinner and discussing *Seabiscuit.*"

"Oh yeah." I leaned forward and lifted my cast off the table with both hands, setting it gently on the ground and reaching for my crutches. "Thanks again for waiting to go riding until I'm free of this plaster prison."

"Not a problem," Tess said. "We didn't want you to miss out, especially since you're the one who picked the adventure." She glanced at my hair. "I like this latest color better than the last. What's it called?"

"Magenta marvel. Before it was bubblegum pink."

"Y'all keep changing Becca's hair color every couple weeks and pretty soon there won't be any hair left on her head," Annette warned.

"No worries. It's only temporary — nothing permanent and no peroxide, so it won't do any damage," Annie said. "I've used it in the past and not had any problems."

"Well, I hope so." Kailyn flipped her liquid gold locks away from her face. "That would be terrible if your hair fell out. I can't imagine anything worse."

"I can," Annie said. "Malnutrition, infanticide, illiteracy ..."

Kailyn's face turned red.

Annie's our resident activist and some would say, bleeding heart. But I see her as kind and compassionate. A real Mother Teresa type.

If Mother Teresa had piercings and tattoos.

Already at her young age, Annie's been to Guatemala, Costa Rica, and Rwanda, where she's helped build clinics, dig wells, and bring supplies to orphanages and those in need. She even helped in the aftermath of Hurricane Katrina when she was barely a teen.

Kind of puts the rest of us to shame.

Except now, Annie's the one bearing the shame. "I'm sorry, K," she said. "I didn't mean to be so didactic."

"Di-what?"

"Moralizing," Tess said.

"Sometimes I just can't help myself. But that doesn't give me an excuse to be mean," Annie said. "Forgive me?"

"Of course I forgive you." Kailyn pointed to the WWJD bracelet on Annie's wrist.

It always blows me away that Annie and Kailyn share the same religious beliefs. Thankfully, Annie's not one of those perky Christians. She keeps it real. What really blows me away is that every single one of the Getaway Girls is a Christian. Except me.

I'm surrounded.

Jenna's not. A Christian, I mean. But Jenna's in Napa now, so I'm the only pagan in the group—which is strange, since I'm the one who founded the book club in the first place. I sure didn't advertise for Christians. It just wound up this way.

I've told my friends not to preach at me or try to convert me, though, and they respect that. Usually. But sometimes I get the sneaking suspicion that they're praying for me.

As long as they don't drag me down to the river for baptism or sacrifice a goat in the living room, we're good.

"Hey, where's Paige tonight?" I asked as I hobbled to the dining room table.

"It's open house at Cyd's school," Tess said.

Cyd, short for Cydney, is Paige's fourteen-year-old foster daughter. I have to hand it to her: taking in a teen, and a troubled one at that, as a first-time mom. I sure couldn't do it. But then, I've never been a kid person.

I'm not big on animals either. At least domesticated ones.

In the wild is another story altogether. I could see myself

living with a bunch of animals someday—of the four-footed variety. Just not wolves. I don't care what that psychobabble book says about women running with them.

"Hey, are y'all ready for some day-at-the-races food?" Annette asked. "We've got pork tenderloin with Jack Daniels sauce, new potatoes, and raspberry cheesecake for the high rollers, and for the little people, hot dogs, French fries, and M&Ms."

"Well, I'm definitely one of the little people," I said, "but if I eat all that stuff and not run it off—which I can't thanks to this stupid cast—I'll turn into Jabba the Hut."

"Don't worry. There's carrot sticks and apples too."

I neighed and pawed at the floor with my good, cast-free foot.

Chloe groaned and Kailyn rolled her eyes.

"This woman needs a life and soon," Annie said. "She's likely to throw a saddle on my back and ride me down the hall for excitement."

"Yeah. She already lunged at me when I dropped a sugar cube into my tea," Chloe teased.

"We need to find some other intellectual pursuits for our housebound member," Tess said thoughtfully. "Should we pull out Cranium or Scrabble?"

It was Kailyn's turn to groan. "I hate those games. They make my head hurt." Her face lit up. "I know. Let's play charades!"

"No thanks, drama queen," I said. "You have an unfair advantage. Besides, aren't we supposed to be discussing *Seabiscuit*?"

"Oh yeah."

"Well, ah'm not discussin' anything on an empty stomach," Annette said. "Let's fill our plates first. Becca, do you want a hot dog or pork tenderloin?"

"Or are you just sticking to carrot sticks?" Annie asked innocently.

"I'll have carrot sticks *and* pork tenderloin, thank you very much," I said. "Might as well pretend I'm a high roller."

After everyone loaded their plates, it was quiet as we all chowed down—the silence punctuated only by an occasional "Mmm," "Yumm," or "This is delicious."

Tess gestured with her fork, a new potato on the end of it. "So, who was your favorite character in the book? Human, that is."

"Charles Howard, Seabiscuit's owner," Annette said, without hesitation. "That man was larger than life. He started from nothin', made his millions in the fledgling automobile industry, and then moved into horse racin'."

"And what a lifestyle he led with his young, glamorous wife." Envy filled Kailyn's voice. "Can you imagine?"

"He was something," Tess said, "but I preferred the trainer, Tom Smith. The last of a dying breed from the West. He had an almost mystical way with horses and was the first one who recognized the Biscuit's greatness."

"You have your own mystical way with horses," Chloe said.

"What's this?" Annie said, swiveling her head to stare at Tess. "I didn't know you had horses."

I stared too. "Have you been holding out on us?"

"No," Tess said. "I haven't had a horse in years."

"Growing up, Aunt Tess won all sorts of blue ribbons for her horsemanship," Chloe said. "Mom showed me the pictures. Said her sister was the best around—she had a special connection with her horses. Never lost a competition."

"Serious?" Kailyn said.

"Really?" Annie asked.

"My, aren't you the dark horse?" Annette said. "How long

have we known you and you've never said a word, Miss National Velvet?"

"There was nothing to say. It was all so long ago. Ancient history."

"But don't you miss it?" I asked. "The horses? The riding? I've always thought riding would be a rush." I looked down at my cast. "And I still plan to do it once I'm out of this stupid thing."

"It is a rush," Tess said. "There's nothing like it." She got a faraway look in her eyes. "I guess I do miss it sometimes."

"Then why'd you stop?" Annie asked.

"Things change." Tess shrugged her shoulders. "I got married and became a mom. And my boys became my focus."

See? Another reason not to have kids. They stop you from doing the things you want.

"Also, horses are expensive. Not very practical when you're a widow raising two boys on your own." Tess sent us a wry smile. "The stabling fees alone every month were almost what I was paying in rent at the time."

Whoa. Who knew? Guess I won't be buying a horse anytime soon.

"But your boys are grown and almost out of the house now," I said. "Besides, James is loaded, so why not have horses again?"

Sergeant Etiquette Annette released a gasp while the rest of the room stayed silent.

"What? What'd I say?"

Chloe shook her head. "You can dress her up, but you can't take her out."

"Actually, you can never dress Becca up," Kailyn said dryly, "and right now you can't even take her out." She inclined her head to my cast.

"Good thing," Annette said. "But when we finally do, let's make sure to put a muzzle on her."

"But Becca's blurts are part of her charm," Tess said.

"Charm?" Kailyn's eyes shot up to her perfectly arched eyebrows. "I don't think I've ever heard that particular word applied to my roommate."

"True," Annie said. "But we love her anyway."

"Yes, we do," Chloe said, giving me a fond smile.

"Just don't give me a group hug," I said. "Or I might have to hurt you with my crutches."

I donned my book club leader hat. "Now let's get back to our *Seabiscuit* discussion. As far as favorite characters go, I liked Red Pollard best. Remember after he broke his leg and the doctors told him he'd never ride again? He proved them wrong. Same as the Biscuit." I recited from memory. "'We were a couple of old cripples together ... all washed up. But somehow, we both had a pretty good idea that we'd be back.'"

I tapped my crutches at my side and intoned in the Governator's action-movie voice. "I'll be back."

"That's what we're afraid of," Chloe said.

"Yeah, we were kind of enjoyin' this enforced respite," Annette drawled.

"Speak for yourself." Annie munched on an apple. "I'm missing our outdoor adventures."

"Me too," Tess said.

"Not to worry. I'm committed to healing and getting out of this cast."

"You can't commit to anything," Kailyn snarked. "Not even a hair color."

"She's got you there," Chloe said.

"That's just because I'm bored with being cooped up and need a change," I said. "Now, returning to our book club discussion ..."

"But what about last year when you signed up for line dancing and dropped out after only two lessons?" Kailyn asked.

"Yeah, or when you were going to become a Big Sister but changed your mind at the last minute because it was too much of a commitment?" Tess said.

"And then you quit your job at Dunkeld's."

So. Not returning to the book club discussion after all.

"*And* you never date a guy more than two or three times," Annette added.

"Your romances have an expiration date of seven days, tops," Tess said. "You never give any poor guy a chance."

"So I don't feel like getting tied down. What's wrong with that?"

"Nothin'." Annette said. "Except you're as bad as a guy with your flavor-of-the-week dating life."

Chloe nodded. "When we were roommates, I could never keep track of your revolving-door dates. I'd just start to get to know one guy and then bam! He was gone and you were on to the next one."

"And that's a problem, why?"

"It's just a symptom of a deeper issue," Tess said. "Your inability to commit. Can you name the last guy you dated longer than a week?"

I shuffled through the dating card file in my head. Chad ... Tyler ... Nick ... Dusty ... "Will."

"Will?" Annie asked. "As in Ferrell?"

I'm supposed to remember his last name too? No way. Too many guys. After a while, they all start to blend together.

I may not wear one of those purity rings like Kailyn, but I'm not into sleeping around. Just dating around. No strings that way.

"I'll bet you couldn't date a guy for an entire month," Kailyn said.

"Sure I could. And have."

"Riiiight. Not since I've known you." Kailyn turned to Chloe. "What was the longest Becca ever dated a guy when she was *your* roommate?"

"Let's see ..." Chloe scrunched up her forehead. "A week and a half—no, I think it was two weeks total, if I remember right."

"See?" Kailyn shot me a smug look. "I rest my case."

"Face it, Becca," Tess said. "You have a problem with commitment."

I pushed away my cheesecake. "So I don't want the whole white picket fence, husband, and kids thing, what's wrong with that?"

"Nothing." Chloe helped herself to a bite of my cheese-cake. "We're not talking marriage"—a dreamy haze settled over her face—"although it *is* pretty wonderful. But we're just concerned that you can't commit to anything for any length of time."

"Okay, I'll prove it to you. Kailyn, what did you say? That I couldn't date a guy for an entire month?"

She nodded, her mouth full of cheesecake.

"So the next guy who asks me out," I said, "I'll date for a whole month."

Annette snorted. "A month's nothin', honey. That's just three or four dates. Shoot, it takes longer than that to break in a new pair of shoes."

"Make it three months and you've got a deal," Tess said.

"*Three months?* That's a prison sentence. Especially if the guy's a dork."

Although ... maybe I could turn this to my benefit. "A deal

suggests that I get something from this. What exactly do I get out of dating one guy for that long?"

"A relationship, if you're lucky," Annette said.

"Even better, maybe a marriage proposal." Kailyn went all fluttery and gooey.

"I'd just as soon stab myself in the eye with one of your stilettos."

"And soil my shoes?" Kailyn stuck her foot out and admired her Jimmy Choos. "Heresy."

Usually I don't know brand names, besides Birkenstocks, but when Kailyn brought those distinctive red high heels home, she held them up to her cheek and murmured, "Jimmy Choo, Jimmy Choo, Jimmy Choo ..."

"You should know by now never to use the M-word in regards to Becca," Chloe said.

"You're right. I don't know what I was thinking. Lost my mind for a minute."

"Becca has a good point, though," Tess said, giving me a thoughtful look. "She should get something from this too. Something concrete."

Annie stretched her arms over her head, causing her white *I don't "get" poetry* T-shirt to ride up, exposing her taut midriff and Celtic cross tattoo. "Yeah. Nothing so nebulous as a relationship."

Tess snapped her fingers. "I've got it. If Becca fulfills her end of the bargain — dates the next guy who asks her out for three months — then she gets to choose the next three books we read *and* the next three adventures we go on. And we *all* have to go. Wherever, *whatever* she wants."

"Whatever she wants?" Annette squeaked. "Look what happened the last time. I don't know about y'all, but I surely don't want to break my leg."

"Me either," Kailyn said. "I can't afford to." She fluffed her hair. "I'm going to be playing Cecily in *The Importance of Being Earnest* and I can't be hobbling around stage in a cast."

God forbid.

"Well, I'm game," Annie said. "Bring it on."

I knew I liked that girl.

Inwardly I rubbed my hands together in glee. At long last, I'd get the club to read *A Perfect Storm* and go deep-sea fishing. They'd always vetoed it before. And maybe ... kayaking at the bottom of the Grand Canyon ... hiking to Machu Picchu ... canoeing down the Amazon ... the possibilities were endless. And all I had to do was date some guy for three months?

Or maybe not even ...

I did the math in my head. "Tell you what: I'll date him for three months *or* twenty-five dates, whichever comes first." I could easily shave three months down to two if I threw in a couple quickie coffee dates during the week in addition to the standard weekend date. But of course I wasn't going to tell them that.

"You've got yourself a deal." Tess extended her hand to mine.

Who shakes hands these days besides suits? At times, cool as Tess is, her age shows through. But I shook her hand to seal the deal while the others looked on and smirked in agreement.

I'll be wiping that smirk off before they know it. I just need to find a guy to ask me out who's not a total loser or some kind of sex fiend.

And where exactly am I going to do that?

4

A thoroughbred racehorse is one of God's most impressive engines ... He pursues speed with superlative courage, pushing beyond defeat, beyond exhaustion, sometimes beyond the structural limits of bone and sinew. In flight, he is nature's ultimate wedding of form and purpose.

Seabiscuit

Before I find a guy though, I have to find a job. I'm broke with a capital B. And Kailyn and Annette already paid my half of the rent this month, which I so don't want to become a regular thing.

Everyone thinks I'm flaky and irresponsible, but I'll show them. I glanced down at my cast. Although who's going to hire me with a broken leg?

I checked Craigslist, Monster, and Sacbee.com. Nada. Then I called around to a couple temp agencies, but when I went in for interviews, with Kailyn as my chauffeur, and they saw my cast, I never got a return call back.

"You should go back to Dunkeld's," Chloe said when I called her to whine about my jobless state. "Alastair has gone through a few different people since you left, but he says none of them knows books like you do. Or authors. He'd hire you back in a heartbeat."

"But then I'm going backwards, not forwards. And I wanted something a little more challenging and exciting."

"I think you'll find it plenty challenging navigating through the bookstore on crutches. Besides, right now it's about getting a paycheck, right? This isn't your forever job, just your right-now job."

"I guess you're right," I admitted. Grudgingly.

"Otherwise, there's always sign waving," Chloe said.

So I went back to my old boss, Alastair Dunkeld, and groveled. And it wasn't as humiliating as I'd feared. It helped that Patrice Hawthorne, one of our local authors who put the H in high maintenance and whose signings I'd been setting up for the past three years, came into the bookstore café while we were talking.

"Becca!" She charged over, her zebra-print scarf flapping beneath her seventy-something turkey neck. When she got to our table, she leaned down and hugged me. "I'm *so* glad you're back."

Not one word about my cast. But that's Patrice.

"Me too." I tried not to breathe through my nose. She was always a little heavy-handed with the perfume. Patrice released her fragrant stranglehold on me with a sniff. "The girl who took your place was an illiterate, incompetent imbecile."

Heavy-handed with the alliteration too.

"She'd never heard of any of my books," she continued. "I've written twenty-two erotic historical romances, you know. And *then*, to demonstrate her further ignorance, she asked if I wrote *fiction novels*. I smiled sweetly at her and explained, with remarkable composure and restraint, I might add, that a novel, by definition, *is* a work of fiction, and that there is no such thing as nonfiction *novels."*

Patrice sighed and smoothed her silver chignon with her age-spotted hand. "She just gaped at me like a guppy. That child had absolutely no idea what I was talking about. And she had a college degree. Whatever do they teach them in schools these days?"

Clearly not enough, by your standards. But cut the poor kid some slack. There are worse things than not knowing that fiction and novels are one and the same. Far worse.

AIDS and cancer immediately spring to mind.

Her patrician face darkened beneath her ivory face powder. "But that wasn't the worst of it. She didn't know the first thing about setting up a proper signing. She hadn't ordered enough books, didn't post the appropriate signage, and had the nerve to serve something called Nutter-Butters and Kool-Aid in dreadful little Dixie cups for refreshments!" Patrice drew herself up to her full, regal height. "I ask you, do I look like a Nutter-Butter woman?"

"Never. You're dark chocolate truffles, English shortbread, and Earl Grey."

Patrice pointed an imperious, bejeweled finger at my boss. "Alastair, this girl is a jewel. Don't let her go again!" Then she swept out, her zebra scarf billowing behind her.

I got a dollar-an-hour raise and started back to work that same day.

Not all the authors I worked with were prima donnas. I thought back to all the authors who came into Dunkeld's. I liked best the first-timers—eyes filling at the sight of *their* book in the bookstore. They'd reach out and trace their name on the cover with a trembling hand, unable to believe that at long last, their dream of becoming a published author had come true. It always reminded me of that J. M. Barrie quote: "For several days after my first book was published I carried it about in my pocket, and took surreptitious peeps at it to make sure that the ink had not faded."

Unfortunately, some first-time authors weren't as humble. Or gracious.

In fact, they were arrogant pains in the butt. Often they were unknowns with vanity presses or a publishing house I'd never heard of—usually because the publishing house was in their garage.

They came in demanding shelf space, signings, advertising, press coverage, and my undivided attention. Everything was all about them, and their amazing book that was going to *change people's lives*: melt away pounds, cure debilitating depression, find the love of their life, divorce the love of their life, get rich buying and selling real estate, make a killing on the stock market, and provide a natural, homeopathic cure for hemorrhoids.

Even more painful were the excruciating "memoirs" from bad, wannabe writers convinced that everyone would want to read their poorly written, mind-numbingly detailed—and BORING—tales about their great-great-grandparents who came over from the Old Country with barely two nickels to rub together, but by golly, they worked their fingers to the bone, pulled themselves up by their bootstraps, and made better lives for their kids. And those same kids had to walk five miles to school in the blinding snow with cardboard in the bottom of their holey shoes, but dad gum, they soldiered through to get an education, worked hard, and made things better for their kids.

They'd be better off banding together and combining and condensing their magnum opuses into *Chicken Soup for the Bootstrap Soul.*

I've got nothing against people who pull themselves up by their bootstraps to improve their lot in life. I'm a bootstrap girl myself. But many of these so-called authors didn't even know basic rules of spelling, punctuation, and grammar—including how to construct a simple sentence.

Verbs are always good.

I used to scream, "Unless you're a guy named Frank with an Irish mother named Angela and you can take the most wretched, miserable childhood and turn it into a thing of terrible beauty with prose that shimmers and cuts deep to the heart and soul, don't waste my time with your freaking book."

In my head, of course. The scream, I mean.

Outwardly, I was the perfect community relations coordinator. But after the umpteenth self-published author brought in their pound of unintelligible family history, I called a local, royalty-published author who'd had a modest success with what the newspaper called a "sweet and charming" memoir and asked if she'd be willing to give a quarterly workshop at Dunkeld's on "Writing Your Family History." We couldn't pay, but it would introduce new readers to her book, and of course we'd have extra copies on hand available for purchase and signing at the end of each workshop.

It was a brilliant move. The author's sales increased and the number of self-pubbed memoirists who'd inundated me with promo bookmarks, pens, and schmaltzy glowing press releases decreased considerably.

Thank you, Jesus! (Even though I don't go to church, I can still thank Jesus.)

I had a bad taste in my mouth about local writers until I met Margaret Coleman. Ah, Margaret. I smiled just thinking about her.

Sweet, sixty-something Margaret has written about a dozen books—nonfiction and fiction—and had some modest success. Enough at least for her publisher to keep giving her contracts. Yet most people had never heard of her.

I'd read several of her books—cozy mysteries were her passion—and they were good. Really good. Funny and fascinating with a delightful, older heroine who reminded me a little of Agatha Christie's Miss Marple—if Miss Marple had lived in California's Gold Country and driven a Harley.

Margaret's books were better than a lot of the stuff that came through our doors, and it frustrated me that they didn't sell more. I did what I could to help out: hand-selling her books to customers, setting up specialty signings and mystery nights where customers would try and solve a mystery to win a book, but it didn't make much difference.

Then I had a brainstorm.

"Why don't you start blogging?" I remember suggesting to her once. "Or get on MySpace and Facebook? That's what lots of artists do now. It's a great way for them to connect personally with their fans and build word-of-mouth. I could help you set up your MySpace page and—"

Margaret had politely declined. "Life's too short," she'd said. "I'm sixty-four years old, and I certainly don't want to spend all my free time and energy tied to the computer. I'd much rather spend it with my grandkids. Besides, I only have so many words in me, and I'd rather put them on the page for my readers."

"But this would be a way to gain *new* readers," I'd argued. "And more readers mean more book sales. And more sales are what you need to get on the bestseller list. That, or Oprah. Oprah means mega sales."

"Oprah would never read one of my novels," she'd said with a chuckle. "They're too sweet and cozy for her. She likes more suffering and angst in her fiction. But as far as I'm concerned, there's enough suffering in the world already. My books are for people who want an escape from their troubles.

"Besides," she'd said with an airy wave of her hand, "I gave up on the dream of becoming a bestselling author years ago. Becoming rich and famous is not why I write. I write because I can't *not* write. And honestly? I have lots of writer friends who blog, hold contests on their websites, and do the MySpace, Facebook, Twitter marketing dance, and they don't see any difference in their overall sales. Most have worst sales than I do.

"There's no magical marketing formula to creating a bestseller," she'd confided. "If there was, all the publishing houses would use it."

At least she didn't say it was up to God or anything.

Before I met Margaret, I used to fantasize about writing a book someday. What English major doesn't? I had dreams of being the next Harper Lee or Anne Tyler and writing a heartbreaking, intelligent, and bestselling literary work of staggering genius that would take the publishing world by storm.

The *New York Times Literary Review* would be stunned by its stark honesty, simple beauty, and haunting lyrical prose and would hail me as the newest shining star in the literary firmament. My publisher would fly me to New York, where he'd wine and dine me and throw me a glittering book launch party, attended by *Publishers Weekly, Library Journal,* and all the smart, respected literati of the day. I'd rub shoulders with Joan Didion, Anne Lamott, and Ian McEwan. Even the reclusive J. D. Salinger would come out of seclusion to meet me. (If he's still alive, that is. Last I heard, he was.)

Afterwards, my publisher would send me on a coast-to-coast book tour to the big chain bookstores where the lines would stretch around the block—the likes of which hadn't been seen since Harry Potter. Naturally, as a true writer of the people and one whose humble beginnings included clerking in a neighborhood bookstore, I'd insist on doing signings at the smaller, indie stores as well.

But after listening to Margaret's stories, I realized my publishing fantasies were all Hollywood and not real life.

"Honey, I'm just happy if my book earns out its advance," she'd told me as we talked over lattes in the café. "Most don't. And the only book tour I went on was when my first book, *Murder in Modesto*, came out. And I paid for it. Or rather, we paid for it—that was our vacation that year.

"Harold filled the car with unleaded, five cases of books, and five hundred bookmarks that I'd had printed up, and we set out on a four-day tour with stops in Lodi, Stockton, Manteca, Modesto, and Turlock—with a side trip to Fresno thrown in to see my mother. We stayed in Motel 6s and ate at Denny's, and when we came home, we had four-and-a-half cases of books left, 317 bookmarks, and we were out more than two thousand dollars."

"Two thousand bucks? I thought Motel 6s were cheap."

"They are. But the books weren't free. Or the bookmarks."

"You have to pay for your own books?"

"Every author does. We get a discounted rate—usually fifty percent—but at six or seven bucks a book and thirty to forty books in a case, it adds up."

"How does anyone ever earn a living as an author?"

"Most don't," she'd said. "Most authors have to supplement their royalty checks—if they're lucky enough to have their advance earn out—with teaching and speaking engagements. And even then, most of us need a second job to pay the bills, or if we're lucky, a supportive spouse with a full-time job and benefits. Being an author isn't the glamorous life everyone thinks. For every J. K. Rowling or John Grisham who storms the bestseller list and earns millions, there are thousands of unknown authors toiling away in obscurity just trying to pay the rent."

"You can't go into writing for the money or fame," she'd gently said. "You have to write because you love it. But loving it doesn't mean you're going to earn a living at it."

Margaret recited, "'You would-be Thomas Wolfes and Gertrude Steins out there should understand one thing above all: likely you ain't gonna make no money as a writer. Real money, I mean. The kind of money that makes a mother clap hands when her progeny marries you …' Larry King said that in *None but a Blockhead*."

"Larry King of *Larry King, Live*?"

"No. Larry L. King, the literary journalist and playwright."

I was thinking again about what Margaret said as I checked the system for the release date of her next title. "'Experience is a dear teacher, and only fools will learn from no other,'" I murmured.

"Ben Franklin, right?"

I glanced above my computer screen to see a thirtyish artist type with a shaved head, dark-rimmed glasses over Guinness-stout colored eyes, and a scruffy soul patch giving me a knowing look.

"No." I hate it when people catch me talking to myself. "Thomas Jefferson."

"I don't think so. Definitely Benjamin Franklin."

This guy does not know who he's dealing with. I'm not called Quote Chick for nothing. "Wanna bet?"

"As long as we're not talking money, you're on. So, what should we bet?"

I looked at the book in his hands—a glossy, hardcover pictorial of Africa that wasn't cheap. "Are you planning to buy that?"

"Considering it, but it's a little expensive. Thought maybe I'd check it out from the library instead."

"I have a better idea. If I'm right and it's Jefferson, you buy the book. And if you're right—"

"If I'm right and it's Franklin," he interrupted, "I don't buy the book and you have coffee with me." He smiled. A smile that revealed a slightly crooked front tooth.

"You're on."

That was easy. Alastair's going to be stoked I sold such an expensive book. Maybe I'll get a bonus — one of his infrequent employee gift cards which I can use to buy Kailyn's birthday present. My turn to smile. I typed the quote into Bartleby.com.

"I don't believe it," I muttered.

"What's that? I can't hear you."

You can hear me just fine. But I guess you want me to say it. "It *is* Franklin. You were right and I was wrong. Satisfied, Mr. Know-it-all?"

"Actually, the name is Ben. Benjamin Franklin Colby. Nice to meet you, Becca."

"I never told you my name."

He inclined his bald head to my nametag.

"Oh. Well. Yeah. So are you related to the great Ben or what?"

"No relation. My folks are just fans."

"And what? They brought you up on flashcards of everything Ben ever said? Or did they just plant a Founding Fathers chip into your DNA?"

"Not quite. I have what amounts to an almost photographic memory, so most things stick pretty well. Especially if it's something I'm really interested in."

"And you're really interested in Ben Franklin."

"Wouldn't you be if you were named after him?"

If I was named after him, I'd suffer from an identity crisis. Hold off on the snark a minute, Sherlock, and think, would you? Sometimes you can be so clueless. Does the word *bet* ring any bells? This is the first guy who's asked you out, stupid.

If you have coffee, you'd only have twenty-four dates to go.

"So, how soon would you like to go get that coffee?" Ben asked.

I could sense my inner scorekeeper start to smile.

"I get off in twenty," I said, after checking the time on my cell. "You could meet me back here and we could grab coffee in the bookstore café. They make great lattes."

"You're on." He flashed me his crooked-tooth smile above his coffee-colored soul patch. "I'll just go put this expensive book back on the shelf and do a little browsing."

After he sauntered off, I pulled up Chloe's number on my cell and punched it in. "Hey, Clo, any chance you can pick me up half an hour later today? I have a few things to do before I can leave."

"No prob. It'll give me a chance to run a few errands. See you at 5:30."

A half hour would be plenty of time for my first date with Mr. Benjamin Franklin Colby.

"So how'd you break the leg?" he asked as I crutched alongside him twenty minutes later.

"Skydiving."

"Sweet. I was afraid you were going to say something boring like tripping over the curb, which would then just make you clumsy instead of interesting."

He thinks I'm interesting? Maybe twenty-five dates won't be so bad after all. "I've never been clumsy," I said. "And boring's not in my vocabulary."

His eyes shot to my hair. "I can see that."

"What about you?"

"What about me?"

"Boring or interesting?" Although his shaved head spoke volumes.

"You tell me," Ben said. "I broke my leg hiking in the mountains of Peru two years ago."

"Where?"

"Right tibia."

"No, I mean where in Peru?"

"On the way to Machu Picchu, the Incan city."

There is a God after all.

I sent a dazzling smile to my new three-month date as we settled into a corner of the café where I could prop my cast up on a chair. "What else do you do when you're not correcting quotes, trekking to ancient cities in Peru, and breaking your leg?"

"For work or for fun?"

"Fun first."

"A girl after my own heart. Let's see"—he stroked his scruffy soul patch—"I like to surf, sail, and sometimes dive for abalone off the Mendocino Coast. And a few years ago I went to Australia and got to go scuba diving on the Great Barrier Reef. Something I'll never forget." He got a faraway look in his Guinness eyes, then fixed his gaze on me. "Have you ever been to Australia?"

"I wish! Someday ..."

"You'll love it. Great country," he said. "New Zealand too. We stopped there on our way back to the States and had a blast backpacking, bungee jumping, and then going black-water rafting in these cool glow-worm caves."

Is this guy for real? Maybe he has a big red S tattooed on his chest.

"And you?"

"Huh?"

"What do you like to do for fun?" he asked. "Besides skydive?"

"Just about anything outdoors. Hiking, camping, rafting —although mine is white water, not black water. I also like to snorkel and scuba dive, but the most exotic place I've been—outside of Paris, that is—is Cabo."

I thought back to Chloe's aborted wedding to Chris the jerk and how Tess and I went with her on her Mexican cruise honeymoon instead, where I taught her to snorkel. "Cabo's where I got to pet a nurse shark."

"Serious?"

"Yeah. It was really cool."

"I'm jealous," he said. "I've always wanted to do that."

"Yeah, well, I've always wanted to go to Australia, New Zealand, and especially, Machu Picchu. Are there any other exotic places you've been to?"

"Does Africa count?"

"Does it *count*? It's only at the top of the list of the Top Ten exotic places to see before I die." I blew out a wistful sigh "What'd you do there? Climb Kilimanjaro? Go on safari? Dive off the coast of Zanzibar?"

This enforced dating thing was looking better and better all the time.

"No Kilimanjaro, safari, or scuba diving yet," he said, "although I plan to return someday and do all three. Actually, when I was in Ethiopia last month, I went with a group who were teaching the locals how to make and use portable solar cookers."

Whoa. Adventurous *and* humanitarian. Wait'll I tell Annie.

"Forgive my ignorance, but what exactly are solar cookers?"

"An alternative to cooking with wood—by using the sun's

energy as fuel," he explained. "Solar cookers help prevent de-forestation and pollution. They also offer young girls in Third World countries the opportunity to go to school, rather than spend so much of their time helping their mothers collect wood."

I'm down with that.

"This group you went with, was it the Peace Corps or something like that?"

"Something like that. Peace was another one of our goals," he said. "I went with a missions group from my church."

Oh my God, they're everywhere.

5

Africa is mystic; it is wild; it is a sweltering inferno; it is a photographer's paradise, a hunter's Valhalla, an escapist's Utopia. It is what you will, and it withstands all interpretations. It is the last vestige of a dead world or the cradle of a shiny new one....

It is all these things but one thing—it is never dull.

West with the Night

"You're a Christian."

He nodded.

"Figures."

"What? Do you have something against Christians?" He smiled and held up his palm. "Wait. Let me guess ... one of them thumped you over the head with a Bible, only it slipped and got you in the arm, leaving you with a chip on your shoulder. Am I close?"

"No. Yes. I don't know."

All I know is I didn't plan to be stuck dating one for the next three months.

Although I didn't say that out loud.

So why do you have to? my inner self asked.

A deal's a deal.

But who's going to know?

I promised.

Like I said, who's going to know?

I will. I may be a flake, but I keep my word.

It's your funeral. Or would that be baptism?

Shut up.

"Did you just tell me to shut up?" Ben asked.

"No." I could feel my face turn the same color as my hair. "I was talking to myself."

"Do that often?"

"Depends."

"On what?"

"The company."

"Ah. Sounds like my cue to leave." He started to stand up.

"No, don't leave." Only twenty-four more dates to go.

He sat back down and quirked an eyebrow at me.

"I'm sorry. I didn't mean that."

"Which part? The don't leave or the company part?"

"The company. Sometimes I speak before thinking."

"I have that same problem," he said.

"Wonder what causes it?"

"Brutal honesty? Or maybe"—the corners of his mouth turned up—"as my grandmother says, a deplorable lack of tact?"

"I was going to blame it on my pain meds."

"That's always a good excuse. I've used that one a few times myself."

All at once I saw Chloe enter the store. Had it been half an hour already? She spotted me and waved.

There wasn't much time.

"Would you like to go to dinner?" I blurted out, feeling a sudden sweat on my brow.

"Dinner?"

"Yeah, you know, that thing you do every night where you put food in your mouth and chew?" I snarked. I smiled to show I was being funny.

"Sounds vaguely familiar."

Chloe was getting closer.

"So would you?" I asked. "Tonight?" Two dates in one day would leave me with only twenty-three more to go.

"Sorry, I've got plans tonight."

Don't tell me he has a girlfriend. That will ruin everything.

He doesn't have a girlfriend. If he did, he wouldn't have asked you to coffee, good Christian that he is.

"Tomorrow?"

"It's a date," he said. "Where'd you like to go?"

"Oh, we can work out the details tomorrow." I grabbed my crutches and pulled myself to my feet just as Chloe entered the café and began to make her way toward us. "Just call me here in the morning." I lowered my voice. "And leave the Bible at home."

"Of course." He stood up. "I wouldn't want to add a chip to the other shoulder."

"Becca, are you ready?" Chloe asked.

"All set. Let's go."

Ben turned around. "Chloe?"

"Ben!" She hugged him. "Welcome back! How are you?"

"Great." He returned her hug. "And you?"

"Good. Really good."

I looked from one to the other. "You two know each other?"

"I certainly hope so," Chloe said, giving him a smile. "I don't usually go around hugging strange men. My husband wouldn't like it."

Ben smiled back and released her. "No, he wouldn't."

"Ben's in Ryan's men's group," Chloe explained. "They meet for breakfast every Wednesday."

Of course they do. Just kill me now.

"Sorry I missed the wedding," he said.

"You had a good excuse. Africa's a bit far." Chloe looked at me and then back to Ben. "I didn't realize you two knew each other."

"We don't. Didn't," I said. "We just met."

"An hour ago," Ben added. A flicker of recognition flared in his eyes. "Wait—is this your old roommate?"

"The one and only," Chloe said.

He gave me a speculative look. "I've heard about you."

"Then you're one up on me." I frowned at Chloe. "Just what have you heard?"

"Nothing bad. Just that you're a bit of a daredevil who likes to take risks," Ben said. "And that's okay. I like to take risks too. I'll call you in the morning. Looking forward to tomorrow night." He gave Chloe another hug. "Good seeing you. Marriage agrees with you. Tell Ryan I'll see him Wednesday."

"Will do." Chloe watched Ben leave, and then turned to me, eyebrows raised. "Tomorrow night? What's happening tomorrow night?"

I shrugged. "We're going on a date."

"You and *Ben*?"

"Anything wrong with that?"

"You do realize he's a Christian, don't you?"

"Yeah. The missions trip to Africa and the men's group with Ryan kind of clued me in."

Unfortunately.

"Is this my same former roommate who vowed she'd never, ever go out with a Christian because they were too"—Chloe ticked off on her fingers—"boring, earnest, and goody-goody?"

I lifted my shoulders. "A deal's a deal."

Chloe's eyes widened. And then her face split into a wide Julia Roberts grin, and she began to laugh.

"What's so funny?"

She shook her head and laughed even harder. So hard, tears trickled down her cheeks.

"And you say *I* make a spectacle of myself in public?"

Chloe gasped and swiped at her eyes as another fit of giggles overtook her.

"You need to be committed. Seriously."

"Well, someone does," she said, her laughter finally under control. "The next three months are going to be very interesting."

I'll say. But if Ben-boy thinks he's going to get me to convert, he's got another think coming. Not gonna happen. Not in this universe.

Or the one beyond. Or any of the ones Dr. Who has traveled to.

I'm a *Dr. Who* groupie. So sue me. Sci-fi isn't just for guys. Girls can like it too. And what's not to like about *Dr. Who*? Time travel. The Tardis. And David Tennant—best Dr. Who ever.

When I got home, I hobbled straight to the wall calendar on the pantry door and marked a big fat 1 on today's date with a red Sharpie. One down, twenty-four to go. Then I popped in the next episode of *Dr. Who* that I'd only seen twice, and settled down to bliss.

Once the Queen Victoria and the werewolf episode ended, I began mapping out the next twenty-four dates with Ben. Hmm, where can we go to dinner tomorrow? Since I invited him, that means I pay, so it needs to be on the cheap. Not fast food cheap, though. Thanks to Jenna's organic and vegetarian influence, I try to limit my Mickey D's and Taco Bell consumption to only once a month.

Besides, fast food on our first dinner date? Not so much.

Especially if I hope to rope him into twenty-three subsequent dates. I rifle through my coupon stash until I find the one I'm looking for: a two-for-one at my favorite Mom-and-Pop Thai-Vietnamese restaurant. Interesting and exotic, but not trying too hard. And definitely affordable. Plus, they have the best pad thai around. And if all goes well, maybe I can squeeze in two more dates this weekend.

Doing what? my nosy inner self asked.

I don't know. Going to the movies? A play? One of those Second Saturday art exhibit thingies? Although … the latter involves a lot of walking. Too bad I'm grounded. Otherwise, we could really have some fun together over the next three months: hiking, sailing, scuba diving … I slapped my cast in disgust, just as the front door opened.

"Ow!"

"What's wrong?" Kailyn hurried into the living room, her hands full of packages which she dropped to the floor as she approached the couch.

"Nothing." I rubbed my palm. "Just hurt my hand."

"Stop hitting your cast! Do you want to reinjure yourself and be stuck in that cast even longer?"

"Hindsight explains the injury that foresight would have prevented."

"Who said that?" Kailyn asked.

"Anon."

"Anon?"

"Ymous."

She wrinkled her forehead.

I spelled it out.

"Very funny." She picked up a white bag and rustled it invitingly. "I brought your favorite—chicken Caesar salad from La Bou."

"What do you want?"

"Why do I have to want something?" Kailyn made her eyes all big and innocent. "Can't I just be a nice roommate and buy you dinner?"

"You could, but I know better."

"Well-l-l, I was hoping maybe you could help me run my lines again," she admitted. "I have to be off book by tomorrow's rehearsal and I'm so not ready." She sighed, and then brightened as a thought struck her. "Hey, want to come to rehearsal with me tomorrow night? We could run lines in the car."

"Sorry. No can do. I've got a date."

"You do? What's his name? Is he cute? What's he like? Where'd you meet him?"

"I met him at work today, his name is Ben, and I guess he's kind of cute—nice eyes. But he's not your type; he shaves his head."

"Eww." Kailyn fluffed her blonde locks. "How come?"

"I don't know. It's just his style. He has a soul patch too."

She made a face. "What about an earring?"

"No. At least I didn't see one. But maybe. I'll check tomorrow and let you know."

"What's he do? Is he blue collar or white collar?"

"I don't know. I didn't ask. Could be either." I thought of Ben's erudition, his humanitarianism, and all his travel, which couldn't come cheap. "Maybe white collar?"

Stereotype much?

Maybe he's a plumber. Or a contractor. Those guys earn the big bucks. And speaking of big bucks, are you forgetting that he put the coffee-table book back because it was too expensive? Maybe someone needs to rethink their assumptions.

Oh, put a sock in it.

"He looks kind of artsy. And he didn't seem to have a lot of money, so maybe he's a musician? Or a teacher?" I shrugged. "Guess I'll find out tomorrow."

"You're so laid back. I always find out what a guy does before I go out with him."

"That's because you size up every man who asks you out as potential husband material. And I could care less."

"You will someday," she said.

"Wanna bet?"

We ate our salads on the couch, using our laps as tables. When we were finishing up, Kailyn passed her script to me. "Okay, you be Gwendolen again. Start with the line 'I beg your pardon.'"

I finished chewing my crouton, then recited, "I beg your pardon?"

"Dearest Gwendolen," Kailyn said in her best upper-crust English accent, "there is no reason why I should make a secret of it to you. Our little county newspaper—"

"Actually, it's country," I said.

"Oh, right." Kailyn resumed. "Our little country newspaper is sure to chronicle the fact next week. Mr. Ernest Worthing and I are engaged to be married."

I stood up politely as the stage direction called for, although it was a little awkward with my cast. "My darling Cecily," I said in a bad imitation of a British accent, "I think there must be some slight error. Mr. Ernest Worthing is engaged to *me*. The announcement will appear in the *Morning Post* on Saturday at the latest."

Kailyn stood up politely as well. "I am afraid you must be under some misconception. Ernest proposed to me exactly ten minutes ago." She held out a book that was supposed to be her diary so I could see for myself. Gwendolen's self.

I pretended to examine the diary carefully through an imaginary lorgnette as I continued reading. "It is certainly very curious, for he asked me to be his wife yesterday afternoon at 5:30. If you would care to verify the incident, pray do so." And with a flourish, I produced my own imaginary diary. "I never—"

The phone rang. "Should I answer it?" I asked.

"Nah, probably a telemarketer. Let's keep going." Kailyn leaned down and scooped up her last forkful of salad.

"Okay, let me find my place again."

While I was looking, the answering machine kicked in and a giggling Chloe's voice punctured the air. "Hey, Bec, I just called to say have fun with your first Christian date tomorrow."

Kailyn choked and spit out a crouton. "You're going out with a Christian?"

6

Beer is proof that God loves us and wants us to be happy.

Benjamin Franklin

My date surprised me the next night by ordering a beer with his green curry.

"You drink?"

"Sometimes."

"I didn't think it was allowed."

"Why?"

"Because you're a missionary."

"Not full-time," Ben said. "I go on short-term mission trips. The rest of the time I'm a graphic artist."

I knew he was an artsy type.

"Besides, missionaries can drink. Occasionally."

"They can? I thought it was against church law or something."

"Depends on the church," he said. "Jesus' first miracle was turning water to wine, plus the Bible says a little wine is good for the stomach. It also says don't drink to excess or be a drunkard, which is why I limit myself to one."

My mother's alky face flashed before me. "Amen to that."

"Amen? There's hope for you yet."

"Don't bet on it."

"Speaking of bets, want to make another?"

I was reminded that Ben first became date fodder at the bookstore as the result of a bet. What was up with this guy? "Boy, for a Christian, you sure have a lot of vices: drinking, gambling ... what's next?" I was going to say "sex" but thought that might be a bit much this soon.

"And for someone who's not a Christian, you sure seem to have a lot of ideas about what Christianity is," Ben said. "Where'd you get your information, anyway?"

"*Footloose* and a few churches I visited when I was little. The rules were pretty clear." I ticked them off on my fingers: "No drinking, dancing, gambling, sex before marriage, or R-rated movies. Better yet, not going to the movies at all, unless it's old Disney or a biblical epic with Charlton Heston. And it goes without saying that you have to be a registered Republican," I added.

"I'm an Independent," Ben said, "but I voted Democrat in the last election."

"And you call yourself a Christian? Better watch out."

"Well, Jesus wasn't a Republican or a Democrat, so I'm in good company."

That's what I'm sayin'. Jesus was cool. I could hang with him.

"So ...," Ben said, "you're down to twenty-three now?"

"Twenty-three?"

"Dates. Only twenty-three more to go before you win the bet."

I dropped a prawn from the fork that was halfway to my mouth. "I'm going to kill Chloe."

"Sheathe your sword, oh avenging one. Chloe didn't tell me. She mentioned it to Ryan, and he happened to mention it to me when we were shooting hoops last week."

"Last week?"

"Yep. Before we ever met."

"Oh."

What's up with that? He seems to be taking it well.

"You're not mad?"

"Nope." He gave me a lopsided grin. "My ego was a little bruised when I put it together that you were the Becca who'd made the dating bet. Here I thought I'd dazzled you with my erudite wit, charming personality, and great looks."

But you had. Only I didn't say that aloud. I inhaled a forkful of noodles.

"Ryan said you'd never be able to do it."

"Ryan doesn't know me very well," I said around the mouthful of noodles, feeling one slide out and dangle on my chin.

"That's attractive."

I wiped my chin with a napkin.

"Want to prove him wrong?"

"What?"

"Want to prove Ryan wrong?" Ben repeated. "I'll help you win the bet."

"Why? What's in it for you? I already told you you're not going to convert me." Potlucks and denim jumpers are so not my thing.

"I can't wait to see what hair color you come up with each week."

My gaze shifted to his shaved head. "Sounds like someone has hair envy."

"You got me," he said. "So … we on?"

"We're on."

"Two down, twenty-three to go. Just one thing though — I get to pick the dates."

I knew there'd be a catch. Looks like I'll be borrowing one of Annette's jumpers.

Ben ordered a container of pad kee-mow, also known as drunken noodles, to go, then asked if I'd like to go on a drive with him since it was still early.

"Do I have a choice, date-picker?"

"Not really."

When we got to his car, he hurried over to the passenger side to open my door.

"Save the chivalry for a real date," I said. "So not my thing. I'm perfectly capable of opening my own door." I struggled with my crutches.

"Are you?"

"Yes." I leaned one crutch against the side of the car and hopped to the door. "It just takes a little longer."

As we headed for the freeway, we debated the merits of *Dr. Who* versus *Star Trek*. I learned Ben's been a Trekkie almost from the womb, but I stuck to my Dr. Who guns. No Captain Kirk or Picard will ever steal the place the Doctor holds in my heart.

Now there's a man I'd date forever.

Fifteen minutes later we exited an off-ramp that led to an older neighborhood where the aged wooden houses were smaller and kind of shabby, yet distinct — a nice change from the suburban sprawl sameness of beige stucco boxes all in a row.

As we approached a run-down trailer park, I held my breath while my childhood flashed before my eyes. But Ben didn't slow down, and as he turned a corner where a cluster of skateboarders busted some moves in the parking lot of a convenience store, I breathed again.

A few blocks later he slowed down and pulled into the driveway of a tiny tan bungalow with a freshly mown lawn and rosebushes flanking the gleaming white front door. Ben turned off the ignition and announced, "We're here."

"Where exactly is here?"

"Where I live."

And I thought Christians were supposed to be different.

He's still a man, inner self reminded me. And men are all the same.

Good thing I took that self-defense class.

Ben unfolded himself from the driver's seat and grabbed the takeout. "Coming?" He glanced at my cast. "Do you need some help?"

"No. I can't stay long though."

"This won't take long."

You bet it won't. My hand closed around the pepper spray in my pocket.

I hobbled behind him up the walk to the front door, and as he turned the key in the lock and pushed the door open, he called out in a loud voice, "Gran, it's me."

He lives with his grandmother?

Guess I won't need the pepper spray after all.

Inside the door, I was greeted by an ape. A carved wooden one atop a rattan table that was also home to an intricately carved giraffe. And between the two animals stood a wood-framed picture of a little boy in his underwear playing in the dirt with a stick.

"That you?"

Ben nodded. "In the middle."

"Thanks for clarifying. At first I thought you were the one on the end."

"No problem. Everyone makes that mistake."

"What mistake is that, Benjamin?"

I turned around to find myself towering over a gray-haired mite of a woman who couldn't have been even five feet tall and eighty pounds tops. She was leaning on a cane and smiling up at us.

"The ape mistake, Gran."

"Well, you always were a little monkey — climbing everywhere and getting into everything." Her eyes, the same rich Guinness brown as her grandson's, twinkled as she turned to me. "And who is this colorful young lady with the cast on her leg?" Her hand trembled on her cane and her head shook a little too, like someone with Parkinson's.

Ben moved to her side, offering her his arm. "Why don't we go sit down in the living room and do the introductions there?"

"Where are your manners, Benjamin?" She frowned at him. "You should help the young lady. She's the one in a cast."

"True," he said. "But she's very independent and likes to do things on her own."

"Sounds like me in my younger days." She smiled at me, then took Ben's arm and gave an appreciative sniff. "What's in the bag? Certainly smells delicious."

"You'll have to guess," he teased as he led her across a woven rush rug to a rattan sofa with tropical print cushions.

I crutched after the family duo and lowered myself into an overstuffed chair next to the couch, setting my crutches down in relief.

"Gran, this is my friend, Becca," he said, once he'd settled her comfortably on the sofa and moved her cane to one side. "Becca, this is my grandmother, Adelaide."

"Nice to meet you, Adelaide."

"It's lovely to meet you, dear. And lovely to hear my name

again." She released a wistful sigh. "No one ever calls me Adelaide anymore. I'm always Mom, Mother, or Gran."

"I'll call you Adelaide if you like," Ben said.

"You do and I'll wallop you with my cane, young man. I'm Gran to you. Always have been, always will be."

"Yes, ma'am."

"Becca, are you comfortable enough?" she asked. "Would you like a footstool?"

"Oh, no thanks. I'm good." Adelaide reminded me of Aunt Bee from Mayberry, minus the bulk.

"How did you break your leg, dear?"

"It's my ankle, actually. I broke it skydiving—didn't land the right way."

"Ah, I see that my grandson's not the only daredevil in the room." She sent him a loving smile and as she did, her eyes landed on the takeout bag again. "Benjamin, what's in there?"

"Guess." He rustled the bag.

Adelaide sniffed the air. "Definitely Chinese. Kung pao?"

"Close but no cigar. I got you your favorite—drunken noodles."

"Wonderful! Thank you, dear. And Becca, don't get the wrong idea. I'm really a teetotaler in every other way," she said. "I'll have it for lunch tomorrow. Now put it in the fridge quick, Benjamin, before it spoils. And when you come back, bring that plate of Snickerdoodles on the counter and some napkins."

Ben's eyes lit up and he sprinted from the room, leaving behind the lingering scent of garlic and basil in his wake.

She chuckled. "Benjamin loves my Snickerdoodles. Has ever since he was a little boy." Her eyes raised to my head. "And I love *your* hair. What a dramatic red. Reminds me of some of my Masai friends."

"You've been to Africa? Did you go with Ben last month?"

"Oh no. I can't travel the way I used to, unfortunately." Her lined face grew wistful. "We lived in Africa for years—starting out in Nairobi and then moving to a smaller farming village miles from the city."

"'I had a farm in Africa at the foot of the Ngong Hills,'" I murmured.

"Isak Dinesen. Wonderful storyteller. But the book's better than the movie." Adelaide leaned toward me and whispered, "Although that Robert Redford was pretty handsome."

"No argument there." I glanced at a trio of wooden elephants on the round table between us. "So what did you do in Africa?"

"My husband and I were missionaries with Wycliffe."

"Wycliffe?"

"Wycliffe Bible Translators. They translate God's Word all around the world—into every language that needs it."

But what if they don't need it?

I kept my skepticism to myself though. No need to be rude to a sweet old lady.

Casting about for another subject, I spotted her cane. "I wish I could trade in my crutches for a cane—it'd make it easier to get around." I leaned forward for a closer look. "Wow, that's awesome. Cool carvings."

She picked up the carved wooden stick and ran her fingers over it lovingly. "Another souvenir from Africa. It's really come in handy these past few years."

Ben rejoined us with a plate of cookies and three steaming mugs, which he set on the coffee table. "Gran, I made you some of your cinnamon tea."

Great. A tea party. One of my favorite things.

"I made you coffee, Becca. Hope decaf's okay."

"Thanks." Unleaded's not my first choice, but it's better than tea.

I took a sip. Way better. "So, how long have you lived here, Adelaide?"

"Almost twenty years. We moved back to the States when my husband got sick. He went home to Glory two years later."

"I'm sorry."

"Don't be, dear. At least, not for my Matthew. He is well, at last." Adelaide seemed to have a faraway look in her eyes. "He is living still, only now with Jesus."

Yeah right. He's not really dead — Matthew lives on in heaven. Even if that's true and he's now with the cool dude, to me, it's a poor substitute.

In spite of her delusions, I attempt to show my caring side. "You must really miss him."

"I do. But I wouldn't wish him home for anything." Adelaide smiled. "How unloving that would be. It reminds me of an old African proverb." She pointed to some framed writing on the wall.

I followed her finger and read aloud. "I pointed out to you the stars and all you saw was the tip of my finger."

Huh?

"My time with my husband was only the tip of God's finger, but his eternal life is more like the stars," she said, "infinite, awesome, and designed by the Creator. How could I ever ask my Matthew to leave all God has planned for him to return to this?" The elderly woman shook her head. "No. Better for me to enjoy the time I have left here. I've been given much."

She winked at Ben. "Especially the gift of my grandson. It was a good day when his parents decided to send their little monkey to me from deep in the African bush country."

"It was a red-letter day for me too, Gran." Ben patted her hand.

She smiled at him and sighed. "Then, when the time comes, I'll go to be with Jesus and my Matthew. I can't wait."

For some reason, I didn't like to hear Adelaide talking about her own exit from this life. I didn't know many — actually, any — old ladies, and she was pretty cool. Even if she was ultrareligious. I mean she didn't blink twice at my hair. In fact, she even liked it.

I wanted to know her better. Spend some time together. Maybe even bring her some drunken noodles myself.

What was happening to me? I was getting all soft and sappy.

Maybe I just longed for some family connections. I never knew my grandparents. My father had cut all ties with his family long before he married my mother, she'd told me, so there went any relationship on the paternal side. And then he cut his ties with us too.

As for my maternal grandparents, they died when I was little.

Maternal. Yeah, right.

> When I look back on my childhood I wonder how I
> survived at all. It was, of course, a miserable childhood: the
> happy childhood is hardly worth your while. Worse than
> the ordinary miserable childhood is the miserable Irish
> childhood, and worse yet is the miserable Irish Catholic
> childhood.
>
> *Angela's Ashes*

I didn't have an Irish Catholic childhood. Mine was more
Woodstock meets *Leaving Las Vegas*.

The only times we went to church were when my blood
mother Earlene's latest husband had dumped her and split with
the grocery money, leaving us with nothing but a package of
Top Ramen, half a box of Cheerios, and a carton of spoiled
milk.

Earlene would drag me to the nearest down-home Bible-
belt church, dressed in my shabbiest clothes — usually ill-
fitting high-water pants and a holey, stained T-shirt — and
weep at the cruel hand fate had dealt her and how she couldn't

even afford to buy milk for her little girl since her good-for-nothing husband had run off and left us with nothing.

She'd hug me to her hot, fleshy body that reeked of Johnnie Walker Red and sweat mixed with baby powder. Fat crocodile tears would roll down her cheeks, dripping into the ample cleavage that spilled out of her too-tight tank top and push-up bra. "What am I going to do, how am I going to feed my poor baby?" she'd wail. "I don't mind about me, but she's just an innocent child."

The small-town preacher would pat my head or her hand — careful to avert his eyes from her plunging neckline — and assure her that God had brought her to the right place. "Judgment is mine, sayeth the Lord," he would thunder in a loud, Bible-thumping voice, "and the Lord will judge that no-account who abandoned his helpless wife and child. Jesus commands us to take care of the widows and orphans, and we will take care of you."

Then he'd call the good ladies of the church together, explain our pitiful situation, and they'd lead us to the food pantry and clothes closet where I'd score cleaner, better-fitting T-shirts, pants, and dresses.

Always dresses.

Those church ladies kept wanting to put me in frou-frou dresses like I was a doll or something. Once, two plump ones, clad in pastel polyester dresses — one pale yellow, the other, a lavender floral — showed up at our broken-down trailer with a plate of cookies and bags from the local Jumbo Mart. Beaming, they proceeded to unload bag after bag of dented cans of generic pork 'n' beans, ravioli, corned beef hash, lima beans, and the canned ham with the key that I always loved to turn to open.

I haven't been able to eat lima beans since.

They saved the best for last. At least that's what they told me. Giddy and giggling, the pastel ladies jointly reached into another bag and with a triumphant flourish pulled out a fancy pink-and-white striped dress trimmed with ruffles and lace and a great big bow that tied in the back.

Welcome to my nightmare.

It had only just begun. Next, they pulled out a pair of white tights and brand-spanking-new shiny white patent-leather shoes, which they insisted I put on then and there.

Preferring my worn Keds or bare feet, I protested, but Earlene put on her gushy voice dripping with sweetness and goo. "Oh sweetie, you'll look like a little angel in that beautiful new dress. Go on now, put it on so Mama can see her pretty little angel."

The sweetness didn't extend to her eyes.

She gave me the look. The do-what-I-say-or-you'll-get-a-whipping-once-they're-gone look. I'm not sure what was worse, the whipping, or the frou-frou dress. But since Earlene was a wild whacker with the wooden spoon, I went for the frou-frou.

Yanking on the white tights over my dirty, scratched legs, I winced as they came into contact with my scabby knees. Maybe, if I was lucky, I'd bleed on the new tights, rendering them unwearable.

No such luck.

I pulled the dress over my head, and Earlene zipped me up and tied the big bow as I shoved my feet into the too-tight shoes, feeling like one of Cinderella's ugly stepsisters.

"Why, she looks as pretty as a picture," lavender lady gushed.

"You're just a little doll," cooed yellow lady, pinching my cheek.

I tugged at the scratchy lace collar and turned to look in the mirror. A deranged Holly Hobbie glared back at me.

"Thank the ladies for your pretty new outfit." Earlene put her arm around my shoulder and pinched me on my shoulder blade where they couldn't see.

I flinched. "Thank you."

My bio-mom hugged me to her in an artificial display of maternal love and gushed, "We can't thank you enough for your generosity. That was so sweet of you," all the while trying to usher the pastel ladies out the door.

"Wait, we have a little something for you too, honey." Lavender lady reached into a final bag and pulled out a mint-green, high-necked polyester blend dress with a white Peter Pan collar. She held it out to Earlene, beaming.

"Oh, you shouldn't have," Earlene said.

"Hold it up in front of you," yellow lady urged. "We thought that color would be perfect with your complexion."

Earlene gave them a sickly smile and held up the dress against her shoulders.

"It's perfect," lavender lady said. "And just the right length too."

The dress that skimmed Earlene's calves was the longest hemline to ever cross our trailer doorstep.

At church on Sunday, with both of us decked out in the dreaded new dresses, the pastor had Earlene and me stand up to show the good people of the congregation the results of their largesse.

Applause and scattered "Praise the Lords!" sounded throughout the little country church while I burned with humiliation.

Thankfully, we weren't there long.

Pretty soon Earlene had met a new man and we were on the road again. As we sped down the highway, she'd crank up that Willie Nelson song and sing along at the top of her lungs, eager to start her new adventure with her new man in a new town.

Enjoying her free-spirited style, the new man would usually sing along lustily. But a year or two would pass, and new guy would grow tired of her drunken binges, jealous rages, and having to be dad to a kid that wasn't his. Sooner or later he'd leave too, and before long, we'd be broke again.

Earlene could never hold a job. Her bosses grew tired of her showing up to work drunk or calling in sick when she was hung over. She'd get fired and collect unemployment for a while, but when that ran out, we'd go on the dole that had nothing to do with pineapples.

The government dole. Welfare. Earlene's favorite job.

Then she didn't have to go to work at all and could stay home and drink all day. Of course that wasn't the sob story she'd tell the church. Earlene would always play the victim role, crying how she'd unfairly lost her job or her man to a younger piece of eye candy, and her with a little girl to support. She'd drag me along by my scrawny wrist as her pathetic single-mom prop and beat her push up breasts at the injustice of it all.

We'd replay our drama with Earlene in the starring role. "What am I going to do? How am I going to take care of my little angel?" she'd wail, perfecting her performance.

"You know what you need, sister?" the reverend would say. "You need the Lord!" A slight variation on the theme.

And improvising on cue, Earlene became born again.

And again.

And again.

Guess it didn't take the first time.

Then the church would throw open its food closet doors and publicly pat themselves on the backs at how they helped out the poor and unfortunate.

Us.

I haven't been poor and unfortunate in a long time. And I determined at an early age to never play the victim card. I'm not into navel gazing.

So I grew up in a dysfunctional family? So what? Who didn't?

The Brady Bunch. Yet even then, Marcia, Marcia, Marcia, came out with that sizzling memoir full of sex and drugs.

As far as I'm concerned, the past is the past. I'm all about the present. And the future.

Wonder what my future will bring?

8

Before they went to bed, Francie and Neeley had to read a page of the Bible and a page from Shakespeare. That was a rule. Mama used to read the two pages to them each night until they were old enough to read for themselves. To save time, Neeley read the Bible page and Francie read from Shakespeare.

A Tree Grows in Brooklyn

What's up with all the raised hands?

I looked around the auditorium that looks like no church I've ever seen. No pews, no stained glass, no organ, not even a wooden cross up front. Just rows of padded folding chairs, a band onstage, and a big movie screen with words on it.

And lots of raised hands. Do they have to ask permission to go to the bathroom or something?

Yes, I'm in a house of worship. I swore I'd never darken the doors of a church again after my childhood experiences, but thanks to Ben and my stupid bet, here I am.

As I was getting ready this morning, my fashionista

roommate, who was thrilled that I was at long last going to church, but tried hard not to show it, offered style advice. "Why don't you wear that cute blue skirt I got you for your birthday?" Kailyn suggested. "I have a white top that would look darling with it."

Darling? Not a word in my vocabulary. And definitely not a fashion choice.

"No thanks. I'm just going to wear my black skirt and a black T-shirt." I'd rather have worn my black jeans, but I didn't feel like cutting the one leg to accommodate my cast, so I was stuck with the skirt. I'd initially planned to wear my red tee, but decided if I had to darken the church doors, I might as well wear the appropriate color.

Kailyn, clad in a banana-colored sundress and matching sandals with a cutesy daisy in the center, lifted her eyes to my now-purple hair which I'd had Annie come over and color last night. "Are you going Goth?"

"No. I just thought my red T-shirt would clash with my hair, so I decided to go for something a little more subdued."

"If that's subdued, then Cher is Amish." She glanced at my hair again, which I'd spiked even more in honor of church. "Speaking of Cher … have you ever thought of going the wig route instead of dyeing your hair every few weeks?"

"Nah. Wigs itch. Besides, they're so fake. I'm more a natural girl."

"Right. Most natural types I know dye their hair regularly." She seemed to stare at my hair a bit too long before she picked up her pink Bible and purse. "Well, I need to run pick up the muffins for Sunday school class. Have a good time."

"You too. Maybe we can compare church notes afterward," I snarked.

"Anytime." Her face got all serious and intent. "Just let me know." She click-clacked away in her daisy sandals.

With all the Christians in our book club, I figured they'd all go to the same place on their Sunday morning God dates. But I was wrong. Each went her own way: Presbyterian, Episcopalian, Catholic, Baptist, Nazarene. I needed a GPS to figure it out.

And something called emerging, I think Annie said. Whatever that means.

Who knew there were so many different kinds of churches? Ben's church, Creekside Calvary, where I'm sitting now, is called "nondenominational."

I sneaked a look over at my date. His hands were up and his eyes closed as he sang.

Interesting anthropological ritual. Although not one I cared to try.

I kept my hands close to my sides. And while everyone else was swaying to the music that resembled a Kenny G concert, I surreptitiously scoped out the congregation. As expected, there were a few Stepford wives and some Italian leather, but not a lot. It was, however, pretty white. I spotted a few Asian faces in the crowd, no African Americans, and only one Hispanic — an elderly, apparently God-fearing woman who frowned at my inattention. Quickly, I swiveled my gaze back to the front and locked eyes with the fortyish pastor.

Uh-oh. I'm in for it now.

The mellow lead singer strummed a final chord on his guitar and as the preacher strode to the podium, I slunk down in my chair, steeling myself for the fire and brimstone you're-going-to-hell sermon like the ones I heard as a kid. The pastor shone a beatific smile at the crowd and quietly said, "Let us pray." Then, in a soft, soothing voice that sounded like he was telling a bedtime story rather than getting his flock all fired up, he began, "Father ..."

I tuned out. So not my thing, the patriarchal bit.

Instead, I started daydreaming about Machu Picchu, mountain climbing, and Africa. I recalled the line from *The Snows of Kilimanjaro*, "And there was never another time like that first time in Africa." And I longed for *my* first time in Africa and the chance to see Kilimanjaro's summit, "wide as all the world, great, high, and unbelievably white in the sun."

That song about Kilimanjaro rising above the Serengeti filled my head, and my mind wandered to Hemingway, Isak Dinesen, and her farm in Africa ...

Pretty soon my eyelids began to feel heavy. This getting up early on a Sunday was so out of my sleep comfort zone. Good thing they were praying. One more bent head wouldn't be noticed.

"Good morning, church!" a new voice boomed out, jerking me awake.

So much for not being noticed.

I focused on the stage, where an enthusiastic white-haired guy in a Hawaiian shirt, jeans, and high-tops was having an ADD attack. This dude, who was easily past sixty, just couldn't keep still. He bounced and weaved all over the place like the Energizer bunny.

Or Robin Williams on speed.

Someone must have taken an extra dose of their Centrum Silver this morning.

The congregation murmured back a good morning, and even from my seat way in the back I could see his eyebrows rise. The jumbo screen helped.

He tried again. "Good morning, church!" he boomed.

Definitely Robin Williams.

"Good morning!" they shouted back.

"That's better. I thought maybe you were all still sleeping."

I wish I was.

The crowd chuckled.

"But why would you want to be asleep on this glorious day that the Lord has made? Let us rejoice and be glad in it."

Scattered "Amens!" broke out around the audience.

"Let's give the Lord a hand!"

Doesn't he already have one?

Applause thundered through the auditorium.

Clapping for Jesus? Wonder how the J-man feels about that?

The enthusiastic white-haired dude — whom Ben whispered to me is Henry, the associate pastor — then proceeded to deliver a litany of announcements and platitudes to which I tuned out. Finally he passed the preaching baton back to Pastor Jeff, the guy with the bedtime story voice who beamed at the crowd and began talking about brotherly love.

As he droned on about loving thy neighbor, I returned to my adventure daydreams. Maybe next summer I could convince the Getaway Girls to take a trip to Machu Picchu. If we started saving now, we could probably afford it.

Can you see Annette and Kailyn schlepping around some ancient Incan ruins, my inner wet blanket says. Or Chloe? Remember, hiking's involved. Besides, Chloe will probably be pregnant anyway.

Africa, then.

Yeah right. Isn't that a little too exotic for your girly roommate? Besides, Africa's a big continent. Where exactly?

Anywhere. Kenya. Rwanda. Maybe Ethiopia. I can ask Ben about it.

Ben. I slid a glance at him and saw that he was absorbed in his paperback Bible, highlighting words in yellow. I looked to my other side where a middle-aged woman was highlighting words in orange. Noticing I didn't have a Bible, she offered me her heavy, hardbound one so I could follow along.

Shaking my head, I mouthed the words "That's okay,"

making sure to include a friendly smile so she wouldn't think I was dissin' her. When she smiled back and returned to her highlighting, I pulled out my black pen and began doodling on the church bulletin.

Until all at once I realized the minister was talking to me.

"Some of you may not usually attend church, or have never been to church before," he said. "You're only here because someone's dragged you, kicking and screaming."

Ben slid me a small smile. At least he didn't turn in his seat.

Polka dots of sweat broke out on my forehead as I flashed back to those childhood churches where the preacher made us "Come on down!" before God and the entire curious congregation.

"Well, don't worry," the reverend said. "We're not going to make you come onstage and confess all your sins." He paused. "We save that for your second time."

Ba-dum-bum.

The crowd laughed.

"Seriously. We're glad you're here," he continued. "Welcome. We'd love to get to know you better, so please fill out the welcome card in your bulletin and put it in the offering basket when it comes around. We promise no insurance salesman or Amway folks will come to your door and sign you up."

The crowd laughed again.

Stand-up comedy? In church? Who knew? He's no Seinfeld, but then Seinfeld's Jewish, and I doubt this guy's ever had a Matzo ball. Or even corned beef on rye. Strictly white bread all the way.

But no way was I filling out a welcome card. Sure, no Amway dudes would show up, but someone would. Or at least call. It's all about the follow-up. Memories of the pastel ladies flashed before my eyes.

The white-bread Jerry wrapped things up with another Father prayer and then the band returned to the stage and ended the show with a "We Will Rock You"—type anthem. Except the lyrics included repeated utterances of "God" and "awesome" instead.

As we stood to leave, the woman beside me who'd earlier offered me her Bible flung her arms around me and pulled me close in a Yogi Bear hug. "Have a blessed day," she chirped in my ear.

For the first time in my Dr. Who—loving life, I wished I could be one of the dreaded Daleks, rasping out in that evil, electronic voice, "Exterminate!"

Finally Yogi released me and gave a small wave to Ben behind me as she left. "God bless you," she sang out.

"I didn't hear you sneeze," I muttered, folding my arms in front of my chest.

The corners of Ben's lips curved up.

"You should have warned me," I said. "I'd have brought my no-hugging sign."

His eyes shifted to my crossed arms. "You did."

Ben passed me my crutches and as we left the auditorium, there was a hug crush at the double doors as one person after another embraced the beaming men of God who stood on either side — the Hawaiian-shirted Henry and the Seinfeld wannabe.

"Great sermon today, Pastor."

"You really nailed it, brother! Keep up the good work."

"Good message. One I really needed to hear today."

Blah, blah, blah.

At last it was our turn.

Thankfully, ADD Henry is busy bouncing amongst a family of four, so we got the main man instead.

"Hey, Jeff." Ben did the church clinch thing.

I'd never seen so much hugging in one place. Or between guys.

Ben gave his pastor pal two brisk back slaps before they released. "How's it goin', brother? Did you play a little Guitar Hero last night?"

"Oh yeah." He riffed on an air guitar. "I really rocked out to some Metallica. You need to get online and see who wins ..."

Metallica? So. Maybe not so white bread after all.

"Dude, I kicked your butt last time," Ben said. "You sure you want to go there again?"

"I'll take my chances." He smiled at me. "And who's this? And how did you break your leg?"

"Sorry," Ben said. "This is my friend Becca, and she broke her ankle skydiving. Becca, this is our pastor, Jeff."

I gripped my crutches tighter and steeled myself for another hug.

"Hi, Becca." He lightly touched my hand in greeting and I breathed a sigh of relief. "Are you one of Ben's missionary friends?"

"Me?" I snorted. "Not likely."

"Sometimes God uses the most unlikely people," he said with a smile.

I started to say something else, but remembered I was in church, so just smiled back instead.

Ben and I headed outside with the masses, and everyone milled around a coffee bar in the courtyard where two teenaged baristas were whipping up lattes, mochas, and hot chocolates. "Would you like a coffee?" he asked.

"I'd sell my soul for a latte."

His left eyebrow lifted, but before he could respond, a high-pitched voice squealed, "Ben!" Out of the corner of my eye, I saw an orange blur fling herself at him.

A wide smile creased Ben's face as he enfolded the blur in his arms. "Luce! I thought you were in Arizona."

The blur turned out to be a beaming chubby chick about my age with a dandelion fluff ball of hair. She wore a tentlike orange dress and clunky black clogs.

Quick, Charlie Brown, tell Linus the Great Pumpkin has escaped.

"I got back late last night," pumpkin-girl continued. "I was going to call, but I didn't want to wake your grandmother."

"Thanks. She tells me she needs her beauty sleep these days." He released her and turned to me. "Becca, this is my friend Lucy; Luce, this is Becca."

"Hi, Becca," Lucy warbled. And before I could drop my crutches and cross my arms, she attacked me with an enthusiastic hug. "Welcome! It's so great you came, especially today of all days."

"Why's that?" I stiffened and shifted a little to extricate myself from her perky orange clutches.

"I'm sorry." She pulled back, her eyes filled with dismay as she glanced at my cast. "Did I hurt you?"

"Nah. I'm good." Especially now that you're not hugging me anymore.

"Oh, praise God. You'll have to excuse me. Sometimes I just don't think." She gave me a goofy grin. "But I'm so glad you came today of all days—it's the last chance to sign up for the women's retreat. You almost missed it."

I snorted.

Lucy's perkiness was replaced by a look of puzzlement. Ben just smiled.

"Sorry," I said. "Allergies."

"Oh, aren't they just the worst? I have them too. I practically live on Sudafed. Would you like one?" She rummaged in a large brown purse. "Otherwise I have some echinacea in here somewhere." At last she pulled out a container that she extended to me with a flourish. "Here you go."

Noticing my bemused expression, she glanced down at her hand and giggled. "Oops. Those are Tic-Tacs."

Talk about eternal sunshine of the empty mind.

One thing's for sure: This Lucy's nothing like Charlie Brown's cartoon nemesis.

"How did you break your leg, Becca?" she asked.

"Skydiving."

"You're kidding! Wow are you brave. I could never go sky-diving. I'd be afraid my chute wouldn't open or I'd break my leg or something." Then she realized what she'd said and burst out laughing.

A few people walked up and Ben introduced me to more of his friends—mostly twenty and thirtysomethings. And all women.

He's obviously a chick magnet. Which is a little strange. Yeah, he's cute, but he's no Johnny Depp. And then I recalled Kailyn's oft-repeated refrain that single men are at a premium in Christendom.

I did a preliminary scan of the perimeter, and it looked like she was right. The women way out-populated the men. And naturally these women all wanted to know how I broke my leg. I was tempted to put a sign around my neck that read: *Broke my leg skydiving.*

Another happy church girl, this one in a Sarah Palin red power suit and pearls whom Ben introduced as Stepford woman, I mean Mindy, joined the group.

"Are you coming to the potluck Tuesday, Ben?" she asked.

"Depends … Are you bringing your famous chicken enchiladas?"

"Of course."

"Then count me in. I'll bring the chips and salsa."

Mindy's gaze slid to me, lingering on my hair. She gave me a nod and a small smile, and then turned the full force of her charm on Ben. "Why don't you bring your friend too?"

"Becca? Would you like to go?" Surreptitiously Ben flashed the number two with his fingers. And then again. Twenty-two. Only twenty-two dates to go.

I gave him a sweet smile. "Sure. Sounds fun. I'm always up for good grub."

"Great!" Mindy said. Although I could tell she didn't mean it. "What would you like to make?"

"Oh, I don't cook. But I could bring more chips. Or margarita mix, if you need drinks."

Perky Lucy, standing beside her, paled.

"Chips will be plenty," Mindy said with a bright smile. "We've already got the drinks covered."

"Well … if you're sure. I want to do my part."

"I'm sure. But thanks."

Ben handed me my latte, which I inhaled, and we all stood around chatting for a few minutes until a middle-aged guy with a plastic nametag that said *usher* hurried over and told Ben he needed some help.

"Excuse me," Ben said, "duty calls. I shouldn't be long." He glanced at me. "Will you be okay, Becca?"

"No worries."

Dude, I've gone skydiving, mountain climbing, backpacking in the extreme wilderness, and scuba diving. I think I can handle a little churchyard chat.

He followed the usher dude inside and I resumed conversation with Mindy, Lucy, and the rest of Ben's church chick posse. "Have any of you seen the latest slasher flick?" I asked. "It's a little bloody, but has some great action scenes. Especially when that demon-possessed guy is running after the priest with a chainsaw."

As expected, I cleared the courtyard.

I glanced at my watch. And in only thirty seconds too.

When I looked back up, I saw a guy with greasy hair and acne approach wearing striped high-water pants and an avocado-green polyester shirt. So not quite clear.

He held out his hand and stretched his mouth into the semblance of a smile, revealing an overbite. "Hi. I'm Lewis. I haven't seen you before."

Poor guy. Someone needed to introduce him to Scope and a better thrift store.

Lewis's bad breath almost knocked me over, but as a former refugee from the high-water pants closet myself, I smiled and shook his sweaty hand. "I'm Becca. And you haven't seen me before because this is my first time here."

I started to withdraw my hand from his, but he gripped my hand even tighter and fixed me with a penetrating stare. "Have you been washed in the blood of the Lamb?"

"No. I'm sort of a vegetarian."

"Do you know Jesus?" His stare became even more penetrating as he crushed my hand in his.

Man, this dude's really intense.

I tried to lighten the mood. "Guy with long hair and sandals? Turned the water to wine? Sure."

"The Lord will not be mocked!" He loomed over me.

Great. The one day I leave the pepper spray at home. Who knew I'd need it at church?

I looked around for Ben. Nothing like leading a lamb to the slaughter. Bet or no bet, I so did not sign up for this. I took a deep breath and prepared to yank my hand free from psycho polyester guy and kick him where the sun don't shine. With my casted leg, of course.

"Lewis!" Ben appeared behind him and clapped him on the shoulder, causing the budding Norman Bates to drop my hand. "How's it going, brother?" He embraced him and did the standard male double-pat-on-the-back thing.

These people will hug anyone.

"Hey, Becca, can you give us a few minutes?" Ben asked as his psycho pal stared at me and mumbled something about the TV show *Lost*.

"No prob. Take your time."

All the time you need. Just keep Norman away. Far away.

I crutched over to a bench that backed up to a high wall of shrubbery where I could extend my cast with no fear of someone tripping over it. I closed my eyes, willing myself to relax, and leaning back, I tilted my face to the sun. Might as well catch some Z's while I waited.

Only I started hearing voices. And on my first visit to church too. Feminine voices.

"Did you see that girl Ben brought to church today?"

"The one with the purple hair?"

"And the cast?"

"And the Goth outfit?"

"How could you miss her?"

I smiled to myself.

"What was he *thinking*?"

"Oh, Ben's always taking in strays," said a voice I recognized. Mindy.

Strays? Not on your life, Mindy-Lou.

"It's the missionary in him," one of them said.

"But missionary dating is not from the Lord. Ben better watch out he doesn't find himself unequally yoked."

Yolked? Personally, I like my eggs scrambled.

"I know. We should pray for him. And her too. Can you believe she watches those horrible slasher movies? Clearly she doesn't know the Lord."

"That's for sure. If Ben's not careful, she could cause him to stumble."

What do you mean? He hasn't tripped over my cast once.

"That's right. And none of us wants to see our brother backslide, do we?"

"Ben's not going to backslide," a high-pitched voice I recognized as Lucy's said. "He's strong in the Lord. And besides, I liked Becca. And her hair. I wish I was brave enough to dye mine." She giggled. "But I'd just look like Barney the dinosaur on a bad hair day. And remember, God looks at the inside, not the outside. I don't know about you, but with this body of mine, I'm grateful for that." She giggled again and I heard a light rustling sound. "Well, I'd better go get the sign-up sheet for the retreat. I'm so glad you're all coming. We'll have such a great time of prayer and fellowship. Bye. I'll see you later."

I heard her clump away in her clogs.

"Well, I feel convicted," one of the voices said.

"Me too."

And me? I'm thinking I always did have a soft spot for Barney the dinosaur. Except for that cheesy "I Love You" song he sang.

9

This was the summer when for a long time she had
not been a member. She belonged to no club and was a
member of nothing in the world. Frankie had become an
unjoined person who hung around in the doorways, and
she was afraid.

The Member of the Wedding

"So how was it?" Kailyn asked when I limped through the
front door.

"Interesting ..." I power-crutched my way over to the
couch and eased myself down onto it. By the time I'm done
with these crutch workouts, my arms will look like Madonna's.

Scary.

Kailyn's eyes gleamed. "Was it a good sermon?"

"Oh, I didn't pay attention to the sermon." I plopped a
couch pillow onto the coffee table and lowered my cast onto it.
"I'm talking about the stuff after."

Annie, who usually hangs out with us on Sunday after-
noons, emerged from the bathroom in jeans and a T-shirt that

proclaimed *Jesus loves me and my tattoos.* "Hey, Bec, how's it goin'? How was church?"

Kailyn responded before I had a chance. "She said it was interesting—although not the sermon. The *stuff after.*"

"Ah. The fellowship."

"Fellowship?"

"Talking. Socializing. Sharing." Annie helped herself to a Diet Sprite from the fridge. She popped it open and took a big gulp.

"There was plenty of sharing," I said. "Although much of it was in a foreign language. What the hell does backsliding mean? And some kind of egg yolks that aren't the same size?"

Annie sprayed soda out her nose and Kailyn yelped with laughter.

"What? What'd I say?"

They continued to laugh.

"What? Anybody? Anybody? Bueller?"

"It's yoked: y-o-k-e-d," Kailyn spelled out, "not yolked. Unequally yoked."

"And that means what exactly?"

"That a Christian shouldn't be yoked together with—or married to—an unbeliever," Annie said as she wiped up the Sprite-spattered floor.

"*Marriage?* Serious?" I stared at her. "Who said anything about marriage? This was just a date. And not even a romantic one. You know how I feel about the institution of marriage."

She lifted her shoulders. "I'm just sayin'."

"It's from biblical times," Kailyn explained. "A yoke was this thing that joined two animals together at the neck so they could plow the fields together."

"Thanks, Webster. I know what a yoke is. And no one's going to be putting one around my neck anytime soon."

As in ever.

"Usually it referred to oxen," Annie said, "but the Bible also talks about not plowing with an ox and a donkey."

"Why do I get the feeling I'm the donkey in this illustration?"

"Or as it says in the King James," Kailyn chimed in, "the ass."

"Figures."

I'm beginning to think I was a jackass to ever take this bet. Clearly Ben has an ulterior motive for going along with it. Maybe he's trying to add another born-again notch on his missionary belt. Or maybe Christians have merit badges like the Boy Scouts. How many do they get for another soul saved? Could it be that whole pyramid scheme thing? I've heard lots of Christians are big into Amway.

I'm so not buying any soap.

"And backsliding? Translation, please."

"Ooh, backsliding is bad," Kailyn said. "It means to fall away from the faith and back into sin and eventually, to abandon your Christian faith altogether."

"It's not that harsh. Backsliding is more like sliding or slipping back into old ways or bad habits that you had before you became a Christian," Annie explained.

"Like what, for instance? Smoking? Swearing? Sleeping around?"

"Depends on the person. It's different for everyone. Whatever pulls them away from God and their walk with him."

"Their walk? Where are they walking to?"

"Sorry," Annie said. "More Christianese. A walk with God means your daily life with God—applying your beliefs into your everyday life."

"This Christianese stuff is a whole other language. And my limited French and Spanish is no help at all. You really need a translation or some kind of guide."

"That's a great idea!" Annie said. "We should make up a guide—like one of those Idiots guides: *The Idiot's Guide to Christianese.*"

"Who are you calling an idiot?"

"Only in love, my friend. Only in love."

"Well, *I* think we should call it *The Getaway Girls Guide to Christianese.* That sounds a lot nicer." Kailyn grabbed a pad of paper and started writing. "Let's see, we've already got fellowship, unequally yoked, backsliding, and the Christian walk. What else?"

Annie ticked off on her fingers. "Convicted, causing someone to stumble—"

"Hey, what's that last one mean? I heard that today too."

"It's like doing something that will make someone stumble off the straight path," Kailyn said.

"I thought that was backsliding."

"Making someone stumble is more like doing something that will tempt someone into something they shouldn't do or that they struggle with," Annie said. "Like serving wine at dinner when one of your guests is an alcoholic."

"Yeah, or having a serious make-out session in front of a bunch of singles who are trying to do the celibate thing," Kailyn said.

The celibate thing was something my roommate and I had discussed before. Chloe too. But that whole waiting-for-marriage bit was too out there for me. Especially since I didn't plan to ever make that long white walk down the aisle.

"All right, I've got stumbling down now." I lifted up my cast and positioned it more comfortably on the pillow. "You guys definitely need to make up that guide. Then I can just flip through it as needed during the Ben dating experiment."

"And you can help us with it too, Bec," Annie said. "Every time you come home from one of these church dates, just write down the words you don't know and we'll add them to the guide."

"Deal. Now, can we stop with all the Christian stuff already and watch a movie?"

"How about *The Ten Commandments?*" Annie's mouth curved upwards into an impish grin.

"You read my mind. But why stop there? Let's make it a Charlton Heston double feature and watch *Ben-Hur* too. You know how I like my action flicks."

Kailyn jumped up and headed to the DVD tower, where she started flipping through the Bs. Yes, she's organized our DVDs alphabetically. She can also be a little literal sometimes.

"Stay in the Bs, but skip right past *Ben-Hur*," I instructed. "If we're going to do a movie marathon, I want the Bourne trilogy instead."

"Not again," Kailyn said. "I mean, Matt Damon's really got the tortured-amnesiac-assassin-thing down, but I can't handle all that violence. How about something more peaceful? Like *Howard's End?*"

"Ennhh." I made the annoying *Jeopardy* buzzer sound. "Pick another category. Boring, talky English films not allowed. Although ... if you want something English that's not boring, I have just the thing."

Kailyn made a face. "I'm not watching *Dr. Who*. You know I don't like sci-fi. Too confusing."

"But so exciting." I stared off into space. "What I wouldn't give to be one of the Doctor's traveling companions in the Tardis. Flying through space to other universes. Meeting cool aliens. Fighting Daleks. Saving the world."

"Daleks?" Kailyn furrowed her brow. "I think we're going to need another guide: *The Getaway Girls Guide to Sci-Fi*."

I really don't see anything romantic in proposing. It is
very romantic to be in love. But there is nothing romantic
about a definite proposal. Why, one may be accepted.

The Importance of Being Earnest

Monday night I tagged along with Kailyn to her *Earnest*
rehearsal. I'm no theater geek, but she wanted me along for
moral support. She was seriously crushing on Drew, the actor
who played her love interest Ernest, but she couldn't tell if he
was crushing on her, so she wanted me to apply my astute pow-
ers of observation and see what I thought.

Yeah, right. Like I'm the big relationship expert. The longest relationship I've ever had with a guy is my current one with
Ben. And that's not even a relationship. Just a bet. Oh well.
Guess it goes along with the roommate territory. Especially
since Kailyn's been playing chauffeur for me for the past several weeks.

I owed her.

Just as long as she doesn't ask me to pass him a note.

After helping me get settled into a seat in the front row where I could stretch out my leg, Kailyn hurried onstage where a cluster of people were milling about.

"Cecily!" A Hugh Grant type replete with the requisite floppy hair enfolded Kailyn in his arms in a welcoming hug.

"Ernest!" She returned the hug and pointed to his back—now facing me—and mouthed the name *Drew*.

Good thing, because in the next moment another good-looking guy strode up to the embracing duo and said, *"I'm Ernest."*

I'd never read the famous period play and had only gone through bits and pieces with Kailyn as she ran her lines, but she said the Oscar Wilde comedy revolved around two men—Jack and Algernon—who use the deception that both their names are Ernest in order to marry the women they love.

O-kaaaay …

"Let's get started, everyone," a female voice called out, who I assumed was Stella, the director. Kailyn had told me she was good, although not lavish with the praise.

For the next two hours I alternately laughed and snorted at the hilarious plot twists and witty repartee. Guess I'll have to revise my opinion about talky English productions. Killer dialogue. And killer Kailyn too. My Barbie-doll roommate was a revelation.

I looked at her with new eyes as rehearsal ended.

"Well, what do you think?" she asked as we were driving home.

"I loved it."

"Not the production—although I'm glad you liked it—but Drew. Do you think he's interested in me?"

Oops. "My bad. I was so caught up in the play, I forgot to watch for that."

"Becca!"

"Sorry. You were great though—the best one onstage."

"Really?"

"Oh, yeah. You rocked. You should be doing this full-time."

"I wish. But it's too hard to earn a living as an actor. Impossible, really."

"You sound like my writer friend, Margaret. She says the same thing about being an author."

"See what I mean?" Kailyn said. "It's tough making a living as an artist."

"But you haven't even tried. And there's a big difference: Margaret's sixty-four; you're twenty-four."

"I'm just being practical."

"Practical is for old folks, not us. We're supposed to follow our dreams when we're young." I was speaking to myself as well as to Kailyn. I just wasn't sure exactly what my dreams were—besides traveling.

"But I want to get married."

"To whom?"

"I don't know. Someone. Unlike you, I've always wanted to get married and have kids and the whole happily-ever-after thing. Like my folks."

So not for me. I plan to make my own happily-ever-after. But Kailyn's not me. In any way, shape, or form.

"So who says you can't?" I asked. "But isn't that supposed to happen naturally? And why be in such a rush, anyway? You're not even twenty-five."

"Now you sound like my singles Sunday school teacher."

"Not in a million years."

"No, really." Kailyn gave me a thoughtful look. "She keeps telling us to trust God and let him provide our mates in his time."

"And I said that *when* exactly? I'm pretty sure the word *mate* has never passed these lips."

"Sorry." She giggled. "That's another Christianese expression. Quick, mark it down before we forget."

I jotted *mate* on a gum wrapper and tucked it into her purse as she pulled into the driveway.

As she removed the keys from the ignition, Kailyn turned to me with a pensive expression on her face. "I wonder if God is using you to tell me something."

"That'll be the day."

Tuesday was busy at work, with a storybook time and a signing by a popular children's author. As a result, the place was crawling with rug rats. They were coming out of the woodwork—and writing on it too.

I removed a red marker from a budding Picasso's hand scribbling on the oak baseboard. "No, no." I smiled and put on my best kid-friendly voice. "We don't write on the walls or the floor. Just the paper, please."

He wailed and began kicking the floor, narrowly missing my cast.

A fortyish woman with perfect hair hurried over, latte in hand. "What's wrong, Evan?"

"She took my marker." He pointed at me, hiccupping through his tears.

"I'll thank you not to discipline my child," she said.

Well, then, watch your kid, lady, or don't bring him out in public if he doesn't know how to behave.

But of course I didn't say that. The customer's always right, Alastair had drilled into me. Instead, I pasted on a rueful smile, nodded to the baseboards, and in my best woman-to-woman-we're-in-this-together-housecleaning voice asked, "Do you know what will remove marker from wood?"

All the while trying not to choke on the domestic words.

"Evan! What has Mommy told you about writing on

walls? You know that's a no-no. Someone needs a time-out."
And she led away her wailing bratspring as he howled anew.

I can't believe people actually want children. I'm with
Scarlett O'Hara on that one. Although *mealymouthed* is no longer a word much in circulation, *brat* still is, and as far as I'm
concerned, that's what most kids are. Along with:

Noisy.

Needy.

Spoiled.

Snot-nosed.

Disruptive.

Besides, the world's already too overpopulated, with barely
enough resources to go around. Why add more people to the
mix? Especially screaming, bratty ones.

No thanks. Not for this chick.

At a display table a few feet away a little girl with a
chocolate-smeared face greedily eyed the deluxe hardcover
version of *The House at Pooh Corner*. Power-hobbling my way
over, I managed to snatch the expensive edition out of reach of
her sticky hands before they closed around it.

The little darling's eyes pierced me with hot fury, her face
turned a mottled red, and she began to bawl. Her mother hurried over and scooped her up, making soothing noises. And
I blew out my breath in relief, cradling the book in a way I'd
never cradle a baby.

Cross my heart and hope to croak first.

Just the thought of all that burping, throwing up, and
pooping? The book in my grip is all the Pooh I can handle.

"So, Becca, do you want to get married?" Ben asked on the way
to the potluck a couple hours later.

I choked on my gum. "What?"

"Do you want to get married?" he repeated.

"No! I hardly know you."

And we haven't even kissed. Or anything.

He laughed. "It wasn't a proposal. I just meant in general: Do you want to get married someday?"

"No. Not interested."

"What about kids? Do you want any?"

"Nope. Although I wouldn't mind a dog."

Ben slid me a speculative look. "So, I'm guessing your folks didn't have the best marriage?"

"Give that man a cigar."

"What about brothers and sisters?"

"What about them?"

"Did you have any?"

"Nope."

"I knew we had something in common besides the broken leg and the daredevil streak," he said. "I'm an only child too."

Oh great, we're bonding now. What's next, the *Mamma Mia* sing-along?

Before he could go all Pierce Brosnan on me, I sent out an SOS. "You sure you want to continue with this dating bet?"

"Yes. Why?"

"I wouldn't want you to get in trouble with your church or anything. Seems some people don't like the idea of your *missionary* dating."

"Some people should lighten up," he said. "And mind their own business."

"Agreed. And that goes for you too, bucko. I'm not your latest missionary project."

"I never said you were."

"But you thought it. You're still thinking it. I can tell."

"Wow. I didn't know you were a mind reader. Guess I'll have to be more careful with my thoughts." His tone turned reflective. "Actually, I don't know what God has in mind; I'm just trying to listen to him."

"What? Are you saying God told you to date me?"

"That would be a yes."

He drove another block and then turned left past a strip mall.

"Was there a burning bush too?" I asked.

"Someone knows her Bible."

"Just *The Ten Commandments*. So ... when God spoke to you, was his voice full of thunder and lightning like when he talked to Charlton Heston? Or was it more like James Earl Jones?"

"Neither. His voice is a still, small voice." Ben murmured, "'God whispers to us in our pleasures, speaks to us in our conscience, but shouts in our pains: It is his megaphone to rouse a deaf world.'"

"Save your C. S. Lewis for Sunday school."

"You've read Lewis? And still you're not a Christian?"

"I've read Tolkien too and I'm still not a hobbit either." I glanced down at my cast poking out of my faded, holey jeans. "A hobbler, maybe, but not a hobbit."

"Ba-dum-bum."

Ben pulled into the church parking lot and found a parking space close to the building. He didn't say so, but I could tell he was making allowances for my cast.

"Am I going to get stoned for not wearing a denim jumper to this thing?"

"Nah, this is a singles potluck, not a home-schooling one."

Two points. Score one for the Christian.

We entered the church gym—another surprise; pumping iron for Jesus—and my nostrils were assailed by the aromas of the food of the gods: Mexican.

It was all I could do not to swoon off my crutches. You can

keep your fancy French food and your New American cuisine of pan-seared Chilean sea bass with a plum reduction sauce or whatever. Just give me some enchiladas or nachos and I'm good.

As we approached the food tables, I could almost hear them groaning under the weight of all those carbs. In addition to Mindy's famous chicken enchiladas, which Ben made a beeline to, there were cheese enchiladas, refried beans and rice, tamales, taquitos, nachos, and every kind of taco imaginable: soft, crunchy, beef, chicken, steak, or fish. Ben parked our blue corn chips and Trader Joe's hot-and-spicy salsa offering next to the ubiquitous seven-layer dip that he informed me was essential to every church singles gathering.

"Becca! Ben!" Lucy's high-pitched voice echoed across the cavernous gym. She bounded over to us in her black clogs, stretch jeans, and polka-dotted tunic, beaming so wide the shine off her teeth nearly blinded me. "I'm so glad you made it! Come on over—I saved you places."

I didn't think it was possible for anyone to register higher on the perk factor scale than Kailyn. But next to Lucy, Kailyn was downright catatonic.

Lucy led us over to a large round table with five other women, including Mindy, and one guy—thankfully, not my Norman Bates run-in of the other day. This dude was middle-aged with graying hair scraped back into a ponytail.

"Everyone, this is Becca," she chirped. "Becca, you met Mindy, Cindy, and Kym at church on Sunday. And this is Char, Leanne, and Donald."

"Not to be confused with Trump," the aging hippie type said. "Although a lot of people make that mistake. I think it's the hair."

Lucy tittered, but the rest of the table stayed silent. Clearly they'd heard it before.

"How'd you break the leg, Becca?" Donald asked.

"Bungee jumping."

Lucy looked confused. "I thought you broke it skydiving."

"I did. I just wanted to mix it up a bit."

She giggled. "Didn't I tell you guys she was a kick?"

Ben pulled out a chair for me and I opened my mouth to tell him not to be so sexist, but then realized this might not be the best time or place. I snapped my mouth shut, deciding to wait until the drive home.

"What do you do, Becca?" Cindy asked as I sat down.

"I work in a bookstore—Dunkeld's."

"Ooh, I love Dunkeld's," Leanne—at least I think it was Leanne—said. Too many new names all at once. "They have that great café with fabulous lattes."

"Yeah. They're the best."

"I've always wanted to work in a bookstore." Lucy got all dreamy-eyed. "But I'd probably spend my whole paycheck on books if I did."

"I've done that more than a few times," I said.

"What kind of books do you like to read, Becca?" Mindy asked.

I noticed the Donald tilting his head to catch my reply.

"Pretty much everything. Except romance novels." I managed to refrain from gagging. "I like mysteries, suspense, literary fiction, and some classics." I thought back to what a struggle *Persuasion* had been when I lived with Chloe.

"I don't read fiction." Char wrinkled her nose like she'd just smelled bad fish. "I like to read things that are true." She leaned forward, an evangelistic gleam in her eye. "Have you read *The Purpose Driven Life*? That's my favorite book. After the Bible, of course."

But I thought you didn't like fiction.

Of course I didn't say that out loud. They'd run me out of this potluck faster than I could say What Would Jesus Do?

"Becca?"

"Huh?"

"I was asking what's the best nonfiction book you've read lately," Char said.

"Oh. That would be *Seabiscuit*," I said. "Hands down. It was one of our book club selections and we all loved it. So much, in fact, we were going to go horseback riding afterwards."

The sting of that missed adventure still rankled. I inclined my head to my leg. "But this damn—uh, darn—cast prevented it."

Smart. Swearing at a church event.

I lifted my head to meet a table of disapproving eyes. All except Ben and Lucy.

"Yeah, *Seabiscuit* was great," Ben said, continuing the conversation as if I hadn't just made a major Christian faux pas. "Good movie too, but the book was better."

"Usually is," Mindy said. "Take *Pride and Prejudice*."

Lucy nodded.

"And *Twilight*," Cindy added.

While the rest of the table debated the merits of various book-into-movie adaptations, Lucy whispered in my ear, "That's okay. I slip sometimes too. Don't worry about it."

I'm not worried. These people need to chill. *Damn* is pretty innocuous. It's not like I put God before it.

Lucy's nice though, for all her Pollyanna perkiness. I smiled my thanks to her and returned my attention to the conversation which had now left movies behind. At least they weren't talking about *The Bachelor*. Thank God.

"There are five books every Christian should read," Donald was intoning in an authoritative voice. "*Mere Christianity*,

My Utmost for His Highest, Evidence That Demands a Verdict, Knowing God, and *Wild at Heart.*"

I recognized a couple of the titles from stocking them at Dunkeld's.

"Well, I thought that last one was pretty stereotypical and sexist," Mindy said.

Go, Mindy.

"Hey, Ben, back me up here," Donald said.

"Sorry, Don. Afraid I agree with Mindy," Ben said. "There's some serious gender stereotyping going on there."

Mindy shot the Donald a triumphant smile.

"Hey, wait a minute," Char said. "You left out *The Purpose Driven Life.*"

"And *The Five Love Languages,*" Leanne chimed in.

"That's for married couples."

"Not just married couples," Mindy said. "It works for most relationships. If people read it before they got married they'd have fewer communication problems after."

Kim gave a knowing nod. "Yeah. Like that *Men Are from Mars.*"

"But that's not a Christian book." Donald frowned.

You've got to be kidding. They're only allowed to read Christian books? Is that another one of the Ten Commandments?

So not workin' for me.

"Well, Christian or non-Christian, I'm not a big fan of self-help books," Ben said. "That whole 'Follow these seven steps and you'll be successful.' Or practice five lessons for lasting happiness. Or if you do these three things, you'll have the perfect relationship. Who comes up with these goofy numbers anyway?"

Now that's what I'm talkin' about. I knew I liked this guy. I smiled at his soul patch.

"Besides, we've already got the best self-help book there is," he said. "God's Word."

Okay, not so much.

The others looked properly chastened—except the Donald, who appeared to be marshaling his thoughts for a rebuttal.

"You're so right, Ben. We don't really need anything else, do we? But still ..." Lucy sounded wistful. "I like Christian fiction. Have you read any, Becca?"

I stared at her, my respect growing. Lucy had managed to steer the conversation to safer ground and effectively block the negative incoming from the SS *Donald*. Everyone's eyes turned to me for a response.

Right. Christian fiction. "You like all that Amish stuff? It sure sells a lot in the store."

"Actually, I've never been big on historicals," Lucy said. "I prefer more contemporary or literary fiction."

Well, color me surprised. I had her pegged as a horse-and-buggy girl all the way. "Like ...?"

"*Gilead, Peace Like a River*, anything by Flannery O'Connor ..."

Who'd have thought? Hidden depths.

"Well, I personally love Amish fiction," Kym said. "There's something really appealing about the simple life and focus on family."

"I hear you," Mindy said. "It's my guilty reading pleasure."

"Mine's *People* magazine," Cindy said.

Just then a freckled fortyish-looking woman with dishwater -blonde frizzy hair streaked with silver rushed up to the table and pulled out a chair. "Hi everyone. Sorry I'm late. The enemy did *not* want me to come tonight," she said breathlessly as she sat down. "He put all sorts of roadblocks in my way. First my oven was giving me problems and then I spilled sauce on my favorite denim jumper and had to go change, then I couldn't find my keys and when I finally did and got in my car, it wouldn't start."

"Sounds like he was certainly trying to stop you from coming," Char said. "But we're glad you made it, Sharon. The Lord must have something really special for you tonight."

Everyone nodded.

"That's what I figured too. And I wasn't about to give the enemy the victory, so I took light-rail instead." She flashed a triumphant smile.

"Good for you."

"That's showing 'em!"

I looked from one face to another, at last settling on Ben. "Who exactly is the enemy?"

Were they talking about one person, a whole nation, or what?

It is absurd to have a hard-and-fast rule about what
one should read and what one shouldn't. More than half of
modern culture depends on what one shouldn't read.

The Importance of Being Earnest

"Why, Satan, of course," Char answered before Ben had a
chance to.

Of course. And I should know that how? Guess I missed
that lesson in Sunday school. Oh wait, I never went to Sunday
school.

"Thanks," I said. "I didn't know if you were talking about
bin Laden, Bill Maher, or Hillary. I must have been sick that
day in Christianity 101."

Lucy giggled. Ben grinned. And the sides of Mindy's
mouth curved up.

The rest of them looked at me like I came from another
planet. Which I wouldn't mind returning to right now. *Tardis,
take me away.*

"I'm sorry, Becca," Lucy said. "We must sound like we're speaking a foreign language or something."

Ya think?

"That's okay. *Stranger in a Strange Land* is one of my favorite books."

Lucy giggled again.

"Becca's new to the whole church scene," Ben explained to the rest of the table.

"Ah." The Donald gave me a knowing nod.

"Everyone?" a familiar voice boomed out. "We're going to bless the food now."

I looked up and saw ADD Henry at the microphone. And then, like the mass crowd wave rippling through a football game, a sea of heads bowed.

"Father God, we just thank you for this food you've provided," he prayed. "And for all that you provide. Just bless the hands that prepared it and bless our conversations too. May our words be pleasing to you."

"Amen," I said, but Henry kept on talking. He sure liked the word *just*.

"And Father, if there are any here tonight who are discouraged or downhearted, maybe struggling with finances, or loss of a job, or difficult family issues, we just pray that you touch them."

I heard some soft sniffles from somewhere behind me.

"Just comfort them, Father. In your name we pray. Amen."

"Amen," everyone said.

"Now let's eat!"

A thundering horde stampeded to the chow—including most of our table.

"Nothing comes between a bunch of singles and their food," Mindy said dryly.

"That's for sure," Lucy said. "Good thing we were sitting

down, or we'd have been trampled in the melee." She glanced over at my outstretched cast. "Becca, if you tell me what you'd like to eat, I'd be happy to fix a plate for you."

What? Like I'm a little kid or something.

I don't think so. I can manage fine on my own.

I started to put those thoughts into words, but as I looked at Lucy, I saw only a desire to be kind and helpful in her open, cheerful face. Over her shoulder, I noticed Ben watching to see how I'd respond.

"Thanks. I appreciate it. And I love everything Mexican, so just pile my plate high and I'll be a happy camper."

Lucy took me at my word and returned a few minutes later with a heaping plateful of tamales, two kinds of enchiladas, tacos, rice, and beans. After setting it down in front of me, she produced another plate with a fat green mound of guacamole in the center ringed by tortilla chips and taquitos which she set next to the first one.

"Serious?" I stared up at her. "I may be hungry, but I'll never be able to eat all that."

"That's okay. Ben and I will help you, won't we, Ben?"

He grabbed a chip and trenched it through the guacamole. "You can bet on it."

The rest of the group returned to the table and it was quiet for a couple minutes as everyone grazed. I had to hand it to Mindy—the girl could cook. Her chicken enchiladas were as good as Ben had said.

Donald took a long swig from his Dr. Pepper, and as he was lowering the can, a burp escaped.

"Nice," Cindy said.

"Eww," Kym said.

Char frowned in his direction.

"Sorry." He raised a fist to his mouth to stifle another impending eructation, his ears red. "Guess I drank too fast."

Draining my Coke, I slapped the empty can on the table, emitting a sympathy burp at the same time. "You're not the only one. Excuse me," I said, smiling sweetly at the prissy trio.

I had laid down the burping gauntlet—would any of them pick it up? This could be fun. Anyone?

"Becca," Mindy said, pretending she hadn't noticed my bodily indiscretion as she segued into acceptable small talk. "Are you from California?"

"No one's *from* California anymore," the Donald said, barking out a short laugh. "Everyone comes here from somewhere else. Texas, Washington, the Midwest ... but mostly *Mexico*." His eyebrows drew together in an almost unbroken line.

"Actually, I'm from Alabama."

"Really? But you don't have an accent," Kym said.

"I haven't been there since I was two."

"Oh, so you were born in Alabama, but raised somewhere else?" Mindy said.

Leanne gave me an inquiring smile. "Where did you grow up? I'm from Minnesota myself, but couldn't handle the winters, so I headed out to the Golden State for college and have been here ever since."

"Me too," Cindy said. "Except it was Michigan's miserable winters I left. Brrr. How about you, Becca? Did you grow up in the Midwest too?"

"Actually, I grew up all over the place. My family moved around a lot."

Visions of broken-down trailers filled my head. All overflowing with Earlene's empty booze bottles ...

So time to change the subject. Maybe something a little controversial to liven things up? "Hey, have you guys read *The Shack*? That book flew off our shelves. We couldn't keep it in stock."

"I loved it," Lucy said. "Made me cry."

"Me too," Kym agreed. "It really spoke to my soul."

The rest of the girls nodded agreement. All except Mindy and Char.

Donald frowned. "I don't see how you can go along with the bad theol—"

Ben held up his hand. "No more *Shack* theology discussions. We've been down that road a million times already."

"Ben's right," Lucy said softly. "We don't need to rehash that again. It ministered deeply to some of us, but not to others, so why don't we just agree to disagree?"

"Agreed," Mindy said.

"And it *is* a novel, after all," Char said. "Fiction. Now if you're looking for a really good book that's true and lines up with Scripture, check out Pastor DoGood's latest. He's spot on."

"He's pretty in-your-face." Cindy grimaced. "I prefer his wife's book."

"But I heard she didn't even write it," Mindy said.

"No. Really?"

"Most celebrities don't write their books." Alastair had clued me into that my first week on the job. "They have a ghost," I said, remembering how bummed I was when I realized that my favorite rocker hadn't penned his own children's book.

"What do you mean, a ghost?" Lucy asked.

"Sorry. My turn to speak a foreign language. Ghost stands for ghostwriter—a real writer who comes along and writes the celebrity's story or novel."

"*Every* celebrity?" Kym asked.

"Maybe not everyone. But come on, do you really think that blonde beach bimbo with the plastic boobs wrote her own book?"

Lucy blushed.

"Then how come the real writer's name isn't on the cover?" Mindy asked.

"Exactly."

Before I could jump on my soapbox and go into a full-on rant about the unethical treatment of talented-but-obscure writers by pop glitterati who fancied themselves literary wunderkinds, Pastor Henry's voice boomed out again.

"Did you all get enough to eat? I know I did." He patted his stomach that was straining the buttons of his Hawaiian shirt. "And now, we're going to have a time of sharing."

"Here I go, guys." Lucy pushed back her chair and gave us a shaky smile. "Pray for me."

"Where's she going?" I asked as she left the table.

"To give her testimony."

"Her what?"

"Her testimony," Ben said sotto voce as the Henry dude continued talking. "Her personal story of how she came to know Christ."

Grabbing my pen, I noted the word *testimony* on a napkin. Then I added *the enemy* as well. I started to fold the napkin and put it in my jacket pocket that I'd slung over the back of my chair, but changed my mind. Who knew how many more foreign words I'd hear tonight?

I glanced to the front of the room, where Lucy was now standing beside the pastor, her eyes closed and head slightly bent. Even from that angle I could see her lips moving.

"Guys, let's pray for Lucy," Ben said softly.

Right here? Now?

Awkward.

Ben bowed his head and everyone else followed suit. "Father, we ask that you calm Lucy and fill her with your strength and peace right now. Give her the words that you would have her say—nothing more, nothing less. And use those words to minister to someone today. In your name, amen."

"Amen," everyone murmured.

At last Henry stopped talking and it was Lucy's turn.

"Hi everyone," she said with a slight bobble in her voice. "You'll have to forgive me because I'm not a speaker. I read somewhere that the fear of public speaking ranks right up there with the fear of death. Well, all I have to say to that is, 'Lord, take me home *now!*'"

Everyone laughed. Except me.

What is it with all these Christians wanting to die?

Lucy continued. "I've been coming to this church for almost two years now," she said, "and I'm so grateful and blessed to be a part of your church family—especially since I don't have a family of my own." A shadow crossed her face. "Well, actually, I do, but they've disowned me."

The eternal sunshine girl? What kind of crappy family would do that?

"Don't judge them harshly," she said as if she were reading my mind. "I'd have disowned me too after all the things I did. I was a mess. You see, I'm a recovering drug addict."

I picked up my jaw from the ground. Lucy?

"I started using when I was sixteen," she said. "My dad had died a few months earlier and losing him just destroyed me. My father was everything to me. And I was his little girl, so the pain and loss were unimaginable. Unendurable." Lucy closed her eyes. "My heart felt as if someone was stabbing a knife into it. Again and again. And then twisting it."

She opened her eyes and looked out at her captive audience. "Some of you have lost loved ones too, so you know what I'm talking about," she said softly. "But just imagine if you didn't have the Lord to help you through—how much harder that would be. I just wanted my daddy back and for the pain to go away.

"But it didn't.

"Then one day a friend introduced me to pot and said it would numb the pain," Lucy continued. "And it did. But unfortunately, I didn't stop there. I started out with pot, but a few months later I'd graduated to cocaine. Crack was my drug of choice, but the rush never lasted long enough. Only for ten minutes or so and then I'd come crashing down. Really low. The only thing that would make me feel better was more crack. Even if it was for such a short time, I needed that total rush again.

"It became this cycle I couldn't break. An expensive cycle," she said. "One that the money I made weekends waitressing at IHOP couldn't sustain. So I started selling stuff to get money. Clothes, jewelry, my iPod ... even my computer. And when I didn't have anything else to sell, I stole from my family."

Someone gasped.

This was like watching an after-school special—except it was more compelling because I actually knew the person.

Or thought I did.

"I started out small, so my family wouldn't catch on," Lucy said. "Ten or twenty bucks from my mom's purse here and there, some CDs from my brother, steaks from the garage freezer ... whatever. And if they asked me about it, I'd just lie and point the finger elsewhere—maybe it was one of my brother's friends?

"But my mom knew. They all knew," she said. "And they tried to talk to me about it, but I wouldn't listen. I'd get really defensive and angry, so they'd back off. By this time my mom had remarried and had a new baby, so she was pretty caught up with that and I kind of flew under the radar for a while. But I was skipping school, doing drugs with my friends, and pretty much screwing up left and right—staying out 'til all hours, failing classes, fighting with my stepfather ... My family tried to get me help—practicing tough love, counseling, a stint in rehab ... but none of it took."

Lucy closed her eyes for a moment, took a deep breath, and released it slowly. "And then one day, shortly after my eighteenth birthday and just a few weeks after getting out of rehab for the second time, I stole my brother's laptop and sold it to buy some crack. I was freebasing in my room and caught my comforter on fire. But not just my comforter—the curtains, the carpet, my clothes. Everything started burning and I freaked out.

"Thanks to my stepfather's fast reaction, the damage was limited to my room," she said. "But that was the last straw. For the sake of the baby and the safety of the rest of the family, they kicked me out. And they were right to do so. I hate to think what could have happened. Imagine being responsible for the torching of your own home. Or the demise of your whole family" Lucy shuddered.

"I stayed with friends for a while," she said. "Druggie friends—which wasn't the smartest move. But when you're a crackhead, you're anything but smart. All you care about is getting high. That's all that matters. It got to the point where I'd do anything just for that next fix."

Lucy looked out at the room with a steady glance. "And I mean anything.

"It's a miracle I didn't contract AIDS or some kind of STD," she said. "I kept spiraling down lower and lower until I hit rock bottom. By then I'd lost everything—my car, my home, my friends, my family, my self-respect ...

"I lost everything," Lucy repeated. "But then I found everything in Jesus Christ when an old friend from high school brought me to church."

"Yes, Lord," someone shouted.

"Praise you, Lord."

"Thank you, Jesus."

Scattered praises swept the room until I felt like I'd been transported back to one of those old-time tent revivals like I'd seen on *Little House on the Prairie.*

It didn't make sense though. The woman I saw before me could not be the same woman who did all those things. I've seen drug addicts up close and personal; I know what they look like. And they're not all shiny and new like Lucy. Even after rehab.

Guess that higher power thing must be workin' for her ...

"Does my story surprise you?" Lucy asked. "Bet some of you are amazed at my past and my present. That's okay, because he is amazing. I hope you will give him a chance to change your life too, whatever your need. His amazing grace is wonderful!" She beamed, tears streaming down her face.

The pastor moved next to her, putting his hand on her shoulder, and asked the room to join him in a closing prayer. I bowed my head, not giving in to my anthropological study as I had in church. Instead, I focused on what I'd just heard from Lucy. Baring her most intimate secrets in front of everyone. When I thought about the woman she used to be and the woman I now knew, I shook my head.

It *was* amazing. Even to me.

You're absolutely the wildest, most unpredictable person I've ever known. Do you always carry on so high-handed?

The Maltese Falcon

I was quiet on the drive home thinking about what Lucy had said. She really put it all out there. Elements of her story — the drug addiction and acting-out behavior — reminded me of my bio-mom. The difference was Lucy seemed sincere and repentant.

Earlene was anything but.

The last time I'd seen Earlene had been four-and-a-half years ago — a prison visit on my twenty-first birthday. She was doing seven years on a host of charges: violating parole, possession of a controlled substance, assault and battery on her latest boyfriend, and God only knows what else.

After that she'd written and called a few times asking for money like she always did, sucking up to me and trying to play the mom card.

It was a little too late for that.

Then she played the born-again card. Said she'd found Jesus in jail.

Yeah right. Like she'd found him all those times before when I was a kid. It was just another one of her cons. And I'd had enough of them to last a lifetime. And enough of her freaky, druggie boyfriends too.

I didn't need that negative energy in my life.

Time to stop enabling and move on. I changed my number. Moved out of state. But if Earlene's latest conversion had even half the impact as Lucy's, I might have left a forwarding address.

"Did you know all that about Lucy?" I asked Ben.

"Yep. Lucy and I are good buds — we pray for each other regularly. She's a great prayer warrior."

Okay, this was getting embarrassing. I was an English major who worked with words all day long. What in the world did *prayer warrior* mean? I pulled my napkin from my pocket and added the expression to my growing list before turning back to Ben.

"How long have you known Lucy?"

"A couple years. I met her the first day she came to Creekside. Her fiancé had just broken up with her and she needed a safe place to come and heal."

"Was the fiancé from her druggie days?"

"No. He was a Christian she met after first coming to the Lord," Ben said. "They started dating and got engaged pretty quickly, when she was still a baby Christian, but then the guy decided he couldn't hang with her past."

Figures. Jerk.

"Tell me he didn't dump her the night before the wedding," I said, thinking of Chloe and her ex as I wrote down *baby Christian* on the crowded napkin.

"No. The week before."

"What a prince."

"I think you mean toad."

Amen.

When I got home Kailyn was painting her toenails and watching *Sleepless in Seattle* for the umpteenth time. My roommate lives and breathes romantic comedies. She's like a little kid who gets fixated on the same movie and insists on watching it over and over again. At least she rotates among her top five: *My Best Friend's Wedding, Sleepless in Seattle, You've Got Mail, French Kiss,* and *When Harry Met Sally.*

I always wonder if it's because she looks a little like Meg Ryan.

With boobs.

"Hey, I've got some more words for *The Getaway Girls Guide to Christianese,*" I said as I clumped into the room.

"Hang on a minute. It's the last scene where they finally meet at the top of the Empire State Building."

I sat down and watched the end of the movie with her. Even I had to admit it was pretty romantic. That Meg and Tom have some serious chemistry.

Kailyn sighed as the credits rolled. "What I wouldn't give to meet the love of my life at the top of the Empire State Building."

"Forget the love. I'd just like to go to the top of the Empire State Building. With all the places I've lived over the years, I still can't believe I've never been to the Big Apple."

"Me either," she said. "You know how you've got that list of all those places you want to see before you die? Well, New York's at the top of my list."

"Could that have something to do with, oh-I-don't-know ... maybe Broadway?"

"You bet. Every theater actor dreams of being on a

Broadway stage someday. And since I know that's never going to happen, I'd be happy just sitting in the audience."

"Why won't it ever happen?"

"Get real," Kailyn said. "Community theater actors never make it to Broadway."

"Even when they're the best community theater actor in town?"

"That's a pretty sweeping statement from someone who hardly ever goes to plays."

"I can still tell the difference between good and bad. And you're really good."

"Well, thanks," Kailyn said. "You don't usually hand out the compliments, so that means a lot." Her eyes grew moist.

Tears twice in one night? Way too much for me.

I pulled the folded napkin out of my jacket pocket to distract her, and as I did, something fell out — some kind of pamphlet. "'The Four Spiritual Laws'?" I read aloud as I picked it up. "What is this and where did it come from?"

"That's a tract. Someone must have slipped it into your pocket at the potluck."

So that's what the Donald was doing by my chair when I came back from the bathroom. Talk about a stealth attack. I crumpled up the laws and tossed them aside, then passed the napkin to Kailyn. "Here's those words to add to the Guide."

"*The enemy, baby Christian, testimony ...*" She looked up from the list with eager eyes. "Ooh, did you hear a good testimony tonight?"

"Depends on what you mean by good."

"Spicy. Juicy. Something a whole lot more interesting than mine. I have such a boring testimony."

"Let me be the judge of that."

"Okay, but try not to fall asleep." Kailyn recited, "I was raised in the church and have been a Christian all my life.

When I was six years old, I asked Jesus into my heart, and he's been living there ever since. The End."

"That it?"

"That's it."

"You're right," I said. "It is pretty boring. Lucy's was way more interesting."

"Lucy? Isn't she the one who looked like a giant pumpkin in that awful tent dress?"

Don't be dissin' Lucy. I might have to take you out.

"She may be a little fashion challenged, but I like her," I said. "And it's not about what she wears or how she looks."

"Don't get all bent out of shape," Kailyn said. "You're the one who told me about the pumpkin resemblance."

"Oh."

Someone's snarkiness is coming back to haunt them.

"Sorry. First impressions and all that. But Lucy's really nice. A little too cheerful maybe, but nice."

"What was her testimony anyway?"

"I'm not sure I should say. It was kind of private."

"It's not private if she told it to a room full of singles," Kailyn said.

"Good point." And I repeated Lucy's story.

"See what I mean?" she said when I was finished. "So not boring. She could have been one of the Spice Girls."

"Only she didn't get her David Beckham."

Or meet her love at the top of the Empire State Building. But that only happened in the movies.

When I went to bed that night, Lucy's story kept replaying in my head. I couldn't get to sleep for thinking about it.

And her.

And the whole evening.

13

Part of her life was made from the tree growing rankly in the yard. She was the bitter quarrels she had with her brother ... She was Katie's secret, despairing weeping. She was the shame of her father staggering home drunk.

A Tree Grows in Brooklyn

"So how's the dating experiment going?" Tess teased at our next Getaway Girls meeting at Annette's the following week. We'd had to put a temporary halt to our book club adventures while I was trapped in my cast. But we still got together to discuss the books and catch up.

"Yeah," Annette said, "are you pulling your hair out yet?"

"Nah, just dyeing it."

Yesterday, having gotten bored of the rainbow hues, I'd had Annie color my hair Amy Winehouse black. I didn't copy Amy's outlandish coif, though. It might work for rehab, but it just wasn't me.

Checking the calendar I saw that Ben and I had been on eleven dates so far, counting a few Starbucks pass-throughs and pizza one night. I thought back to Date Ten where we'd gone to a movie with some of the singles gang—a flick his pastor buddy had encouraged the entire church to see opening weekend to drive up those box office numbers.

"We'll show Hollywood that there's an audience for the kind of movies we want to see," he'd declared from the pulpit. "Family-friendly fare that you don't have to worry about taking your kids to. No sex or swearing. Just clean, wholesome entertainment with a good faith message."

It was clean all right. Wholesome too. But utter cheese. Make that udder.

Could it *get* any preachier?

Someone never learned the word *subtle*. I walked out with goose eggs from the heavy two-by-fours hammered into my skull.

"Oh my," Lucy murmured as we left the theater. "Did any of those folks have acting experience? Didn't seem like it."

"Sure they did," Ben said. "The lady with the big hair was in that eighties sitcom. I can't remember the name of the show, but she was pretty funny."

"Was it the one with the kids and the dog?" Cindy asked.

Yeah, that narrows it down.

"At Bible study they said this was made on a shoestring budget," Kym said, "so they used mostly regular people. Some of them had done church skits though."

" 'Well, all righty then,' " I quoted from one of the movie's pivotal scenes.

Nothing like stealing from Jim Carrey.

"So it won't win any Academy Awards," Donald said. "Still, it was a good message."

Guess he really likes his two-by-fours.

"A little heavy-handed though," Mindy, who works in marketing, said. "It doesn't matter how good the message is if it's delivered poorly."

"Well, the important thing is that this movie clearly presented the gospel," Donald said. "It's playing on hundreds of screens around the country. Just think of how many people it could win for Christ."

"Except it's kind of preaching to the choir," Lucy argued.

"Well, I liked it," Cindy said.

Kym sniffed. "Me too."

"But you're the choir." Mindy turned to me. "Becca? What did *you* think of it?"

Six pairs of eyes swiveled to mine.

There goes my Miss Congeniality banner.

"Well ... I'm glad I didn't pay to see it."

"But did it make you want to become a Christian?" Mindy pressed.

"You know that saying, 'Don't shoot me; I'm only the messenger'? Someone should have shot this messenger."

At book club I asked, "Did any of you see that Christian movie that opened last weekend?"

"Oh yes, we went opening night as a family," Annette said. "Ah loved it!" Her Texas drawl became even more pronounced when she got excited.

"And I hated it," Kailyn said. "Sorry, Mom, but the dialogue was cheesy and the acting laughable. I almost walked out."

There are times when my roommate and I are in perfect harmony. Those times are usually few and far between, but in moments like this I could almost hug her.

Almost. No sense reordering the universe.

"I have to agree with Kailyn," Paige said. "You know what a movie buff I am—"

"Really?" said Annie, whose T-shirt today proclaimed *Jesus is my homeboy.* "I'd never have guessed."

"Um, who was it that wanted me to work their shift at the shop tomorrow again?" Paige said. "As I was saying ... from a movie buff's perspective, on a scale of one to ten, I'm afraid I'd have to give it a one."

"Make that a minus one," I piped in.

Annette bristled.

"Let's stop talking about the movie before we come to blows," Chloe suggested. "I, for one, would much rather hear more about Becca's dates." She bared her teeth at me like one of those grinning monkeys in the zoo. "How's it going with Ben? What do you think of him?"

"He's nice. Kind of cool. And if I wasn't in this stupid cast, we'd be having a whole lot more fun, I can tell you that."

"Please don't." Annette's cheeks pinked. "I'm not sure my tender ears can handle it."

"I was talking about athletic activities. You know: hiking, running, bicycling."

"Oh."

"Get your mind out of the gutter. I'm not going to corrupt some nice Christian boy," I said. "I am sure learning a lot at all these church activities though. It's a whole new world. An alien universe."

Annie hummed the theme song from *The Twilight Zone.*

"Becca's learning a whole new language too. And we're helping translate for her." Kailyn handed Chloe a spiral-bound notebook. "Check it out."

"*The Getaway Girls Guide to Christianese,*" Chloe read aloud. "Love it!" She began flipping through the pages, giggling as she scanned the entries.

"Hey, share with the class," Paige said.

Chloe passed Paige the notebook and she began reading

aloud. *"Causing someone to stumble, backslide, unequally yoked . . .* these are great. Ooh, I have another one for you: *anointed.* Anyone have a pen?"

"What's *anointed* mean?" I asked.

"Chosen," Tess said. "It's usually descriptive of a person. As in: 'Tom's a really anointed worship leader.' Means someone's well-suited for the task, but God's the one who equipped him. Her."

Annette handed Paige a pen and she scribbled down the new word.

"While you're at it, add in *witness,*" Chloe said.

"Spiritual meat," Tess offered.

"Milk," Annette said.

And for the next several minutes the Christianese volleyed back and forth along with the laughter.

Paige waved her hand at us to get our attention. "That's nothing. At this one church I attended for a little while, during worship they didn't use any musical instruments—just sang a cappella. I wasn't sure if it was tradition or what. It was unusual but really pretty. Then I found out that musical instruments were not allowed within that denomination. *But,*" she added, "some of the churches were starting to question that stance and trying to modernize by adding a piano. Once I overheard some women talking about another church within the denomination and one of them asked in a hushed voice, 'Do they have *the instrument?*'"

"Serious?" Annie said.

Paige nodded. "I thought they were talking about some kind of torture device down in the basement."

We all burst out laughing.

"The *instrument?*" Tess repeated. "And this was how long ago?"

"It sounds like something from *Little House on the Prairie* days," Kailyn said.

Paige grimaced. "Which would make me over a hundred and fifty. It was only three years ago. Besides, in *Little House* they had a piano in church."

"Scripture says 'Make a joyful noise,'" Annette said.

Kailyn giggled. "Just not with piano."

"And definitely not drums and guitar," Annie interjected.

"Guess it's all a matter of interpretation," Tess said.

"Speaking of interpretation, are we going to talk about the book tonight or not?" I asked. "Which one are we discussing again? I read them all together, so I can't remember the order."

"*A Tree Grows in Brooklyn*," Kailyn said. "But first we need to catch up on someone else's dating life." She smirked at Paige. "What's going on at Golden Daffodils? Anything blooming over there?"

"Oh yeah. You should see the gorgeous Ecuadorian roses we just got in."

"Very funny," Annette said. "Now tell us how things are goin' with you and that yummy Marc."

"Good. Really good." Paige's face went all soft and gooey. "I'm very happy. Marc's a great guy."

"We already know that," Kailyn said. "You have to give up more than that. We're dying for details here."

"Well, you all know what a help he was to me after my mom died," Paige said. "I don't think I could have gotten through it without him. And all of you too." A lone tear rolled down her cheek.

Tess handed her a tissue.

"Thanks," Paige said. "Marc's really good with Cydney too. He's helped me a lot. I didn't realize being a foster mom would be quite so challenging, but Cyd has some real trust issues—especially with men. I think I told you that her dad abandoned the family when she was eleven?"

We all nodded.

"That's a tough age for a girl anyway—especially these days," Tess said.

"I know," Annette said. "They go through puberty so much younger now. Why, I've heard of some girls getting their period at eleven. Kailyn didn't get hers till she was fifteen."

"Thanks, Mom. Why don't you take out a billboard while you're at it?"

"Oh hush, baby girl. We're all gals here."

"Marc has a lot of experience with girls Cyd's age," Paige said. "His thirteen-year-old cousin came to live with his family for several years. Dicey times. She even had a record. Cyd isn't in *that* league. Not yet, anyway." She crossed her fingers. Then immediately uncrossed them with a quick "sorry."

Like she'd flashed a Satanic sign or something.

"Kids need structure and stability," Paige continued, "so I'm trying to provide that for Cyd. I make sure I'm home from work every day when she gets out of school, and we have dinner together most weeknights with Marc except when I've got class. Usually I cook, but Marc often takes us out to dinner on the weekend. Afterwards, we'll go to a movie or come home and have popcorn and watch DVDs."

"You sound like a family," Tess said.

Paige's eyes filled. "I know. It's pretty wonderful."

"So when's he going to make it legal?" I asked.

"Yeah," Kailyn said. "I think you should have all of us be bridesmaids."

"We're not in any hurry to get married," Paige said. "It's all up to God."

Really? And here I thought it was the guy that did the proposing.

Go figure. I grabbed the *Getaway Girls Guide to Chris-tianese* from Paige's lap and flipped it open to a blank page. Only I didn't know what to write down. This was getting old.

When would I start having all the answers instead of all the questions?

14

I don't mind a reasonable amount of trouble.

The Maltese Falcon

The next day at work I was reshelving some books in the mysteries section — having mastered the art of using only my left crutch when standing so I could have my right hand free to work with — when Margaret approached.

"Hi, Becca," she said. "How's it going?"

Only she didn't say it with her usual enthusiasm.

I looked closely at her. "Hey, Margaret. What's up?"

"Nothing much. Except I just got dumped by my publisher."

"What?" I lost my balance and my crutch clattered to the floor. At the same time I started to pitch forward, arms flailing, but Margaret grabbed me and kept me from falling.

"Whoa," she said. "I've got you. Steady now."

I clutched her shoulders and righted myself.

"Okay?" she asked.

I nodded and tried to slow my heartbeat back down to normal.

Alastair rushed over. "What happened? I heard something fall." His eyes slid to the crutch on the ground. "Are you okay, Becca? Margaret?"

"We're fine," she said. "But I think Becca should probably sit down."

"I'm fine. I don't need to sit down. If you could just get me my crutch?"

"Of course." He picked up my instrument of torture and handed it to me. "Where's your other one?"

I jerked my head toward the Cs where earlier I'd leaned it against a row of Agatha Christies.

Alastair retrieved that crutch too and handed it to me with a stern look. "Go take a break and get some coffee. And from now on, no more shelving for you. I don't need you breaking your other leg. I hate filling out workers' comp paperwork."

"I'm sorry," Margaret murmured as we made our way to the café. "I didn't mean to get you in trouble. I didn't mean to startle you either."

"That's okay. No harm, no foul. Alastair's just blowin' smoke. But never mind about that. What happened with your publisher?"

"I'll tell you in a minute. Let's get you settled first and then I'll get us some coffee." Margaret pulled out a chair from the first table we reached and relieved me of my crutches, bustling about and pulling out another chair so I could prop my cast on it.

"You really don't need to fuss over me. I'm fine."

"I know. I can't help it." She smiled. "I'm a mom."

Earlene never fussed over me a day in her life. She definitely didn't bustle.

"Now let me go get our coffees and I'll be right back. You like latte, right?"

"Right."

Margaret returned a few minutes later with a latte, a mocha, and two fudgy brownies. "Nothing like a little comfort food to make things better," she said. "And as far as I'm concerned, chocolate is the number one comfort food." She picked up her brownie and bit into it with gusto, following it with a chaser of mocha.

"Ah." She blew out a contented sigh. "That's better."

"Okay, so now will you tell me what happened?"

"It's a common enough story in publishing. Just not common for me," Margaret said. "My last book didn't earn out its advance and the numbers on my current book are low, so the publisher decided to cut their losses and cut me loose."

"But didn't your latest mystery release just a couple months ago?"

"Four-and-a-half months, to be exact."

"They haven't even given it a chance." My hackles rose on behalf of my friend. "What do they expect? It's not like you're J. K. Rowling or Stephenie Meyer."

"Exactly," Margaret said. "I'm a dinosaur. Who wants to read books about little old ladies when they can read about exciting boy wizards or teen vampires?"

"I do. And there's plenty of others who do as well."

"Not enough," she said. "Oh, well. C'est la vie. I've had a good run. Thirteen books over a dozen years is nothing to sneeze at. Especially at my age."

"That's for sure. But I still can't believe they did this to you."

"I'd be lying if I said I wasn't disappointed," Margaret said. "But publishing is a business. And as P. D. James said, 'Publishers don't nurse you; they buy and sell you.' I don't blame them. They have to earn a living too. I'm just glad my husband has a good retirement plan."

An hour after Margaret left, I was still thinking about the

injustice of her publisher dumping her without warning—the same way Chloe's former fiancé had dumped her the night before the wedding. And the more I thought about it, the more I fumed.

And in the midst of all that fumigation, an idea emerged.

After my near mishap in mysteries earlier, Alastair had confined me to the information desk where I was now pounding the keys of the computer with a vengeance typing a letter to Margaret's publisher. This was my second attempt. I'd thrown away the first draft that began, *Dear Idiots, Do you have your heads up your butt or what?*

By extolling the virtues of Margaret's books and telling her publisher how much our Dunkeld's customers loved her cozy mysteries, I hoped that my tiny influence in the bookstore world might make them reconsider firing her. I didn't hold out much hope. But still, I had to try.

I continued pounding away.

"Becca?" a timid voice squeaked.

"What?" I said through clenched teeth, dragging my eyes from the computer screen to discover Lucy's pink face before me.

"I'm sorry. You're busy. I can come back later." She turned to leave.

"No, that's okay. Hang on a sec. Just let me save this." I hit Control S and stuck the missive in my drafts folder to finish later.

"So what are you doing here?" I asked.

"You mean besides interrupting your work?"

"I'm sorry I snapped at you. Bad day."

"I can relate," Lucy said. "Work was a bear today, so I took off a little early. Thought I'd treat myself to a new book." She grinned. "That always makes me feel better."

I thought God was supposed to do that.

What? No Christianese solution for me to jot on a napkin?

"I usually stop at the bookstore near my office," Lucy said, "but I decided to come to Dunkeld's in hopes of seeing you."

"Why?"

Rude, much? "I mean, that was nice," I said.

"Well, I did have an ulterior motive."

I knew it. Don't tell me, let me guess. You're the designated emissary sent to tell me I should stop seeing Ben before I corrupt him and he falls off the straight-and-narrow Christian path.

"I got your number from Ben and was going to text you," Lucy said, "but my mom always said that we're getting too technological and impersonal in our daily communications and losing the personal touch, so I thought it might be nicer to come invite you in person."

"Invite me to what?"

"Sorry. I do babble on, don't I?" She giggled. "A few of us are having a movie night at my apartment tonight and I wanted to see if you'd like to come." Lucy held up her hand. "And before you answer, I promise it will be nothing like the last one we saw." The corners of her mouth curved up.

I refrained from saying or even thinking something snarky. "Is this a girls-only movie night, or guys and girls?"

"It's coed. Ben was going to call and ask you, but I told him I wanted to." Lucy gave a slight frown. "He said I was supposed to tell you the number twelve. I asked him twelve what, but he said you'd know what he meant."

"Inside joke. Don't worry about it." I smiled. "I'd be happy to come tonight."

Especially since this brings me almost halfway to my goal. Only thirteen more dates to go. Lucky thirteen.

"So what new book did you get?" I asked.

"Actually, it's really not new. It's an old friend." Lucy held up *To Kill a Mockingbird*. "But my other copy was falling apart."

"I love that book." I recited, "'Remember it was a sin to kill a mockingbird ... mockingbirds don't do anything but make music for us to enjoy ... they don't do one thing but just sing their hearts out for us.'"

"That's one of my favorite quotes," she said.

"Mine too."

"I'm sure glad God brought you into my life." Lucy beamed. "I think we have a lot in common."

Well ... maybe not a lot ...

"Would Ben be one of those things?" I asked. "Were you guys ever involved?"

"Me and Ben?" Lucy giggled. "Oh no. Ben's my dear, precious friend and brother in Christ—nothing romantic. Never romantic." Her voice softened. "Ben was the first person to befriend me when I came to Creekside. He's the one who showed me it was possible—healthy, even—to have men friends. Men who didn't want something from me. I'd never known that from anyone else before."

Hmm. I wonder if Ben thinks of me just as a friend too. He hasn't made any moves yet.

Maybe it's his mission in life—to befriend every woman he meets.

He's got a different mission. Remember? He's collecting born-again notches on his missionary belt.

No. Forget that. I waved the idea away.

Maybe that was unfair to Ben. I'd certainly misjudged Lucy.

"Hey, I get off in a few minutes, but first I have to stop by the children's section and pick up all the checks and credit card receipts for Alastair," I said. "Want to come with me and then maybe grab something to drink in the café while I wait for my ride home?"

"Sure. But do you need to go home first before coming over for the movie?"

"Only if I want to eat."

"Would you like to have dinner at my house?" Lucy asked, her voice timid. "Nothing fancy, just pasta with clam sauce and salad, but then you could ride over with me."

"Sounds much better than my TV dinner. Thanks." I called Kailyn and told her she didn't have to pick me up, and then I crutched over to the children's department with Lucy chattering beside me all the way.

Thankfully, the brats quotient was low when we arrived. Only a couple of rug rats on the premises—a toddler entranced by Dr. Seuss and a skinny boy in threadbare jeans who looked about nine or ten.

The last thing I needed to round off my day was a bunch of screaming kids.

"Hey, Brandon," I said to the teenaged clerk at the register. "How's it going?"

"Pretty slow today. I'm counting down the minutes. Only twenty more to go."

"I've only got five," I said in a singsong voice.

"Rub it in."

As I removed the checks and credit card receipts from the bottom of the cash drawer, Lucy browsed the nearby picture-books rack.

"Look, Dad," I heard the skinny kid say. "It's the Chronicles of Narnia. The *whole* set. All together."

I glanced over and saw enormous eyes in an enraptured elfin face.

The boy reached out and placed the palm of his hand reverently on the glossy boxed set. "Can we get 'em, Dad? Please? They're my favorite books in the whole *world*."

"I'm sorry, Son," said the slight man next to him whose

jeans had also seen better days. "I wish we could, but they're too expensive. We can go and check them out of the library next time we go, though."

I braced myself for the tantrum that usually accompanied a parent saying no to their little bratspring—complete with red face, screaming, and kicking.

"Okay, Dad," the kid said quietly. He stroked the cover and gave it a last longing look before placing his hand in his father's and following him away.

I watched them leave, a curious wrench in my gut.

"Becca, quick, can you ring this up?" Lucy asked.

I turned to face her and she thrust the Narnia set at me. "What?"

"Hurry," she said as she scribbled something on a slip of paper and slid a fifty-dollar bill my way.

As I rang up her purchase and Brandon bagged it, Lucy dropped the scrap of paper into the bag and beseeched him. "Can you do me a huge favor? Could you run after that little boy please and give this to him? Tell him it's from a friend, but don't say who."

He gaped at her. So did I.

"Hurry, before you lose him."

Brandon grabbed the bag and sprinted away.

"Well, that was a nice thing to do," I said as I handed Lucy her change. "But how come you didn't give it to him yourself?"

She ducked her head. "Scripture says don't let your left hand know what your right hand is doing."

"Huh?"

"Giving should be anonymous," she explained, her cheeks pink. "I wouldn't even have done it in front of you, but I had to act fast."

"And you say that's in the Bible? Has it always been?"

"Yes. God's Word is the same yesterday, today, and forever."

Is that right? Guess those church folks my bio-mom and I met back in the day had a different translation.

"Besides, the gift's not from me," Lucy said. "It's from God. He's the one who told me to give it to that boy."

Great. Another one who has God on speaker phone.

"Please keep this between us," she said. "Don't say anything to anyone."

Lucy is an odd duck. If I'd done something cool like that, I'd want a pat on the back, not obscurity. Wouldn't most people?

Like the celebrities who get their pictures taken feeding the homeless in soup kitchens at Thanksgiving. Or presenting a personal check on air to a TV talk-show host after a hurricane. Great PR. Keep those kudos coming. Who doesn't want the love?

But no photo-op if you did it Lucy style.

And then I remembered how earlier in the year when I couldn't pay my part of the rent, Annette and Kailyn had stepped up to the plate and taken care of it. Quietly and without fanfare. And Chloe had done the same thing in Paris when I came up short.

They must know the left hand, right hand translation too.

15

Next to trying and winning, the best thing is trying and failing.

Anne of Green Gables

The movie we watched that night over at Lucy's was *Chariots of Fire*, an eighties' film I'd never seen about a couple of British runners who competed in the 1924 Paris Olympics. Watching them as they ran made me long to be running again myself. I'd competed with Jenna in a couple California marathons and my legs were itching to start moving again.

One leg was a little itchier than the other.

But the doc had given me strict instructions not to scratch inside my cast, saying there was the risk of breaking the skin and causing an infection. Only one more month and I'd be free. And once I was, I planned to go running in slow motion on the beach with this *Chariots* movie theme on my iPod.

Cool music. Cool movie too. Although I couldn't believe it when one of the runners, Eric Liddell, nicknamed "The Flying

Scotsman," refused to compete in a race on Sunday because it went against his beliefs.

Dude! I wanted to scream at the screen, this is the *Olympics*. Do you know how many people would have killed to be in your shoes? Inwardly I raised my hand.

Run the stinkin' race already.

I wasn't the only one who felt that way. So did most of his countrymen—including his future king. But Liddell, a devout Christian, stuck to his convictions. And in the end, they allowed him to run another race another day—the 400 meters, for which he won the gold medal.

The way this guy ran was wild—and went against all conventional running wisdom. I've never seen anything like it. All flailing arms and throwing his head back. Wild, but glorious. Add in the stirring music and the voice-over in his great Scottish accent, "I believe God made me for a purpose, but he also made me fast. And when I run I feel his pleasure," and I was a puddle on the floor.

This was better than all the *Rocky* movies put together.

I excused myself to go to the bathroom so no one would see my wet cheeks. Once inside, I closed the door and stared at my tear-streaked face in the mirror. What's up with that? I never cry at movies.

Never. I didn't cry at *Titanic, Ghost,* or even *Bambi*.

Of course they weren't sports movies. I splashed cold water on my face and returned to the others.

"Now *that* movie might make me want to become a Christian," I said.

Ben and Lucy's eyes lit up. And so did every other pair of eyes in the room. The Donald beamed and reached for his ever-present Bible and stack of tracts.

"Cool your jets there, Bible-man. I said *might*."

As Ben drove me home from Lucy's later that night, I

studied his profile—not that he noticed. He seemed to be lost in thought about something. I'm beginning to wonder if he might be gay. The guy hasn't made a single move since we started dating.

Not even a kiss.

Is that against the Christian dating bylaws or something? Or is he just not that into me?

Be honest. Are you really that into him?

Well … he's cute. And interesting. And smart. And he's definitely got the outdoor adventure thing going for him. Or at least he says he does. It's not like I've gone on any exciting adventures with him—other than potlucks, which are so exciting I can hardly stand it. Maybe it's just all talk.

Or maybe it's because you're out of commission with your cast and he's being nice by not suggesting sporty dates so you won't feel left out.

Hmm. Guess that would fit with his nice persona. Hey, maybe that's why I'm not into him. He's too nice. Usually I like my men with that element of danger. Excitement. When I first met Ben, I thought he had it. But now? The only danger surrounding Ben was a Bible-thrashing threat from the Donald.

"Hey, I have a proposition for you," Ben said all of a sudden when he stopped at a red light.

So … not gay after all.

"Fire away."

He leaned toward me.

Here comes the kiss.

"How would you like to have one of our dates count as a date, even though it technically wouldn't be with me?" Ben said.

Or not.

"I mean I'd be there, but you wouldn't be with me," he said.

"You pimpin' me out here?"

"Just with Lucy."

"Lucy's gay?"

Even in the car I could see Ben's face flush. Or was that just a reflection from the stoplight?

"No," he said. "Lucy's part of our church women's ministries, and this weekend is their annual tea or fashion show or something. She's in charge of a table. Her cohort bailed close to zero hour and ... well ... I suggested she ask you to help her out."

"Me?" I snorted. "I hate all that girly stuff. I'm the last person she should be asking for help. What about Mindy or Cindy? Or Kym?"

"Mindy's already hosting her own table, Kym's doing something else that day, and Cindy's going to be out of town."

"So I *am* the last person."

"Just about. Unless I put on a wig."

I glanced over at his bald head. "She must be really desperate."

"She is. But she also really likes you and said she wouldn't be as nervous if you were there too for moral support."

I sighed. Afternoon teas had to be one of my least favorite activities on the planet.

If you can even count going to tea as an activity.

The Getaway Girls had already roped me into a couple: once at a fancy hotel in San Francisco and another time for Tess's bridal shower. Although I must admit the food was good—scones are a great invention—all the frou-frou stuff that went along with it left me cold.

"You'd be able to mark one more date off the calendar," Ben said, his tone cajoling.

"How exactly can I do that?"

"Because I'll be one of the servers. The men of the church

are serving the women. So, technically, you and I will be out together." He grinned. "And I can come pick you up too."

"How come Lucy didn't ask me herself?"

"She thought you'd turn her down."

"She'd have been right."

And then I thought back to how Lucy had given the little boy at Dunkeld's the Narnia books and how nice she'd been to me ever since we met.

Even when I wasn't.

"Okay, it's a date. Tell Lucy to call me later with the details."

Those details included an invitation that said "Hats required."

Great. A bunch of grown women playing dress up. However, as one who always goes by the book, I wore a hat.

Lucy, who had a floppy straw hat plopped atop her dandelion-fluff hair, giggled when she saw me. "So you're an A's fan, huh?"

"Big time. I have a matching jersey too, but I didn't think it tea-worthy. Although the green does flatter my eyes."

At least the tea was in the gym, so I felt more at home. Or at least thought I would when Lucy first told me the locale. But seeing it now, the place looked nothing like a gym. Not with all the pink and white linens, lace, china, and flowers. Tons of flowers everywhere. Mostly roses, and mostly pink. As if it were some giant baby shower or something.

One woman had even brought a pink Oriental rug to go beneath her table and cover her section of the gym floor — the free-throw zone.

Paige's mom would have loved it. She was all about pink.

Lucy and me? Not so much. We'd put our heads and our resources together — I borrowed heavily from the Getaway Girls — and come up with our own twist on the traditional tea.

"How dramatic," the table hostess next to us said when we finished decorating. "I don't think I've ever seen a black tablecloth at a tea before."

"We're going for a more Asian look," Lucy said.

To that end I'd borrowed Tess's simple white Japanese china with a bamboo motif, some small red lacquer boxes from Kailyn, and as the finishing touch, had Annie create one of her exotic tropical floral displays for the center of the table. I'd thought of bringing a little Buddha I had in my room but decided that probably wouldn't go over very well.

Dueling deities.

"Oh my," exclaimed each woman who arrived to take her assigned seat at Lucy's table. "How: [fill-in-the-blank] unusual, different, contemporary ..."

Our tablemates were all middle-aged and married, with the exception of one very pregnant young wife and mom-to-be named Tara.

The women all peppered her with questions.

"When's the baby due?"

"Have you decided on a name?"

"Do you know if it's a boy or a girl?"

Blah, blah, blah.

Really having some fun now.

Lucy caught my eye and smiled. No wonder she wanted backup. We single chicks had to stick together.

"Hi." The middle-aged woman on my right pointed to her name tag. "I'm Judi," she said. "I like your hat. We're big A's fans in our family too. Have you been coming to Creekside long?"

Her hat was a plain straw one without embellishment—no ribbons, lace, or silk flowers like the rest of the table's. Judi had laugh lines around her eyes and looked to be in her late forties.

She was wearing a tan scooped-neck T-shirt above a gauzy Indian skirt.

"Becca," I said, indicating my name tag. "And I'm just visiting."

"Oh, that's nice. Where do you usually go to church?"

"I don't."

"Been there, done that," Judi said. She leaned in. "There was a period when my husband and I stopped going to church altogether. We'd gotten way too overloaded with activities and responsibilities and got to the point where we were completely burned out. We needed to just step back for a while and refresh and renew. It's healthy to do that now and then." She gave me a warm smile.

I decided not to burst her bubble.

"Ladies," a voice said into the microphone. "Can I have your attention, please?"

All eyes focused on the speaker, who was clad in billowing waves of spring flowers topped off by a green floppy hat with a silk sunflower in the center and who introduced herself as Renee. "We have a lot of new faces here today, so we're going to get started with our icebreaker game," Renee said.

"When you came in, one of our hostesses taped a piece of paper to your back and told you not to look at it or to tell one another what it said. On that paper is the name of a famous woman of faith. Your job is to find out whose name is on your back, but you can only do so by asking questions of your table-mates that end in yes or no. All right?"

Nods and murmured assents rippled through the room.

"Okay, you can get started."

"Becca," Lucy said, as the rest of the women at the table began to stand up, "we don't want you to have to keep getting up and down like a jack-in-the-box with your leg, so why don't you just stay seated and we'll all come to you instead?"

My doctor had recently changed my cast. The original one had gotten loose as the swelling in my ankle decreased, plus he'd wanted to make sure I didn't have any sores or blisters forming. I didn't, but I was glad he'd swapped it out for a new black one. The old green one had been getting a little rank.

That would have really made the tea ladies' noses turn up.

"That's a good idea," said the tea lady in green on my left whose name tag read Linda. "Let me see who you've got."

I turned my back to her.

"Ooh, that's a really good one," she said. "Now let me show you mine." As Linda turned in her seat, I read a single name on her back: Esther.

Who's Esther? And how come she doesn't have a last name?

"So am I alive or dead?" Linda asked a little too eagerly. This woman clearly loved to play party games.

"I think we're just supposed to ask yes or no questions."

"Oh that's right. I'm sorry." She giggled. "So, am I alive?"

I have no stinkin' idea.

Lucy must have seen my dismay because she glided behind Linda and looked down at her back. She shook her head at me.

It's not only Ricky Ricardo who loves Lucy.

"No," I said. "Am I?"

"Yes," Linda said. "Very much so."

"Am I a famous singer?"

"No," she said. "Okay, my turn again. Have I been dead a long time?"

Lucy nodded behind Linda's back.

"Yep."

"Am I Mary, the mother of Jesus?"

"Nope." Not unless your middle name's Esther.

Tara waddled over. "Can I see you guys's backs?"

We obliged.

"Those are both really good ones. Here's mine." She turned around and said over her shoulder. "I already know that I've been dead a while and that I was married."

Another one-word name: Ruth.

"I thought I might be Queen Esther," Tara said, "but I'm not."

My face must have given it away.

"Am *I* Esther?" Linda asked.

"You got it."

A pleased smile stole over her face. "She's one of my favorite women in the Bible. Okay, Becca, ask some more questions."

"All right. I know I'm alive and that I'm not a singer. Am I a famous actress?"

"No way," Linda and Tara chorused.

"Am I old?"

"Nope."

"Define old," Tara said.

"Over sixty."

"Definitely not."

"Well, then I'm not Hillary Clinton."

They both looked horrified.

"I should hope not," Linda said.

Remember where you are, stupid.

"Sarah Palin?"

"No, *I'm* Sarah," the blonde fifty-something woman across from me said with a broad grin. "And look—I even wore my red suit today."

"*I* know," I said. "I'm Tina Fey."

"No." Linda frowned. "We already said you're not an actress."

"Okay, ladies," Renee's voice over the microphone interrupted. "I hope you've all found out who you are by now, but we do need to continue with our program. If you'll all take your seats, in a moment we're going to ask the blessing."

I reached behind me and yanked off my paper so I could see who my mystery woman was. "Beth Moore? Who's that?"

Several pairs of stunned eyes met mine just as Ben arrived to pour water. He winked.

Oh, you are so dead. You owe me big-time for this, bucko.

It went downhill from there.

First they sang a bunch of songs I didn't know — although one sounded a little familiar. And then there was a skit about someone called the Proverbs woman who bought and sold a lot of stuff and wore purple.

Maybe she was the one who originally founded that Red Hat Society.

On the hat front, pregnant Tara was scoping out mine. "I wish I'd had the guts to wear a baseball cap," she said, "to be that relaxed about following the rules." She pulled her flowery boat off her head and fanned herself with it.

I thought I *was* following the rules.

And then we had lunch. Tea, I mean. Tons of little sandwiches. And every single one of them boasted a mayo mix — tuna salad, chicken salad, salmon salad, and roast beef — the latter with garlic mayo.

I hate mayonnaise. It's not that I'm allergic to it and will blow up and die like people who are allergic to peanuts or shellfish or anything like that. It's just slimy and gross and makes me gag.

Somehow I didn't think gagging would be cool to do at this fancy tea.

After the first bite, I tried to discreetly spit the chicken salad into my napkin, but there's nothing discreet about spitting. Then I tried the salmon, hoping it was made with cream cheese.

Nope. More mayonnaise.

I gulped a drink of water.

My stomach began to burble and I shoved my chair back as I reached for my crutches. "Excuse me," I said, as I bolted for the bathroom.

Only it's a little hard to bolt when you're on crutches. I wasn't sure if I was going to make it, but I managed to keep everything down until I got inside the restroom.

And then I hurled. All over the mirror.

The sight made me retch again. I gripped my crutches tight, trying to keep my balance.

I heard the door open behind me. "Becca, are you okay?" Lucy asked. She hurried over to me. "Oh, you poor thing. Let me help you."

She led me over to the loveseat in the corner and helped me sit down, leaning my crutches against the wall. "You just rest a second now and I'll get you some water." Lucy hurried back over to the sink where she wet a paper towel and filled a Dixie cup with water. "Here you go," she said, handing both to me. "Drink that slowly and you'll feel better. Then wipe your face and just relax here for a few minutes."

"Yes, ma'am." But I did what she said. Then I closed my eyes as I let my stomach settle.

When I opened them a few moments later, I saw Lucy cleaning the mirror.

"You don't have to do that," I said, starting to rise. "I'll clean it up."

She waved me back into my seat. "Honey, if I had a dime for all the times I cleaned up puke when I was usin' I'd be a rich woman now. Besides, I'm the one who roped you into coming. If it weren't for me, you wouldn't be in this mess. The least I can do is clean up."

Lucy met my eyes in the mirror. "Thank you again for

helping me out. I really appreciate it. I know this is out of your comfort zone."

You don't know how far out. "That's okay," I lied.

After she finished beautifying the bathroom, Lucy sat with me until the waves of nausea ended and we could return to our table.

At last the main event. The speaker for the day. A forty-something woman from the Bay Area, who'd formerly lived in the South and had written a couple of humorous marriage books, Renee said. The speaker, Catherine-something-or-other, was wearing a cream-colored linen suit with black piping and a sophisticated black fedora.

Then she threw all her sophistication out the window.

"I don't know about you," she said, "but I've been sitting too long. It's time to do a little moving. Come on, ladies, get out of your seats. Stand up. Yep, this means you. Let's all stand up and wriggle our fingers." She demonstrated by holding out her hands in front of her and wriggling her fingers as if she were typing at breakneck speed on a laptop.

The room followed suit.

"Good," she said, still wriggling her fingers. "Now let's throw them away!" And she flung out her hands.

Giggling, the estrogen-filled room did the same.

"Now wriggle our wrists and throw them away!"

Like proper lemming ladies they wriggled their wrists and threw them away.

"Now wriggle our arms and throw them away."

I'd like to throw *her* away.

"Very good, ladies," she said. "Pat yourselves on the back. And now I want you to march, march, march. Let's all march in place. Get that circulation going."

And here I thought I left kindergarten behind. Besides, no way was I planning to stomp on my cast.

"Okay, ladies, you can sit down," she said. "Don't you feel better now?"

A murmur of feminine assent, punctuated by giggles and laughter, swept the hot-flashing room.

Just shoot me now.

"Well, I know I feel better," she continued. "Because now I know you won't fall asleep during my talk."

More laughter.

This chick should write for *Saturday Night Live*. She's better than Tina Fey. Yeah right.

And then she launched into a mini-memoir, telling us how her father had been a successful businessman and her mother, a happy homemaker, and how they lived in a beautiful house in the nice part of town, yada, yada ... until one day tragedy struck.

"My daddy lost his white-collar job and couldn't find another one," she said, "and the bank was about to foreclose on our McMansion. But praise the Lord, just in the nick of time, Daddy got another job and we didn't lose our house."

Oh, play me a violin, honey. Is that the best you've got? Try living in a one-bedroom trailer with cockroaches and a drunken mother and only peanut butter and a sack of potatoes to eat.

"As the head of the household, Daddy took responsibility and made sure things were right for his family," she said. "And I knew then and there, that that was the kind of man I wanted to marry someday. The kind of man the *Lord* wanted me to marry." She looked out over the room. "Can I see the hands of all the single ladies, please?" she asked.

Why?

"Come on, ladies, don't be shy," she coaxed. "We were all single at one time or another."

Yeah, and some of you will be single again.

A smattering of hands raised. Nine. Ten. Eleven. In a room of well over one hundred.

I kept my hands in my lap.

"Now don't you fret, you single girls. I know how hard it is to wait. But I'm here to tell you that the Lord has a plan for your life," she said. "And he has a *man* for your life! You just have to trust him and wait for him to bring about his purposes. God's timing is never late. But he *wants* to bless you. He's *waiting* to bless you. You just need to believe and pray. And the Lord will give you the desires of your heart. The man of your heart. Now you don't lose hope now, ya hear?"

I stole a look at Lucy.

"I'm sorry," she mouthed.

Not as sorry as Ben's going to be.

16

A woman without a man cannot meet a man, any man, of any age, without thinking, even if it's for a half-second, Perhaps this is *the* man.

The Golden Notebook

"You are so dead," I said to Ben once we got in the car. I yanked off my baseball cap and slapped him on the arm with it.

"Ouch! That hurt."

"Good."

"What's wrong?" He gave me an innocent look. "Didn't you have a good time?"

"Oh yeah, great. I can't decide if my favorite part was playing the women of faith guessing game, wriggling my hands and *throwing* them away, puking in the bathroom, or listening to that sexist drivel."

"You threw up?"

I ignored the note of concern in his voice. Once I go into full-on rant mode, there's no stopping me.

"Even the restrooms were sexist," I said. "*Ladies* room. I mean, come on, people, join the twenty-first century already."

"Um, what's wrong with ladies room?" Ben asked.

"I'm no lady!"

"Duh."

I smacked him again.

I'm not sure I can hang with this dating experiment or not.

"This is so freaking not worth it," I said.

"Are you backing out?"

"Maybe."

Ben shook his head. "I can't believe you let a few women in hats and a little sign on the door defeat you. Especially since you're more than halfway there."

There is that.

"I thought you had more stamina than that," he said.

"I do. But right now, I just can't deal with another church date."

I tried to call Jenna when I got home to vent about my ludicrous afternoon, but it went straight to voicemail.

Like always.

"Where in God's name did that woman come up with that tripe?"

I was still fuming about the tea and the sexist message the next night at dinner with the Getaway Girls. Annette liked to cook for us every now and then, and since Kailyn and I weren't domestic divas in the kitchen, we never said no to a free home-cooked meal.

"Well, it certainly wasn't in God's name," Chloe said.

"I mean seriously. Do all Christians really believe that the be-all and end-all of life is marriage?" I asked. "And that a woman is not complete without a man? Are we living in the Dark Ages or what? This is the twenty-first century!"

"Preach it, Becca," Annie said, punching her fist in solidarity above her *Got Jesus?* T-shirt.

"Ah know it's the twenty-first century, girls," Annette began, "but some Christian women believe that marriage is the highest calling—"

"I thought that was motherhood," Paige interrupted.

"Well, that's the saying," Tess said. "But bottom line, as a Christ follower, following him is the highest calling. Not marriage or even children."

Annette nodded, which surprised me. She was always expounding on the virtues of home, hearth, and happy marriages. And her twenty-nine-year marriage to Randall bore witness to her strong beliefs.

"I'm surprised they chose her as their keynoter," Chloe said. "Her theology's a little skewed."

"Lucy said the same thing. She was going to let the powers-that-be know."

"Good," Annie said. "Marriage isn't for everyone. Even the apostle Paul said so."

Amen to that.

Although Kailyn didn't look convinced.

Date Fourteen was opening night of Kailyn's play.

Annie and the rest of the Getaway Girls and their significant others—or not so significant in mine and Ben's case—were attending to support her, which made Kailyn even more nervous.

"I always have opening-night jitters," she said as she got ready to leave for the theater that evening. "But knowing you're all going to be out in the audience watching tonight is even more pressure."

"Relax. You'll be great. You knocked it out of the park in rehearsal. Don't worry."

"Rehearsal's one thing," she said, "a live performance is another."

"Well, what do you usually do before you go onstage?" I asked. "Can I help? I read somewhere that actors have all different kinds of rituals they do to prepare for their performance. Some drink, some meditate, some run their lines one last time."

"I pray. I pace. I throw up."

"Sorry. Can't help you with any of those."

"I know," Kailyn said, "but thanks for offering. My acting coach always said it's good to be nervous. Just channel those nerves into energy on stage. It's when you're not nervous that you should be worried. No energy; flat performance. Well, if that's true, then there's no worry about a flat performance tonight." She scooped up her script and purse and headed for the door.

"Good luck," I called after her.

Kailyn whirled around, her eyes wide. "Never ever say good luck. It's bad luck in the theater. You're supposed to say, 'Break a leg.'"

"Considering the circumstances, I'd rather not." I inclined my head to my cast.

She giggled. "Good point. Well, I better go. I'll see you afterwards."

"*Courage, mon ami,*" I said, rustling up my limited French from our Paris trip.

My roommate didn't need courage. Or luck. Or even a broken leg. Her case of nerves was nowhere in evidence that night. She didn't seem nervous at all. She was so at ease. In fact, she oozed ease. And she was amazing.

The first act was funny—great dialogue—although the actors weren't anything to write home about. Then came act two and Kailyn's first entrance. The play came alive.

She was luminous. Radiant. Those terms are usually applied to expectant moms. "She's got that new mother glow about her. That radiance. Yada yada." Only Kailyn wasn't pregnant.

Unless she'd lied to me about that whole celibate thing.

No, what I was seeing onstage was a whole different kind of creation unfolding before my eyes. When she'd first talked about focusing her nervousness into energy, I'd imagined it in an over-the-top frenetic energy, and I wasn't sure how that would fit with her character. But I needn't have worried. The energy was more like regular life with a bit of a rush.

My roommate was a star. But not in a diva way. I'd heard the term "owning the stage" at one of the rehearsals. Now I understood what they meant. And I wasn't the only one to notice. Even the other performers stepped up their acting game.

I glanced over at Annette and Randall, squeezed in between Paige and Marc and Tess and James, and saw they were beaming with pride. All of us were. That was one of our Getaway Girls up there, and she rocked it.

Afterwards as we all gathered in the lobby waiting for our star to join us, I introduced Ben to everyone.

"A pleasure to meet you," Annette said. "Becca didn't tell us you were so handsome. It takes a good-lookin' man to pull off that shaved-head look."

"Darlin', don't embarrass the man," Randall said.

Ben grinned. "I don't embarrass easily."

"That's for sure. Or you wouldn't be dating me."

Annie extended her hand to Ben's. "I've been wanting to meet the guy who got my friend to go to church. You've succeeded where the rest of us have failed." Tonight she was wearing her favorite T-shirt, *Nobody puts Baby in the corner.*

Ben clasped her hand and shook it. "What can I say? I have the magic touch."

Was that a spark I saw when their hands met? Or was that just Annie's eyebrow ring glinting in the light?

"Magic nothing," Chloe teased. "I believe it's called a bet."

Ryan clapped his buddy on the back. "Ben always rises to a challenge." He winked at me. "And Becca's definitely a challenge."

"Keeps life interesting," I said.

"If you want interesting, you guys should come check out my church sometime," Annie said.

"What church do you go to?" Ben asked.

"Actually, we don't have a name. It's more a home group type thing."

"Oh, a Bible study."

"Sort of. Although it's not just a Bible study; more like a community—modeled on the church in Acts."

"Christianese time-out," I said. "Can you start speaking English?"

"Sorry, Bec—"

"Hey," Tess interrupted, "here comes our star."

Kailyn approached holding a sheaf of yellow roses in her bare arms, her face flushed with excitement. I don't know if it was from the thrill of opening night or because Drew was at her side.

Annette hugged her daughter, while her dad kissed her on the cheek. "You were wonderful, sweetie," Randall said.

"Just wonderful!" Annette echoed.

"Thanks. And thanks for the beautiful roses."

Paige presented Kailyn with another bouquet—this one, multicolored blooms. "Congratulations! You were great. These are from all the Getaway Girls—Marc did the arrangement."

Kailyn breathed in the scent. "Mmm, they're gorgeous. Thanks so much, you guys. And thanks for coming."

"Looks like you got over those opening-night jitters," I said.

"Yeah, once I'm on stage I'm good."

"You were more than good," Annie said. "You totally rocked."

A flicker of impatience, or was it irritation, crossed Drew's face.

Looks like someone doesn't like sharing the spotlight.

Annie noticed also. "You were really good, Algy," she said. "Or should I call you Ernest?"

"Drew would work."

Kailyn's face flamed. "Sorry. Everyone, this is Drew. Drew, these are my friends and family."

"Charmed," he said, still in character with his English accent.

"Are those really cucumber sandwiches you eat on stage?" Tess asked.

"Every performance, dear lady. Our lovely wardrobe mistress makes them for me."

"Ah love cucumber sandwiches," Annette said. "Especially with a nice cup of tea. But if I had to eat them every show I'd blow up like a balloon in no time flat." She giggled.

Drew's eyes flitted to her plump midsection. "That's why I work out every day."

Randall stole his arm around his wife's waist. "You're perfect the way you are, honey. I like a woman with some curves."

"Me too," Marc said, giving Paige a sexy smile.

"Is it hot in here or what?" I asked, stealing Tess and Annette's favorite midlife refrain. I cut my gaze toward Ben, dressed in black T-shirt and jeans. Talk about hot.

If I had to go through with this stupid dating bet, at least some nice eye candy went along with it.

Kailyn noticed too. She zeroed in on my date. "So … this is the famous, yet elusive Ben?"

"Well, the Ben part's right," he said. "I don't know about the rest."

"I'd call it elusive. You've been dating my roommate a while now, but this is the first time we've met," Kailyn said.

"Hey, just how many dates have you two been on?" Ryan asked.

"Fourteen," Ben and I chorused in unison.

"Not that anyone's keeping score," Annie said.

17

It is not a good thing for an artist to marry. As the ancients used to say, if you serve a Muse, you must serve her and no one else. An unhappy marriage may perhaps contribute to the development of talent, but a happy one is no good at all.

Ivan Turgenev

After the play, we went out for dessert — all except Drew, who'd been spirited away by some work colleagues. Technically, I thought dessert should be counted as Date Fifteen since it wasn't on the original evening's date agenda, but Chloe disagreed.

"It's all one night," she said. "That makes it one date."

The other book club members backed her up. They weren't going to give an inch on anything that might make them lose the bet.

"If you'd done something earlier in the day, like gone out for coffee or something and there were a few hours in between," Tess said, "then we'd consider it two dates."

"But since this was a continual, unbroken span of time," Paige chimed in, "it's just one."

"They've got you there, Bec," Annie teased.

"I'd have to agree," Annette said.

Kailyn was the only Getaway Girl who didn't weigh in. I could tell she was bummed over Drew's defection, especially since one of the work colleagues he was busy celebrating with at this very moment included a petite, dark-haired Eva Longoria type who'd latched onto his arm for dear life at the theater. Poor Kailyn. Already experiencing the modus operandi of the entertainment industry without even setting foot in Hollywood.

"Hey, we haven't gone on a big Getaway Girls trip since Paris," I said, dangling a distraction before her. "I think we should plan a trip to ... wait for it ... New York."

My roommate's eyes lit up. "New York?"

"Yeah. For our *A Tree Grows in Brooklyn* adventure. We could go and check out Francie Nolan's neighborhood."

"I think you'll find the neighborhood's greatly changed since Francie's day," Tess said. "That was just shy of a century ago."

"No matter. It's still a good excuse to visit The Big Apple."

"Like I need an excuse," Kailyn said. "I am so there. When do we leave? I can pack a suitcase tonight."

"Now hold on a minute, baby girl," Annette said. "You're getting as wild and impulsive as Becca. I'm not sure the two of y'all livin' together was such a good idea." She smiled to show she was teasing.

Sort of.

"A big trip like that requires planning," Annette continued. "You can't just decide on the spur of the moment to take off for the other side of the country."

"Why not?"

"Yes, why not?" Randall echoed his daughter's question.

"Darlin', don't encourage them."

"Why not?" he repeated. "They're footloose and fancy-free. What's to stop them?"

"Jobs, for one thing," Tess said.

"Money, for another," Chloe piped up.

"Yeah." Paige whistled between her teeth. "New York's pretty expensive."

"It doesn't have to be," I said. "If we all go, we could split the cost of a couple hotel rooms and just bunk together."

"All of us?" Ben said.

"Sorry. No men allowed. This is a girls' adventure only."

"When exactly were y'all planning this big adventure?" Annette asked.

"I don't know. I just now thought of it." I shrugged my shoulders. "Whenever. Next week. Next month. Doesn't matter to me. Although ..." I looked down at my leg. "I guess it'd be more fun once I'm out of this cast."

"I'm afraid I'll have to pass," Chloe said. "I used up all my vacation on our honeymoon." She did her gooey-eyed thing at Ryan.

"I might have to pass too," Tess said. "Depending on when you want to go." She lightly touched her husband's hand. "We have a couple upcoming road trips planned."

James squeezed Tess's hand.

"You've been awful quiet tonight, James," Annette said. "You all right, honey?"

"I'm fine." He grinned. "But when you Getaway Girls get together, I just watch and listen."

"Smart man," Randall said.

"Oh, hush." Annette gave her husband a playful punch.

"Count me in for the trip," Annie said. "That is, if my

slave-driver boss will give me the time off." She sent Marc a sweet smile.

"Well, I don't know," he said. "Golden Daffodils might just wither and die without you there."

"So it looks like this trip might be just the single Getaway Girls," I said.

"I'm afraid I don't know if I'll be able to make it either, what with Cyd and my classes and everything," Paige said.

"I wasn't counting you as one of the singles."

Paige's cheeks bloomed bright pink. Marc's, a lesser shade.

Open mouth, insert foot, stupid.

We all knew it was just a matter of time before Marc proposed. What we didn't know was exactly when that time would be.

"Wait a minute," Tess said, adroitly changing the subject. "Becca, we do have a Getaway Girls trip coming up. Remember? We're going to Monterey and Salinas next month in honor of John Steinbeck and *Travels with Charley.*"

Kailyn stuck out her lower lip. "That's not exactly New York."

"Or Paris," Chloe, our resident Francophile, said.

"Well, I'm just glad that this time when we go camping we'll have indoor plumbin'," Annette said.

"And we won't have to sleep on the ground," Paige added.

"You guys are a bunch of wusses." I sighed. "I sure miss Jenna."

"Me too," Chloe said. "Hey, we should invite her to join us."

"She'll probably be too busy with work. Ever since she got that new job in Napa, she's kind of dropped off the face of the earth."

Jenna's never been good at returning phone calls or email. It's nothing personal. Just not her thing. And I get that. I hate yakking on the phone. Unlike Kailyn, who exceeds her cell minute limits every month.

It would have been nice to have Jenna onboard since our Big Apple group was shriveling by the minute, but even so, I could feel my wanderlust begin to rev into start-your-engines mode. Maybe it was being on crutches so long that had me longing to break free with a new adventure. Or maybe it was too many churchy potlucks and ladies' teas — yes, just a few, but those felt like fifty — that nudged me New York way. But whatever the cause, that night when we got back to the duplex, Kailyn and I spent hours online Googling everything we could find out about New York.

Afterwards, I hobbled into the bathroom to take my every-other-day bath. I'm so not a bath girl — bubbles and bath salts have never been my thing — too smelly and frou-frou — but with a cast, my daily showers were down for the count. My doctor had warned me that I was *never* allowed to get my cast wet, which made bath time really fun.

I'd developed a good system though. I'd rigged up a cast cover, or as I liked to call it, a leg raincoat, out of those heavy-duty black trash bags, which I'd wrap around my leg until it was completely covered. Then I'd stick a durable plastic stool Annette had loaned me into the bathtub, fill the tub with water, sit on the stool with the rain-coated cast resting on the edge of the tub, and bathe.

Worked like a charm. But it was getting old. As I counted down my dates with Ben, I was also counting the days until I could suds under the spray of a bracing hot shower again.

Meanwhile, I was considering trying to patent my leg raincoat and then sell it on eBay.

I could use the cash. For clothes. I'm no fashionista like my roommate, but I'd had to cut most of my pants to accommodate my cast. That was another thing I couldn't wait to get rid of—though there was one good thing that came out of my busted ankle: it got me out of cleaning chores.

Cleaning's never been my thing. When I lived with Chloe, she said she had to take out hurricane insurance just to step over the doorway into my bedroom. And she couldn't understand why I didn't make my bed every day.

"Why bother?" I'd say. "I'm just going to sleep in it again tonight."

We agreed though that as long as I kept my door shut and the common areas free from clutter, we were good.

Kailyn wasn't as accommodating. She insisted that we split the household chores straight down the middle: vacuuming, dusting, loading and unloading the dishwasher, and, the most dreaded task of all, scrubbing the toilet.

Gross. Talk about germ city. When we first moved in together, I tried to bribe her into taking full-time toilet duty by offering to always unload the dishwasher. Seemed like an even trade to me.

Kailyn? Not so much.

However, now that I was stuck in this crummy cast, there was no way I could get down on my hands and knees to scrub the toilet.

Bummer.

Between you and me, I plan to use that get-out-of-jail-free card as long as possible.

The next day at work, Margaret dropped by to visit.

"Thanks for the nice letter you sent to my publisher," she said. "My editor—former editor, that is—forwarded it to me. That was very sweet of you."

Sweet? Not a description that's normally applied to me.

"Did it help?"

"No, but I appreciate your doing it all the same."

"So what are you going to do now?"

"Well, the one thing I'm *not* going to do is wear purple and a red hat," Margaret said. "I liked that poem when I first read it, but I don't need to join a club and wear purple to let my hair down and have fun with my girlfriends. Besides, purple's not my best color and hats don't look good on me."

"I hear ya on that."

"I'm not exactly sure what I'll do, but it's clear that I'm now entering the next chapter of my life, or as Jane Fonda said in her memoir, 'the third act.' And I plan to make it a good one. I'll probably still write, but maybe I'll just write stories for my grandkids."

"But won't you miss the author life?"

I clung to my romantic author illusions. I always thought that would be the life for me. I wouldn't mind basking in a little fan adulation now and then.

"What I *won't* miss about being an author is all the extraneous busy stuff that went along with it," she said. "No more shelling out the big bucks to a professional photographer for a glamorous, yet intelligent-looking publicity photo that doesn't show my crow's feet and double chin; no more printing out thousands of postcards with my book cover and giving them out to everyone I've ever met in my entire life—including the woman next to me in line in the supermarket. No more foisting pens with my latest title printed on them to unsuspecting second and third cousins at family reunions and funerals ..."

Margaret took a deep breath and continued. "And best of all, no more taking out a second mortgage so I can hire a hotshot publicist from New York who will then get me three online reviews and one radio interview in Podunk, USA, with a general listening audience of seven."

Who knew there was so much ancillary stuff to being an author? Margaret kept educating me.

"There's a glorious freedom in not having a deadline," she said. "For the first time in years, a book deadline doesn't have to influence my every waking hour. If I want, I can go out and putter around in my garden, or have lunch with a girlfriend, or go make mud pies with my grandkids."

She was really getting worked up. I patted her hand and tried to make appropriate sympathetic noises the way I'd seen Annette and Tess do on numerous occasions. Unfortunately, they backfired.

Margaret's eyes filled, tears spilling out. "Last year I couldn't see my granddaughter in her ballet school's production of *The Nutcracker*—she was one of the angels. I missed seeing my little angel because I was on deadline. Well, no more deadlines for me. I've had it. I'm done."

I was more than surprised by my friend's revelations. How could she put aside the vocation she had honed and polished so long? "But I thought writing was so important to you. I thought you loved it."

"I did. And I have. Writing used to be my be-all and end-all," she said. "And I have several author friends who share that same passion. You *must* have a passion to write. This is a business filled with rejection, and you need that passion to carry you through those hard times. But at the expense of the people you love?" She shook her head. "I don't think so."

"Really, Margaret. Missing one ballet performance doesn't make you a bad grandma. Life happens. You'll make the next *Nutcracker*." I hated for her to be so hard on herself.

"It's more than that. For my birthday this year, a dear friend invited me on a tour of lovely homes all done up for the holidays by local designers," she said, "but I canceled because I was on deadline. Two weeks later she was gone—dead from a brain aneurysm. And I missed a sweet memory with her because I couldn't take the time to carve out three hours from my writing deadline."

"Three *hours*," Margaret repeated. "I lost my way. I made writing my god—at the expense of everything else in my life. But no more."

She made good points. Points that poked at the inner me. Was I doing what I really wanted to do? In my work? In my life?

No.

"When I was younger it was all about the writing," Margaret said, looking past me as if viewing a memory. "Nothing stood in the way of my writing. And I have a precious husband who supported me in the pursuit of my writing dreams. But now I have a new dream: to spend time with that wonderful man of mine. And to travel. We've wanted to go to Europe for years, but I never made the time. I wouldn't take the time from my writing. And who knows how much time I have left?"

She focused her gaze back on me. "As Ben Franklin said, 'Either write something worth reading, or do something worth writing.'"

Good advice. And exactly what I intended to do. As soon as I ditched this freaking cast.

I didn't want to wait until I was Margaret's age to travel. There was a whole wide world out there to explore and I wanted to see it now, while I was still young. Not just Europe, either. My travel dreams extended beyond those shores to more exotic locales.

One little problem, my inner voice of reality said. You don't have the cash to follow those dreams.

Thanks for the reminder, dream killer.

Anytime.

Maybe I can find some kind of job overseas?

You could always join the Air Force like Annette did. Or the Army.

Yeah, and we both know how good I am at following orders. Besides, when Annette signed up in the seventies, there weren't any wars going on. I may like adventure, but I'm not into getting shot.

Chicken.

You got it.

You could be a nanny, or as they call them over there, *au pair.*

And babysit someone's bratsprings all day long? I don't think so.

Instead, I Googled 'jobs in Africa.' Whoa. Lots of options.

I'm all about options.

18

When one is in town one amuses oneself. When one is in the country one amuses other people. It is excessively boring.

The Importance of Being Earnest

I'm cheating on Ben.

Well, not really. It's not like we're exclusive or anything. He's not my boyfriend. And it's certainly not like there's anything romantic going on between us.

At all.

That's why when Zach, my skydiving instructor with the sexy, gap-toothed smile ran into me at Dunkeld's and asked me out, I said yes in a heartbeat. A heartbeat that skipped whenever I looked at him.

There was some serious heat between us.

Plus, Zach was no church boy. He wasn't the least bit shy about kissing me. And more.

But on a first date? For once I was glad for my broken leg.

Maybe all these churchy friends are rubbing off on me.

In any case, I decided not to tell the girls about my Zach date. They'd think I was being unfaithful to Ben or something.

And in a weird way they'd be right.

I felt a little guilty. Which is crazy. I never feel guilty. About anything.

That's for sure, my inner self snarked.

Watch it.

A few days later Ben and I went on a double date with Ryan and Chloe—miniature golfing, which was a little challenging with my cast and crutches. But I was determined to get back in the swing of things again. Pun intended. All these enforced indoor activities had me climbing the walls.

I had only one concern. "Are you guys going to pray before each shot?" I asked Ben when he picked me up.

"Only the last one." He winked.

We had fun though. Especially when we skunked Chloe and Ryan.

Not that either of us is competitive or anything.

"Way to go, partner," Ben said when we tallied our score.

"You guys make a good team." Chloe smirked at us.

Ben looked uncomfortable.

"Don't go matchmaking, Clo," I said. "Remember, this is a bet."

"That reminds me," Ryan said. "What does the book club get if you lose and they win?"

Chloe looked at me. "We get ... wait a minute." Her brows drew together. "Come to think of it, I don't think we ever said *what* the Getaway Girls would get. We got so caught up in getting you to commit, we forgot to make it a two-way bet."

"Not my problem." I shrugged.

"Don't worry," Chloe said. "We'll correct that oversight as soon as I talk to the rest of the girls."

"Fine by me, but it won't matter. You're not going to win."

That night when I got home, I marked fifteen on the calendar. As I capped the marker, Kailyn came out of the bathroom sniffling, her eyes red-rimmed.

"What's wrong?"

"The play's over and so's my relationship with Drew," she said. "He's dating that little Eva Longoria type from his office, but he hopes we can still be *friends*." She shook her fist. "Well, friend that, buddy."

Then she burst into tears.

"Don't cry over that idiot," I said. "He's a self-absorbed jerk. And a lousy actor to boot. His English accent really sucked."

Kailyn giggled. "It did, didn't it?"

I hobbled over to the freezer and pulled out the Ben and Jerry's, Kailyn grabbed a couple spoons, and we spent the next half hour slurping Chunky Monkey and dishing over Drew's affected enunciations.

Date Sixteen was a daylong Christian conference held on the outskirts of Reno. They probably didn't want the Enemy to tempt the faithful with all those slot machines, blackjack tables, and roulette wheels.

Only slots weren't confined to Reno proper.

When I'd last been to Nevada with Earlene and her latest flavor-of-the-month, every gas station, convenience store, and restaurant in the state seemed to sport the flashing one-armed bandits.

We'd have to give the Donald some dark shades to put on when we made a pit stop. Yes, Donald was joining us on our date. As were Cindy, Mindy, Lucy, and several others. Another group date.

Safety in numbers. Maybe Ben thought I was going to lunge for him over the GPS unit.

I haven't lunged in ages.

Zach doesn't count. He was the one doing the lunging.

Since there were so many of us, we had to caravan in three vehicles. Ben and I got stuck in Donald's big honkin' SUV along with Cindy, Mindy, and Kym. Donald thought it would be fun to do a sing-along.

Except it wasn't "Old MacDonald."

Our driver said he thought it would be a good idea for us to *prepare our spirits* for the day ahead by singing praise-and-worship songs—the same Kenny G elevator music they sang Sundays in church. Since I got the middle row next to the door, I heard the singing in surround sound.

And after the third time of getting hit in the head by Cindy whenever she closed her eyes and raised her hands to sing about Jesus shining somewhere, I started singing "Ninety-nine Bottles of Beer on the Wall."

Ben joined in on the second refrain.

Shocked silence greeted us—although I detected a snigger from Mindy's front passenger seat. "If you don't like this song," I said, "we could plug in my iPod. You guys like hip-hop? I've got the latest Kanye West."

"Or we could just talk," Mindy said, turning around in her seat to face us. "What seminars are you guys planning to attend today?"

"I'm going to 'Dating and Finding a Mate,'" Cindy said. "And 'If You Lead, He Won't Follow.'"

"Me too," Kym said. "Those are some good ones. I also want to check out 'Beauty from the Inside Out' with the former Miss Texas." Her eyes sparkled. "And I can't wait to see the traveling exhibit with the larger-than-life sculptures of the *Last Supper.*"

Sounds a little too *DaVinci Code* for me. Is this like, sponsored by the Illuminati or something?

"I'm going to 'Old Testament Eschatology' and 'Reaching

the Lost with PowerPoint.' Donald started droning on about something called pre-trib and then he and Mindy got into a heated discussion about pre-trib versus post-trib and someone from Armenia named Calvin.

I leaned over and murmured to Ben, "You sure know how to show a girl a good time. I haven't had this much fun on a date in oh, forever."

"Good to hear. I'm all about making my dates happy."

Yeah, right.

I couldn't figure Ben out. The guy hadn't made a single romantic move, and by now, it didn't look like he was going to, so what exactly was he getting from dating me?

Was this all about saving my soul or what? And why did he hang out with this singles group? He wasn't cut from the same cloth as most of them—especially the Donald.

I just didn't get it.

Whatever.

At last we were there.

We pulled into the massive church parking lot and parked next to Lucy's PT Cruiser. She hurried over to help me out of the SUV before Ben even had a chance to unbuckle his seatbelt.

As I settled my crutches beneath my arms, I whispered to her, "Please, can I ride home with you? If you let me, I'll buy you a book. Or dinner. A weekend at a spa ... You name it."

Lucy just smiled.

The parking lot was packed. As I scanned the lot I saw that nearly every car around us sported some kind of bumper sticker: *Christians aren't perfect, just forgiven*, lots of the Christian fish symbols, even some fish eating fish with feet.

Ah. Meant to be a clever anti-Darwin statement. I was surprised, however, to see several cars still had plenty of McCain/Palin stickers, now peeled back and fading.

Give up already.

"Come on, guys, the next shuttle's arriving," the Donald said.

"Shuttle?"

Ben nodded to a distant speck on the horizon. "It's a bit of a hike to the church, so they provide shuttle service."

Is this a church or an airport? But I guess that's better than having to walk that far on these crutches.

As we shuttled through the sea of cars, the Donald said, "This is one of the fastest growing churches in America. Attendance has tripled in just the past two years. Wait'll you see it. It's amazing."

That's one word for it.

We passed by several other buildings in a complex that was the size of a shopping mall and then finally pulled up to the main building. I stared up at the multistoried marble-and-glass edifice thronged with people pushing through the massive doors. "Dude! That's the biggest church I've ever seen. And I've been to Notre Dame."

Inside was even more of a revelation.

Everything was all new and shiny. And mostly white. White walls, white ceiling, white doors, white marble floor flecked with gold. Soft elevator music piped through hidden speakers.

We walked over the sparkly marble floors past the giant koi pond and waterfall in the lobby. Theater-sized projection screens were embedded high in the center of each wall. Color was provided by a constant stream of nature images flashing across the screens: sunsets over the ocean, snow-capped mountains, flaming fall foliage, red barns in waving wheat fields, fighter jets streaking across the sky superimposed over an American flag.

Concerned I'd trip or at least get a stiff neck from looking up, I lowered my eyes and found myself face-to-face with a huge oil painting of a silver-haired guy in steel-framed specs and a gray suit a shade darker than his hair.

"Who's that?" I asked. "Someone famous?"

"Oh, that's our pastor," said a beaming middle-aged woman in a watermelon-colored suit sporting a white stick-on tag that read "Can I Help?" She was all spritzed and shellacked. Her hair didn't even move as she inclined her head to us. "Pastor Douglas. We just love him. You'll get to hear him speak at the opening session ... in about twenty minutes."

Shellack woman zeroed in on my cast. "Would you like a scooter, dear? Those crutches must be uncomfortable. We have scooters for our elderly or handicapped members."

"Thanks," I said. "But I've gotten used to them. They're like another appendage."

A posse of shellacked, smiley women advanced on the next set of arrivals. It was like the Cybermen episode of *Dr. Who*, except instead of clomping forward in shiny metal suits, this Jamba Juice army dressed in watermelon, peach, and strawberry and rounded off their uniforms with matching pumps.

"Please visit the booths in our north wing," the first cyberwoman, I mean shellack woman, said. "We have so many different things ... it's a cornucopia of treasures."

During the opening ceremonies with the silver-haired, silver-tongued Pastor Douglas, he urged all the attendees to "seek his face."

I thought God was invisible. Or is he just hiding?

Would he play hide-and-seek?

So do we ever get to tag him and say, "You're it"?

Wait, we have to capitalize: You're It.

After that illuminating session, we decided to check out the north wing. The Donald wanted to "get oriented."

Ben said, "Let's just get it over with."

I'd expected to see people selling books, music, and some

bumper stickers, but what I didn't expect to see was a huge room filled with booths. It reminded me of the convention halls at the state fair: clothing, purses, backpacks, jewelry. Framed art and figurines.

Then I started to notice specific items for sale: golf balls with Scriptures on them, cell-phone covers with a flashing cross, purple glittery scarves with Bible verses in gold script, throw blankets, pillows, candles ... even Christian edibles: Testamints, Bible Bars, and Apocalypse hot sauce.

It was like shopping for souvenirs at Jesus World.

There was a Fruit of the Spirit glass cutting board, biblical action figures, even a bobble-head Jesus. I thought the wash-away-your-sins soap was a joke, but I think maybe they were serious. And then there was the rack of sweatshirts proclaiming *This Blood's for You.*

My personal favorite though was the Jesus ashtray. The picture on the bottom showed Jesus wearing a crown of thorns and the saying around the rim said, "Jesus hates it when you smoke."

Are you kidding me?

The last time I'd seen so much kitsch was when Chloe dragged me to a Sunday flea market out at the fairgrounds.

"Is that what I think it is?" I nodded to a small triangular piece of hard plastic a little bigger than a quarter that had the words "Pick Jesus" emblazoned across the front.

"That's a guitar pick," said the smiling dude behind the booth. "Would you like to try it out?"

"No thanks. I don't play."

Lucy, Mindy, Ben, and I passed by another booth where the woman called out to us that she had some pretty shades of nail polish we might like to try.

"I do need some new polish," Lucy murmured.

We backed up, and the woman, who had the longest set of

nails I'd ever seen — scarlet red with glittery crosses sparkling on them — extended a bottle of bright red nail polish to us. "This is our 'Washed in the Blood of the Lamb'," she said. "It's one of our best sellers."

Lucy made an inarticulate choking sound.

"Sorry," I said, holding up my hand. "I bite my nails."

As we hurried away, Ben's face darkened. "I hate all this Jesus junk," he said.

"What? You don't think a switch-plate cover should have Jesus' face on it?" Mindy said.

"Or your kids should suck on a lollipop of the cross?" Lucy said. "The cross our Lord died upon?"

"Don't even get me started."

"And we're here again, why?" I said to Ben out of the side of my mouth.

"Definitely not for this garbage," he said. "But there's a couple good speakers I want you to hear. I think you'll find them interesting."

Right. Watching paint dry would be more interesting.

Finally at the end of the commercial gauntlet were two booths of books. Now we're getting somewhere ...

Except Ben chose that moment to pull me into a session. Something about finances and firstfruits and something called tithing? I should have brought along my Christianese translation guide.

I scribbled down as many unfamiliar words as I could.

The chick next to me leaned over and whispered, "I know, isn't this message great? Definitely one we all need to hear. You can buy the tape afterwards if you want to listen to it again. That's what I always do. Then whenever I want to hear the message again, I have it right at my fingertips."

At least her fingertips weren't washed in the blood of the lamb.

But that whole thing of giving God money when I can barely even pay my bills? I don't think so. Besides, God doesn't need money. What's he going to do with it? Buy a few more gold harps for the angels or something?

The seminar on people in Africa and other Third World countries who lacked the basic essentials—including water—made me sit up and take notice, however.

"We waste more water in an afternoon watering our lawns and letting the drinkable water drain down our driveways than most Third World families get to drink in a month," the speaker said. "In Africa, thousands of kids are dying daily for want of clean, safe water."

Then he went on to cite a bunch of statistics, including ones that said every day, diseases related to diarrhea cause some six thousand deaths, mostly among children under the age of five. "Diarrheal diseases have killed more children in the past ten years than all the people lost to armed conflict since World War II," he said, attributing the diseases to water, sanitation, and hygiene risk factors.

How can that be in this day and age? That many kids dying because they don't have access to clean water?

"Wait'll I tell Annie about this," I said to Ben when the speaker concluded. "She'll want to know all about it. She's gone on a few overseas mission trips where she helped dig wells to provide water and stuff."

"She has?" Ben sat up straighter in his seat.

"Yeah. I think the wells were in Rwanda. Or maybe it was Costa Rica. Can't remember. She also worked in an orphanage in Guatemala for a while and helped in the clean-up of New Orleans right after Katrina."

"I'm impressed."

"Me too," I said as we exited the seminar room. "In fact, I'm even motivated."

"To what? Become a missionary?" He smirked.

"No way. But to do something tangible. Something meaningful. Something that makes a difference."

As much as I wasn't into kids, staggering amounts of them dying for a basic resource I took for granted was just wrong. Maybe if people sent them bars of that wash-away-your-sins soap it would help.

Ben and I turned away by mutual, unspoken agreement from the Jesus junk gauntlet and opted to go outside instead for some fresh air.

"It was hard to breathe in there," he said.

"You're telling me." I looked over at him. "I'm curious. Why do you go to stuff like this if it's not your thing?"

"I wanted to hear the speakers." He shrugged. "And to hang with my friends."

"But you could do that anywhere. And, not to be harsh, but I find it hard to believe the Donald's really your friend." I rolled my eyes. "I mean, serious?"

"Why not? Friends don't have to be exactly alike to be friends," he said. "Take you and me."

"Yeah, why don't we take you and me? What's that all about anyway?"

The door opened and Mindy and Cindy walked out into the courtyard. "*There* you guys are," Cindy said. "We've been looking for you everywhere."

Saved by the indy twins.

At the end of the day as we rode in the shuttle back to the parking lot, Lucy said, "Ben, would you mind if Becca rode home with me instead and Patrick rode with you guys? We have some girl things we want to discuss."

"Sure," Ben said. "No problem."

I nearly leaned over and kissed Lucy. But I didn't want to start tongues wagging.

Her other two passengers had met up with friends at the conference and were spending the night in Reno, so Lucy and I would have her comfy PT Cruiser all to ourselves on the drive back to Sacramento.

I buckled my seatbelt and pushed the button to move my seat all the way back so I could stretch out my leg. "Thanks for the ride, Luce. I appreciate it."

"Well, I sure hope you'll appreciate this too." She handed me a small, leather-bound Bible. "The best gift I know—the Word of God. I want you to have it."

Normally, snarky remarks would pop into my head, but I found myself strangely snarkless.

"Thanks," I said, genuinely touched. Her gesture had surprised me—unexpected, yet somehow welcome. Like Lucy herself.

And Ben.

Which reminded me. Only nine more dates to go.

As we sped down the freeway, I reminded myself I was in the home stretch. Soon I could ditch all this Christian lingo and fellowshipping and church hopping. I'd win the bet and be free from all the restraints of these past few weeks. It was time to get excited.

So why wasn't I?

19

She began the first of what we later called "my lessons
in living." She said that I must always be intolerant of
ignorance but understanding of illiteracy.

I Know Why the Caged Bird Sings

Our date the next night was better—dinner with Ben's
Grandma Adelaide.

"It's so nice to see you again, Becca," she said after I
crutched my way through the door. Adelaide laid a gentle,
shaky hand on mine. "How are you, dear?"

"I'm good. But more important, how are you?"

"I have my good days and bad days," she said, "but the
Lord always sees me through. Today was a good day. Although
... I need to sit down for a bit if you don't mind." She leaned
heavily on her cane.

"Of course not. I wouldn't mind getting off of these
crutches myself."

"How much longer until you're free of your cast?" she

asked as we all made our way into the living room. "I see you have a black one now. Very chic."

"Just two more weeks. I can hardly wait! The first thing I'm going to do when this puppy comes off is start running again."

"Whoa. Hold on there, Wilma Rudolph." Ben relieved me of my crutches and leaned them against the wall. "You won't be running immediately. Your leg's going to be pretty weak after being in that cast all this time," he said. "You'll need to build up your strength and stamina. It was a good month after my cast was removed before I could start running and hiking again."

"Yeah, well, I'm younger and in better shape than you, marathon man." I stuck my tongue out at him. "I bet you I'll be running laps within two weeks."

"You might want to rethink that whole bet thing. As I recall, the last time you bet me something, I won." He gave me a stern look. "And I think you'd better talk to your doctor before you do anything. Remember, Seabiscuit didn't race until he was completely recovered."

"If you'll pardon my saying, dear," Adelaide said, "if it were me, the first thing I'd want to do after the cast came off is to take a shower and shave that leg. It must be quite the forest by now."

A snarky senior citizen? Who'd have thought? But Adelaide's kind twinkling eyes saved her.

"Yeah, I've nicknamed it Sherwood Forest."

"Well, that's a visual I didn't need," Ben said.

"And you call yourself a world traveler?" I grunted. "In case you didn't know, Mr. Unaware, in many countries around the world, women don't shave their legs. It's considered a sign of beauty."

"Yeah, but I think that involves both legs, Hopalong. Not just one."

"Speaking of countries around the world, I hope you don't mind ethnic food, Becca," Adelaide said. "Since you're so interested in Africa, I thought you might enjoy sampling some of what we ate when we lived there."

"I'm really into exotic foods. I'll eat anything. Except mayonnaise."

"Yeah, mayonnaise is really exotic," Ben said. "It's right up there with chicken feet and Rocky Mountain oysters."

"Chicken feet?"

"That's an Asian delicacy," Adelaide said, "but don't worry. I'm not going to make you eat any strange animal parts tonight. We're having peanut soup, lamb kebabs with yogurt dipping sauce, and couscous."

"Sounds great. I love couscous. Lamb too."

Although Jenna would kill me if she knew I was eating Mary's little lamb.

"I thought of making this Kikuyu side dish, irio," Adelaide continued, "but it's not to everyone's taste."

"I'll say." Ben made a face.

"What is it?"

"Mashed corn, mashed peas, and mashed potatoes all mixed together," he said.

"You don't like mashed potatoes?"

"With gravy, sure—and especially at Thanksgiving. But I prefer my vegetables in their original texture, not all mashed to a pulp."

"It's called puree, Benjamin," his grandmother said.

"Puree. Pulp. Potato, potahto. I don't care what you call it, I don't like it. It's like eating baby food."

"Was he this fussy as a baby too?" I asked Adelaide.

"Worse." She smiled and stood up. "And now that we've

exhausted the topic of what my grandson doesn't like to eat, shall we adjourn to the dining room for dinner?"

Adelaide's African meal was delicious. I would have licked the plate clean but didn't want to be rude, especially since I was hoping to be asked back again.

"Tell me about your job at the bookstore, Becca," she said. "What's it like?"

"Nothing to write home about." I shrugged. "It's just a job. Pays the bills." Then I remembered my outstanding Visa bill. "Usually."

"But what do you do, dear?"

"My title is community relations advisor, which means that in addition to normal bookstore activities—stocking shelves, working the register—I set up events and signings. Basically, I babysit authors."

"You don't sound too crazy about it."

"I'm not," I said. "I used to love it—I mean what could be better than to be surrounded by books and authors all day long? But it's definitely not what I want to do for the rest of my life."

"What do you want to do?" Adelaide asked.

"No idea. Something that makes a difference, though."

"How'd you like to start right now?" Ben asked. "Once you get your cast removed, I mean. Are you any good with a hammer?"

"Pretty good. Why?"

"Habitat for Humanity is building some homes in the area, and I thought you might like to help on one of the next ones."

The succession of rundown rental trailers Earlene and I had occupied over the years filled my head. "Sounds great. Sign me up."

"It's a date," Ben said.

"You sure know how to show a girl a good time," I teased.

"I try."

"I wish I could help too." Adelaide looked ruefully at her shaking hands. "But I'd probably drop a hammer on someone's head."

"Gran, I don't think you need to worry about swinging a hammer to make a difference. You already gave at the office." Ben laughed, then turned serious. "Your whole life has been about giving. Even this tasty meal you've made is a gift."

"I'll say. That was wonderful. Thank you, Adelaide," I said, remembering not to speak with my mouth full.

"I'm glad you liked it. I really enjoy cooking, and it's a treat for me to have guests for dinner. Usually it's just Benjamin and me—when he's home, that is." She wagged her finger at her grandson. "Someone's been keeping him pretty busy lately."

Uh-oh. Did I detect a note of admonition under the teasing?

Adelaide set down her fork and dabbed at her mouth with a cloth napkin. "I think we'll wait a little while for dessert."

"That's a good idea." I undid the top button of my jeans beneath the table.

"What's for dessert, Gran?"

"Remember how we used to eat a lot of mangoes when we were in Africa?"

"Oh yeah." Ben licked his lips. "I love mangoes."

"Well, I wanted to make homemade mango ice cream with pineapple rum sauce," Adelaide said, "but with these shaky hands of mine, homemade ice cream's just too difficult. So ... I thought in a little bit maybe you could run to the store for me, Benjamin, and pick up some peach ice cream instead?"

"Just say when."

"And while we're waiting for dessert, do you think you could tell me a little more about your days in Africa?" I asked. "What you did, where you went, what you ate, what you saw ..."

"I'll do even better than that. I'll show you my scrapbooks."

"Sweet."

Adelaide and I gimped our way over to the couch while Ben pulled down a couple oversized photo albums from the bookcase. She settled herself in the middle of the sofa with Ben and me flanking her on either side, and opened the first album. A faded black-and-white photo of a smiling young couple standing in front of what looked like a lake or some other large body of water stared out at us.

"That's Matthew and me at Lake Victoria the day we arrived in Kenya," Adelaide said.

"Cool. Did you go down the Nile?"

"Oh yes. Many times." She turned the page.

"Wow. Are those hippopotamuses?" I asked, leaning in for a closer look at the large dark creatures in the river.

"Yes, but you don't want to get too close to a hippo," she said. "They're the most dangerous animal in Africa."

"Serious? I thought that would be crocodiles."

"Well, you want to stay away from them too, but hippos have been known to kill crocs and lions, and on land, they can run faster than a person," she said. "It's not that they hunt humans; they're just very territorial, so it's best to keep your distance."

"Thanks. I'll remember that."

She turned the page and pointed to a large bird in the air. "That's a fish eagle. It's been called the voice of Africa because of its distinctive, piercing call." Adelaide got a far-off look in her eye. "It's one of the most beautiful sounds of Africa."

"Sure is," Ben said.

I peered closer. "Looks like a bald eagle."

"Yes, they're in the same family."

"What's that it's holding in its feet?"

"A fish," she said. "The African fish eagle feeds mainly on fish."

Duh. Keep up with the class, Becca.

"The eagle spies its prey and swoops down and plucks it from the water," Adelaide said. "We had the opportunity to see that a few times."

"Yeah, it was pretty cool," Ben said.

I tried—and failed—not to be jealous. Although I'd seen things like this on nature videos and the Discovery channel before, I'd never actually seen them up close and personal in real life.

But I determined to. Someday. And I became even more determined to make that someday soon as Adelaide continued to show me picture after picture from her days in Africa.

Lions and hippos and crocs, oh my. Zebras and monkeys and wildebeest too. Even hyenas.

She turned the page again and a picture of a thin, young, unsmiling dark-haired woman sitting in front of a dilapidated tin shack stared out at us.

"Who's that?" I asked.

"That's me," Adelaide said.

"But it doesn't look at all like you. You look so unhappy."

"I was. Being a missionary—especially in a small village on the other side of the world without any of the amenities I was accustomed to—was a huge culture shock for me," she said. "Especially since I used to be what was called a priss."

"You?" I stared at her. "You're the farthest thing from a priss I've ever seen. Now my roommate Kailyn, there's a priss for you. She wouldn't last a day in Africa. She could barely handle camping last year in the Redwoods."

"Sounds familiar," Adelaide said. "I was never good at camping either, and when we camped on the way to our Kenyan village over fifty years ago, they didn't have air mattresses, porta-potties, or nylon multi-roomed tents. Heavens! We had to lug our heavy canvas Army surplus tent through the bush in the hot summer—all the while keeping an eye out for snakes. I was perspiring so much my clothes were sticking to me, and I got blisters on my soft, lily-white hands."

She glanced at her gnarled, age-spotted hands with a rueful smile. "But I was young and in love and starry-eyed and thought I could handle anything. And although sleeping on the hard ground and sharing space with scorpions and snakes and all sorts of other dangerous critters was scary, it wasn't half as scary as trying to keep house and build a life with my new husband without even such basics as running water," she said. "Not to mention trying to teach the women how to sew and the people how to read. Those first few months were incredibly difficult. I cried myself to sleep more nights than I can count."

"So what made you stay?"

"God. And my patient husband." She grinned. "And the people. Always the people."

"Africa is beautiful and exotic and magical," Adelaide said, "but it was the people there that captured my heart. Especially the children. They have so little compared to us, and yet so much. They were always smiling and laughing and full of joy. The simplest things brought them pleasure—chasing after chickens, the wonder of a new pencil ... so unspoiled."

I thought about the bratsprings who peopled Dunkeld's and pitched a screaming fit when Mommy or Daddy didn't buy them the latest Gameboy.

"And what a joy it was to see them read the Bible in their own language," she continued. "Their eyes would just light up. When I think of all the children in the world who can't read, it breaks my heart."

Her memories mesmerized me. Seeing Africa through Adelaide's eyes made me believe that one person might matter.

One person could change things. Even me.

"If I could," Adelaide said, "I would return there tomorrow. But I'm afraid this old, broken body can't make the trip. The spirit is willing, but the flesh truly is weak." She sent us a rueful smile. "And I know it's not the same Africa I left. I don't have a romantic vision that things will be the same. So many terrible things have happened since then: the famines, the genocides in Rwanda and Darfur, all the problems in Zimbabwe …"

Her face looked suddenly older. "And AIDS has decimated entire populations throughout the continent. It breaks my heart. But what can I do? Once I was among them and could show them God's love. Now, I'm just an old woman."

She looked down again at her folded hands. "What I can do is pray. For the sick and dying. For the dear, dear children. And for change. Only God can change enough hearts to draw folks to Africa."

No wonder Ben was a Christian. Just look at his legacy.

Although I still didn't get how his parents could leave him with Grandma all those years, I looked at the next scrapbook page. "Is that a picture of Ben's folks?"

"Yes, that's my daughter Rachel and her husband, John," Adelaide said. "And that's my little monkey they're holding. You were such a cute baby, Benjamin."

"Thanks, Gran. I notice that compliment is in the past tense. So I take it I'm no longer cute?"

Adelaide gave Ben's arm a soft punch. "Oh, you."

I looked at the bald-headed infant and then over at Ben. "You haven't changed much. Other than the soul patch."

"Oh, I've always had soul," he said.

"Do your folks live here in town? Or are they still in Africa?"

"Nah. Now they're in India. They were in Africa about fifteen years and then came back to the States on furlough, but only stayed a year," he said. "They've been in New Delhi for the past decade."

"Did you live in India too?"

His face changed almost imperceptibly. "No."

"Ben's lived with me since he was six," Adelaide said. "John and Rachel were on assignment to a remote village deep in the bush where there was a huge outbreak of malaria, as well as the stirrings of some political unrest, so for his safety, they sent Benjamin home to live with me."

She gave him a tender smile. "Matthew had gone home to be with the Lord six months earlier, so there was a big empty spot in my heart and in my life—just waiting for God to fill it. And he did. With Ben."

"And your parents stayed there?" I asked.

He nodded, his face inscrutable except for a slight tightness to his jaw.

"That's where they believed God had placed them," Adelaide said. "He'd called them to minister to the lost of that village, so that's what they did."

Ben stood up. "Gran, I don't know about you, but I'm getting a little hungry for your dessert. Want me to go get the ice cream now?"

"Yes dear, if you would, please. I didn't mean to go rattling on."

"That's okay. I'll be back in a few." He grabbed his keys and left.

"Please continue to rattle," I said. "This is great stuff."

"Actually, I've been wanting to talk to you, Becca. And now that Benjamin's gone, it's the perfect time."

Uh-oh. I'm in for it now. Here comes the Mama Bear protecting her cub talk, where she tells me that she likes me, but she'd prefer Ben date a nice Christian girl instead.

And she's right too. But not until I win the bet.

"I love my grandson very much," Adelaide began. "He's a kind, wonderful young man and he takes good care of his old grandmother. But—"

"But you're worried about him dating a non-Christian," I interrupted.

"Actually," Adelaide said. "I'm worried about you."

"Me?"

"Yes. You and Ben have been spending a lot of time together, and I just don't want you to get hurt. I'm afraid my Benjamin's a little lacking in the commitment department," she said, a frown furrowing her forehead.

I burst out laughing. "That's okay. I'm not looking for anything serious either. Really."

So really.

I debated telling Adelaide about the bet but wasn't sure how his sweet, old, missionary grandmother would feel about her grandson being attached—even peripherally—to anything that involved gambling.

Discretion might be the better part of valor.

"Ben and I are just friends," I said. "Nothing more. We just like hanging out together."

"Well, if you're sure ..."

"I'm sure."

And as I said it, I knew it was true. I mean Ben was cool and fun and everything. More cool than I expected a Christian guy to be, but there just wasn't that spark.

The only fire seemed to be between him and Annie. But had I read that right?

"Romance doesn't factor into our relationship." At all. *That* I could say with certainty.

"Well, I'm relieved to hear it. But there's something else I've been wanting to say to you, Becca," Adelaide said softly. "I would be remiss if I didn't tell you that Jesus loves you." She patted my hand. "The hound of heaven is after you, my dear, but you're running from him."

"It's kind of hard to run when I'm stuck in this plaster prison," I joked.

Although I'd really like to right about now. First the Bible from Lucy, now this. Did I have "hell-bound" written on my forehead or something?

"The Lord is a gentleman," Adelaide said. "He doesn't force himself on us. He simply stands at the door and knocks. All you have to do is open the door and he'll come in."

The front door opened.

"I'm back," Ben said.

Whew. Saved by the ice cream.

I couldn't get through my dessert quickly enough.

As we were leaving, Adelaide said, "Benjamin, before you go, can you get me my other cane from the closet, please?"

He gave her a puzzled look, but acquiesced, returning with a basic brown cane with a black rubber handle.

"And if I could hold onto your arm for just a moment?" she said.

"Sure." He proffered his arm.

Adelaide linked her left arm through his. "And now, if you'd give me that cane, I'd like you to hold this one for me, please."

Ben looked even more puzzled as she handed him her hand-carved cane that I'd so admired on my first visit.

"Becca, dear. I'd like you to have this," she said. "Benjamin's going to carry it for you since you've got your hands full with your crutches."

"But I can't take that. That's one of your souvenirs from Africa."

"I've got plenty of souvenirs," she said. "Too many. When you get to be my age, you don't want as much stuff. Someone,

I think it was Sartre, said, 'We are possessed by the things we possess.'"

So you want me to possess it instead.

The snarky thought came automatically. I didn't really mean it.

Adelaide continued. "I have a feeling this is just the beginning of your African collection, my dear."

"I don't know what to say. Thank you so much." My fingers followed the intricate carving along the handle. "When I look at it, I'll always think of you."

"I hope you'll think of Jesus too." Adelaide gave me an impromptu hug. "There is no one better to lean upon, my dear. He will hold you up when you are too weak to stand."

When I got home, I sat down on the couch and propped my cast on the coffee table on top of the now seriously dented throw pillow. I lifted the cane to my lap and inspected it up close. Carved elephants and hippos cooled off in the Nile, and a little higher up, lions chased zebras and gazelles. Above them, monkeys swung in the trees and a fish eagle stretched out its wings.

As I stared at the beautiful carvings, my eyes filled.

I couldn't believe Adelaide had given me such a precious gift. My fingers traced the lion's mane, and for some reason I thought of Aslan from the Chronicles of Narnia. The great lion that died willingly for the stupid Edmund. But then ... didn't Aslan come back to life ... like Jesus?

Lately, wherever I looked, Jesus seemed to be there. Was he waiting, like a gentleman, to open the door? Or chasing me like a hound from heaven? Maybe both. Maybe neither. I didn't know.

But one thing was for sure. That Grandma Adelaide was one smart chick.

I smiled as I ran my hands over the carvings. And then I

noticed something I'd missed earlier. A couple faint letters and numbers etched beneath the eagle's wing: Is. 40:31.

Is forty thirty-one? What kind of existential question is that?

Look closer, dummy. There's a period after the s. Could it be, maybe, oh, I don't know, a Bible verse perhaps?

Is?

I laid the walking stick across my lap and leaned forward to the edge of the coffee table to pick up the little Bible Lucy had given me. Luckily there was an index listing all the books of the Bible. I ran my finger down the list: Genesis, Exodus, Leviticus, blah, blah, blah, Esther.

Whoa, she got her own book? No wonder the chick at the tea was jazzed to have Esther's name on her back.

My finger continued its search for a book beginning with Is: Job, Psalms, Proverbs, Ecclesiastes, Song of Songs, Isaiah.

Isaiah. Bingo. And there was even a page number. Sweet.

I decoded the message from her cane: "But those who hope in the Lord will renew their strength. They will soar on wings like eagles; they will run and not grow weary, they will walk and not be faint."

Cool.

20

I saw in their eyes something I was to see over and
over in every part of the nation — a burning desire to go,
to move, to get under way, anyplace, away from any Here.

Travels with Charley

"I've been healed!" I threw my crutches down on the floor of
the doctor's office once he finished cutting away the black plaster of my cast.

Dancin' the happy dance now. Okay, so maybe not exactly
dancing just yet, but soon ... I reached down to my exposed
right leg that hadn't seen the light of day in forever and gave
it a vigorous scratch.

Ah, heaven. Until my fingers got tangled in the hair.

Adelaide was right. It was quite a forest. But at least the
thickness of the hair covered the whiteness of the leg. My set-
free leg was a skinny, shriveled, pale imitation of my healthy,
tanned left leg.

"I can't wait to get home and shave," I said. "Maybe I'll
even borrow some of my roommate's self-tanning lotion so I

won't blind everyone on the street." I started to bound out the door.

"Whoa," Doctor Helm said. "Not so fast there, Sparky. I think you've forgotten something."

"What?"

"The next step in your treatment. Also known as a walking cast."

Crap. I'd totally spaced on the fact that I was simply exchanging one plaster prison for another. Which totally sucked.

At least this one doesn't require the hated crutches and I'd be able to move around more freely on our next adventure with the help of Adelaide's beautiful cane.

The Getaway Girls were getting away again. This time in homage to John Steinbeck's *Travels with Charley*. It had been ages since we'd gone on one of our book adventures, and I couldn't wait. All the girls together again—except Jenna—and going on a road trip. Yes!

Except at the last minute, Annie and Paige had to beg off—some kind of crisis at the flower shop.

As the remaining five of us set off down the highway in Tess's fancy Winnebago, I felt like bursting into song. Willie Nelson's "On the Road Again" popped into my head, but that was forever tainted by my bio-mom memories, so I replaced it with Dolly Parton's "Travelin' Thru," which the dreadlocked Jason had sung on *Idol*.

Hmm. I forgot there were God lyrics in it. Jesus too. Can I never get away from it? Maybe Adelaide's right and that hound of heaven *is* chasing me.

But he's not going to catch me. I'm a fast runner. Or I will be again soon.

I scrolled forward to a little Springsteen.

It felt good to be traveling again. Sure, it was only to Monterey and Salinas over the weekend, but still, it got me out of town. Rolling down my window, I closed my eyes and let the wind ruffle my hair as I rocked out to "Born in the USA."

A tap on my arm made me open my eyes. Tess mouthed something from the driver's seat.

"What?" I pulled out my earbuds.

"I said I like your natural hair color best," she said. "Your different rainbow colors were fun for a while, but your dark hair looks best with your skin tone."

"Thanks."

"Does Ben like it?" she asked with a little smile.

"I have no idea. You do know that Ben and I aren't romantically involved, don't you?"

"Really? Even after all these dates?"

"Yep. We're not a good match," I said. "No chemistry. Although we work well as friends."

"How many dates left now?"

"Only six more to go to the magic twenty-five, and then victory is mine."

Since dinner with Adelaide and Ben, I had gone on two more dates — coffee at Starbucks and the latest movie from Pixar. Kailyn was really hoping I'd lose the bet. Once Chloe told the others they'd forgotten to extract a concession from me if I didn't follow through with my end of the bargain, they'd put their heads together and decided that if they won the bet, we'd all go en masse to San Francisco for a full weekend of shopping and pampering at some upscale hotel, complete with the girlie works — manicure, pedicure, and a massage.

The massage I wouldn't mind. But a manicure and pedicure? Not so much. And shopping? No freaking way.

Now I was even more determined to win the bet.

"I hope you've got your fishing gear handy," I said to Tess, "because the first thing we're going to do once I win is go on that *Perfect Storm* deep-sea-fishing adventure."

She didn't even blink an eye. "No problem. James has got a full complement of fishing equipment. He and his sons go fishing several times a year."

"Did I hear someone say fishing?" Kailyn asked, appearing between our two front seats from the back of the Winnebago. "Eew, with worms and everything?"

"You use a little bigger bait when you go deep-sea fishing," I said. "Depending on whether you're going trolling or bottom fishing. Bottom fishing is for things like red snapper and grouper, where you use squid or cut-up fresh fish, while trolling is usually for tuna or shark. There you use a combination of live bait—minnows or shad—and artificial bait with bright colors."

Tess looked at me in admiration. "Someone's been doing their homework."

"Google is my friend."

"Did you say shark?" Chloe's head popped up next to Kailyn's. "We're not going anywhere near any sharks," she said.

"Sharks?" Annette's voice floated from the back. "What are y'all talkin' about ugly ol' sharks for?"

"For when we go on our deep-sea-fishing adventure," I called back over my shoulder.

"Who said we're going deep-sea fishing?" Kailyn asked.

"That's part of the bet, remember? Once I win, you have to go along with whatever adventure I choose."

"You haven't won yet," Chloe said.

"But it's getting close. Only six dates away."

"Six?" Kailyn said. "It hasn't been three months yet."

"The agreement was three months or twenty-five dates—whichever comes first, and we've had nineteen dates so far," I reminded her. "So if I were you, I'd start exercising your casting arms for when we go trolling in the Pacific."

"Don't be too cocky," Chloe said. "You never know what's going to happen. Ben could always bail on you."

I narrowed my eyes at her. "Do you know something I don't? Or does Ryan?"

"No. I'm just sayin'."

"Okay, ladies," Tess said, turning on her blinker and pulling into a rest area. "Time for an early lunch. I know it's only eleven o'clock, but I'm really hungry."

"Me too," Kailyn said.

"Make that three." I clambered out of my seat and followed them to the back, where Annette bustled about fixing lunch.

Tess's Winnebago was like the Ritz on wheels.

I released a low whistle the first time I saw inside. "Not exactly Rocinante, is it?"

Steinbeck's modest pickup truck and camper shell that he drove around the US and nicknamed after Don Quixote's horse had maybe a third the size of James and Tess's rolling campground.

Or as I came to think of it, the Luxurymobile.

From what I recall, Steinbeck's camper, where he chronicled his 1960 travel adventures, had a double bed, toilet, small stove and refrigerator, heater, closet, and limited storage space.

In Tess's Luxurymobile there were two sleeper couches in the living room area that made into beds, a fully equipped kitchen with a full-sized fridge, stove, microwave, and sink, and some kind of high-end countertops Annette called Corian.

Also, a complete bathroom with a full-sized shower, sink, and toilet, and a master bedroom with a king-sized bed, closet, and nightstands on either side.

The only thing missing was a Jacuzzi tub and a tanning bed.

We sat down at the dining room table to a lunch of cold salmon salad and sourdough bread.

"I was going to make my famous seafood salad," Annette said, "but I know how much you hate mayonnaise, Becca, so I switched to salmon salad instead, which doesn't have a drop of mayo in it. I use a honey-dijon sauce."

"Thank you," I said. "My stomach especially thanks you."

"Well, after hearin' what happened at that ladies' tea, I didn't want to take any chances."

"What happened at the tea?" Tess asked. "Somehow I missed that."

"Becca ralph—"

"Kailyn, we're eatin' here," her mother said. "I don't think we need to get into the graphic details."

"Enough said." Tess took a sip of her iced tea. "I think I get the picture."

"Picture." Kailyn slapped her hand against her forehead. "I forgot to bring my camera to take pictures for Annie and Paige."

"That's okay, baby girl," Annette said. "I brought mine."

"Yeah, and I have the camera in my phone too," I said.

"Speaking of Annie and Paige," Chloe said. "Does anyone know what the emergency was at the flower shop that made them bail on the trip at the eleventh hour?"

"Yeah." I made a face. "Somehow, the words *flower* and *emergency* don't seem to go together."

"Ah beg to differ," Annette said. "There could be any number of last-minute wedding emergencies. Why, the bridal bouquets could have gotten mixed up and one poor bride got red roses for her special day when she'd ordered pink, or maybe the lavender hydrangeas were still so green it looked like the bride was carryin' a head of cabbage. What about that?"

"What was I thinking?" I said. "That would be a major disaster."

"To most brides, yes," Kailyn said. "Wouldn't you agree,

Chloe? You're the most recent bride in our bunch. If you hadn't gotten the flowers you'd ordered for your special day, wouldn't you consider that a flower emergency?"

"Honestly?" Chloe said. "I was so happy to be marrying Ryan that nothing else really mattered."

Now there's a woman after my own heart. "All that frou-frou junk isn't my idea of a wedding anyway," I said.

"But this," Annette said, stretching out on one of the couches after lunch, "*this* is my idea of camping: air conditioning, comfy furniture, indoor plumbing, electrical outlets, and no sleeping on the hard ground."

"I hear ya on that," Kailyn said. "Give me comfort over roughing it any day."

"You're your mama's daughter, baby girl." Annette's eyes roamed the Winnebago. "Tess, there's just one thing missin': a washer and dryer."

"Actually, James is planning to add those in before our next excursion. I told him it wasn't necessary — that we could just find a local Laundromat wherever we went, but he insisted."

"He's spoilin' you," Annette said. "Just enjoy it."

Tess was a little defensive about the Luxurymobile her new husband had given her as a gift for their six-month anniversary. For years as a widow and penny-pinching single mom, she'd camped only in Northern California with her boys in simple tents and sleeping bags. But James surprised her with the Winnebago, saying he wanted his wife to travel in style. She resisted at first, but he told her that neither of them were as young as they used to be and if they could afford the creature comforts now, why not enjoy them? Why rush themselves into an arthritic state sleeping on the hard ground?

Considering her own lack of extra padding, Tess saw his point. And the concept of upper-crust camping was born.

"Hey, remember our last camping trip?" Kailyn said.

"You mean the one where you fed Rocky Raccoon the graham crackers and then Pepe LePew and his family came trotting out of the woods to scarf up the remaining crumbs?" I said.

Annette giggled. "You really had me worried, baby girl. I was sure we were all goin' to be drenched in skunk spray."

"Me too," Tess said. "And I was prepared to douse us all in spaghetti sauce to try and get rid of the smell since we didn't have tomato juice with us."

Kailyn broke in, her voice tinged with something like admiration. "I was thinking more about when Chloe rescued us from what she thought was a bear and it turned out to be that big black Newfoundland who slobbered all over her."

"Oh yeah," I said. "That was so funny."

"Hilarious." Chloe did that moue thing with her mouth.

"That's when Chloe the timid became Chloe the brave." Tess sent her niece a fond gaze.

"Hey, that's what we needed on this trip," I said. "A dog. Remember what Steinbeck said in the book? 'A dog, particularly an exotic like Charley, is a bond between strangers. Many conversations en route began with 'What degree of a dog is that?'"

"Sorry," Tess said. "I don't have a dog."

"Me either," Kailyn said.

"Besides, Steinbeck was traveling alone," Chloe said. "So he needed him as a bridge to meet people. And we don't. We've got each other."

"Yeah," Kailyn said, raising her glass of iced tea. "Girl power!"

"Getaway Girl power," Annette said, clinking her glass against her daughter's.

The rest of us raised our iced tea in unison. "Getaway Girls rule!"

"I just wish Annie and Paige were here too," Chloe said. "And after losing Jenna, our numbers seem to be dwindling. No more copouts, ladies."

"I agree with Chloe," Annette said. "The next no-show better have an even better excuse than a flower emergency."

Would feeding hungry children in Africa work?

21

When I was very young and the urge to be someplace else was on me, I was assured by mature people that maturity would cure this itch. When years described me as mature, the remedy prescribed was middle age. In middle age I was assured that greater age would calm my fever and now that I am fifty-eight perhaps senility will do the job. Nothing has worked.

Travels with Charley

Two hours later we pulled into Monterey.

Tess parked the Luxurymobile and we headed straight for Cannery Row. Although the Steinbeck classic hadn't been one of our book club choices, several of us had read it and wanted to revisit the stretch of buildings the author had made famous.

"… A poem, a stink, a grating noise, a quality of light, a tone, a habit, a nostalgia, a dream," I recited.

"What's that?" Kailyn asked.

"*Cannery Row.*"

"No, I don't mean where we are. I mean what's that from?"

"Steinbeck's novel *Cannery Row*," I said.

"Okay, Miss English Major."

"The name's Quote Chick."

The stink from the sardine canneries was long gone, as were most of the canneries and the entire sardine fishing industry, but the scent of fish still hung in the air.

Cannery Row bore no resemblance, however, to Steinbeck's "gathered and scattered, tin and iron and rust and splintered wood, chipped pavement and weedy lots and junk heaps ..." Now it was a tourist's mecca with all manner of shiny retail and souvenir shops, amusement arcades, eateries, and art galleries. And at the very end of the row in a former cannery, another famous attraction now occupied center stage: the Monterey Bay Aquarium.

Another reason for our trip.

It had been a couple years since I'd visited the world-renowned aquarium. Tess and Chloe too. But when we learned that neither Annette nor Kailyn had ever been to the nation's finest aquarium, we insisted that a visit be tacked onto our Steinbeck jaunt. Thankfully, our travel guide guru Tess had insisted we buy our tickets online before leaving Sacramento, so we were able to sail right on past the long line at the entrance. We timed our visit for a little after 2 p.m., when the crowds were supposed to be lighter.

Except there's no such thing as lighter crowds on a Saturday in the summer. We entered the central hall with a huge crush of people. I'd wanted to explore the Outer Bay Wing first to check out the sharks and giant tuna, but we were swept along with the throng to the aquarium's most popular attraction: the lovable sea otters in the two-story tank in the main hall.

"Oh, aren't they adorable?" Kailyn squealed.

"Those are just the cutest little critters I've ever seen," Annette said.

We pressed up against the windows, where we had a great underwater view of the playful marine mammals swimming and frolicking in the water.

"If you go up to the second floor, you can see the otters on the surface," a guide said. She checked her watch. "In ten minutes it will be feeding and training time, which is always fun to see."

"Can you remind me where the jellyfish living art exhibit is?" Chloe asked.

"I'm sorry. That closed last year. But you can still see the moon jellies in the Outer Bay exhibit."

"What's a moon jelly?" Kailyn asked.

"They're these luminous jellyfish that are so big, it's like you're looking at the moon in the sky," Chloe said. "They're really mesmerizing. Graceful too."

"Well, let's check them out when we're done with the otters," Tess said. "But let's hurry up and beat the throng so we can have a good view."

There was a pretty big crowd upstairs already, but we managed to find a small opening in front of the tank, where we all squeezed in to check out the furry creatures.

"Aw, look at that little one on its back playing with the ball," Kailyn said. "How cute is he?"

"Too cute for words, baby girl," Annette said.

"Look, Mommy," a little girl next to us piped up, pointing at the tank. "Those two are wrestling."

"Just like you and your brother," her mom replied.

Annette craned her neck for a closer look. "Are those ice cubes they're eating?"

"Yep," Tess said. "I read in the brochure that they like to

crunch on ice cubes because it's like having to crack through the hard shells of the food they usually eat."

After finally tearing Annette and Kailyn away from the otters, we moved on to the Outer Bay exhibit with its one-million-gallon curving floor-to-ceiling tank so Chloe could see her jellyfish. And not only did she see her moon jellies — large, iridescent orbs pulsing through the water like something otherworldly from one of my *Dr. Who* episodes — but also her favorite ocean creature next to Nemo: sea turtles.

"It's almost like they're flying," she said in a hushed voice as she gazed at the giant sea turtles paddling by next to a school of giant bluefin tuna.

"Like they're underwater birds or somethin'," Annette said.

A large dark shape glided by.

"What's that?" Kailyn asked. "It looks like a giant bat or something."

"That's a stingray," I said. "Chloe, remember, we saw one when we were snorkeling in Cabo?"

"How could I forget? Freaked me out."

"Wasn't it a stingray that killed that poor crocodile hunter man in Australia?" Annette asked.

"Yes, but that was a fluke accident."

"Well, fluke or not," Annette said. "I'm just glad there's a thick wall between us."

"You and me both, Mama," Kailyn said.

Annette pointed. "Becca, what's that big golden fish with that thing on its back?"

"Uh, I'm not sure."

"That's a dolphin fish," a nearby guide said. "Also known as mahimahi. They can get as big as six feet long."

"Ah love mahimahi," Annette said. "Although it seems a shame to eat it now after having seen it so up close and personal."

"Jenna would agree with you," I said.

Our former Getaway Girl was always trying to get us to turn vegetarian with her. But it wasn't going to happen. We were a pack of rabid, slathering carnivores in need of meat.

A hammerhead shark swam into view. Talk about carnivores. Too cool. I've always been fascinated by sharks.

Chloe, not so much. She turned pale and stepped back.

My old roommate used to be afraid of everything. But Chloe had really stepped out of her comfort zone and conquered her fears in the past couple years. Except when it came to sharks. She has a serious shark phobia.

"Chloe? You okay?" Kailyn asked.

"Fine. I'm just going to sit down over here."

"I'll come with you," Tess said.

Seeing the sharks and tuna and all the other marine life made me realize how much I missed my snorkeling. I thought back again to when I'd petted that nurse shark in Cabo. What a rush. I haven't had a rush like that in a while. But then I've been pretty landlocked these last couple months.

Not for much longer though. Time for some major changes in my life.

We moved on to the next exhibit — the living kelp forest, where we were able to overhear a tour guide who was talking to a group of Japanese tourists.

"At twenty-eight feet high, our living kelp forest is one of the tallest aquarium exhibits in the world," the guide said. "Each towering kelp plant is like an apartment building, sheltering a host of fishes, crabs, and other creatures. You'll see sardines, leopard sharks, wolf eels, and many other fish weaving among the fronds of kelp, just as they do in the wild."

"Wow. It's like looking through a window to the bay," Kailyn said.

"You'll notice that the exhibit opens up to the sky," the

guide said. "The light streaming through the amber fronds helps the kelp grow more than four inches a day, and a hidden water jet maintains the water motion this plant requires to absorb nutrients from 335,000 gallons of seawater."

Just then a leopard shark swam past.

Sweet.

Chloe backed away quickly, holding her stomach.

Maybe coming to the aquarium wasn't the best idea for someone with such a shark phobia.

For dinner, Annette, who was a big *Forrest Gump* fan, begged to go to the nearby Bubba Gump's.

"Shrimp is the fruit of the sea," she drawled, mimicking Tom Hanks's thick Southern accent as we walked to the theme restaurant. "Pineapple shrimp, lemon shrimp, coconut shrimp, pepper shrimp, shrimp soup, shrimp stew, shrimp salad, shrimp and potatoes, shrimp burger, shrimp sandwich ..."

Kailyn joined in the Forrest fun. "My momma always said, 'Life was like a box of chocolates. You never know what you're gonna get.'"

"That's right, baby girl. That's right."

What we got was peel-and-eat Cajun shrimp, coconut shrimp, cocktail shrimp, shrimp tempura, fried shrimp, and hush puppies.

Lots and lots of hush puppies for Annette. That woman loved her fried food.

The Bubba's décor was heavy on the cheese with the walls plastered with stuff from the movie, but the view was amazing. We were seated by the window overlooking the bay. I meditated on the reflection of the setting sun and the crashing waves while the Getaway Girls chattered around me.

Afterwards, we walked on the beach, where it felt good to move and enjoy the freedom of no crutches — now replaced by Grandma Adelaide's cane. Kailyn kicked off her flip-flops and ran toward the surf, squealing when the incoming tide got the bottom of her capris wet.

I wouldn't have squealed. And I'd have plunged full on into the surf. The only thing that stopped me was my walking cast.

"'Look at that sea, girls—all silver and shadow and vision of things not seen.'" I recited one of my favorite *Anne of Green Gables* quotes. "'We couldn't enjoy its loveliness any more if we had millions of dollars and ropes of diamonds.'"

Kailyn squealed again when Tess pulled the Luxury-mobile into our campground for the night. "It's slumber party time! Let's give each other pedicures and facials. I brought supplies." She sent me a sly smile. "Becca, I brought something special just for you—Washed in the Blood of the Lamb nail polish."

"Oh, goodie. My favorite." I held up my stubby bitten nails. "But only if you paint my fingers as well as my toes."

Chloe clapped her hand to her mouth and ran to the bathroom, looking decidedly green.

"I'm sorry," Kailyn said. "It grossed me out too, but I didn't realize Chloe would react so strongly."

Retching sounds reached our ears.

"I think she might be having some other kind of reaction, baby girl," Annette said. "I surely hope that shrimp wasn't bad, or we're all going to find ourselves with a case of food poisoning."

"Well, I feel fine," Kailyn said.

"Me too." I looked up as the bathroom door opened.

A pale-faced Chloe rejoined us. "I'm sorry, everyone, that you had to hear that. How embarrassing."

"Oh, hush," Annette said. "We're all friends here. If you can't puke with your girlfriends, you need new friends, I say. How ya feelin' now, sweetie?"

"Better. Thanks."

Tess handed Chloe a glass of water. "The girls were worried you might have food poisoning. They're concerned the shrimp might have been bad."

Chloe exchanged a look with Tess, and then took a long drink of water.

"The shrimp wasn't bad," she said. "I'm pregnant."

"What?" It was Annette's turn to squeal.

"Oh my gosh, that's wonderful!" Kailyn said, grabbing Chloe in a clinch. "Come on everyone, group hug."

See what I mean? Perky with a capital *P*.

But this time I joined in on the group hug.

"Congratulations," I said. And I found myself meaning it. "The first Getaway Girl to get pregnant."

"Hey, I resemble that remark." Annette frowned at me.

"Me too," Tess said.

"But that was ages ago. You know what I mean."

"Becca's right," Kailyn said. "Chloe's the first one to get pregnant since we formed the book club."

I could see the wistfulness in my roommate's eyes. Did anyone else?

Maybe I should come up with some kind of diversion or something. But what? I couldn't think of a thing short of falling and breaking my other leg, and that was going a little overboard.

"Wait a minute," Annette said. "Chloe, you had champagne last night."

"No, I didn't. I only pretended to."

"Why?" Kailyn said. "Why not just tell us then?"

"Because I promised Ryan I wouldn't. We just found out the day before the trip and haven't even had time to tell our families yet, other than Tess"—Chloe smiled at her aunt—"who guessed on the drive over. So you have to promise me you won't breathe a word. I wouldn't have said anything now, but I didn't want you all to worry that you were going to get food poisoning."

"How long do we have to keep our lips zipped?" Annette said. "It's hard to keep good news like this quiet."

"Just for a few days. We're having both families over for dinner Thursday night and will tell them all then." Chloe began to rustle around in the kitchen. "And now will someone please tell me where the candy is? I have a serious craving for gummi bears."

The next morning, we headed to Steinbeck's hometown of Salinas, stopping by his gravesite first to pay our respects before heading to the National Steinbeck Center.

Cool museum. The centerpiece of the sprawling center was the John Steinbeck Exhibition Hall, where passages from *The Grapes of Wrath* were displayed on the wall. As we wandered among the exhibits, I was surprised to discover that the Pulitzer Prize–winning novel had been burned twice in Salinas.

I knew it had been banned when it was first released. But burned?

Who burns books?

For telling the truth about the plight of the migrant workers? About starving families? And opening people's eyes to the suffering he'd seen with his own eyes?

I thought of Tom Joad's farewell speech. "Whenever they's a fight so hungry people can eat, I'll be there. Whenever they's a cop beatin' up a guy, I'll be there .... I'll be in the way guys yell when they're mad an' I'll be in the way kids laugh when they're hungry an' they know supper's ready. An' when our folks eat the stuff they raise an' live in the houses they build — why, I'll be there."

And I had a sneaking suspicion where I would be too. I think. I hope. Sooner, rather than later.

I was gratified to read that *The Grapes of Wrath* has been

translated into nearly every language, still sells a hundred thousand paperback copies a year, and is considered one of the most enduring works of fiction by an American author.

As it should be. That and *To Kill a Mockingbird*, of course.

"Hey, look," Kailyn said, interrupting my literary reverie. "There's Rocinante."

We all hurried over to the tiny green truck camper that Steinbeck had traveled all around America in with his faithful companion, Charley.

Except it was behind glass walls.

"Just like the *Mona Lisa* in the Louvre," Chloe said.

"Hey, you gotta protect the great art of the world," I said.

Before we left, we stopped in the gift shop for some bookmarks and paperbacks. Kailyn and I picked up a T-shirt for Annie's collection that bore the Steinbeck quote: *No one wants advice, just corroboration*. And I got one for myself that said, *I guess there are never enough books*.

When we returned to Sacramento, Tess dropped us off at our duplex first. As Kailyn and I said our farewells to the others, I pulled Chloe aside for a moment and looked into her eyes. Would I see fear as she prepared to embark upon this new chapter in her life?

All I saw was joy.

I laid my hand on her stomach and patted it gently. "I'm really happy for you."

"Thanks." She clasped my hand. "Me too."

"And I'm especially happy that it's you and not me."

"I thought you might be." We exchanged grins.

After the Luxurymobile pulled away, I kicked back on the couch and started paging through the copy of *East of Eden* I'd bought.

"Aren't you going to unpack?" Kailyn asked as she pulled her rolling suitcase toward her room.

"Eventually."

"Just don't leave all your stuff in the living room," she said as she disappeared into her bedroom.

"No, Mother, I won't."

I tried to read my book but was having a hard time concentrating. I kept thinking about Chloe and the massive life change ahead of her. I couldn't even imagine. Although ... I was hoping for a massive life change of my own to announce one of these days.

Kailyn's cell blared out Patsy Cline's "Crazy," interrupting my reverie.

She came out of the bedroom a minute later with a funny look on her face. "That was Mom. She and Tess are on their way back over."

"Why? Did they forget something?"

"No," she said. "Paige called her and said she has some news she wants to share with all of us."

Just then my phone rang. I flipped it open.

"Becca?"

"Hey, Annie, what's up?"

"Are you and Kailyn going to be home for a little while?"

"Yep." I nodded at Kailyn and mouthed "Annie."

"Good, because Paige and I want to come on by for a few minutes if that's okay."

"Sure. Annette just called and said she and Tess are on their way over too. You want to give me a clue what this is all about?"

"We'd rather tell you in person."

"Okay. See you soon."

Kailyn clapped her hands in delight as I hung up the phone. "You know what it is, don't you? Marc finally popped the question and they're engaged! Ooh, I can't wait to see

Paige's ring. It's probably gorgeous. Marc's got really good taste."

Kailyn always did like shiny, sparkly things.

Ten minutes later the doorbell rang.

"They're here," Kailyn squealed as she yanked open the door.

"Oh, it's just you," she said when she saw Tess and her mom.

"Well, that's a nice welcome," Annette said. "I love you too."

"You know what I mean. I thought you were Annie and Paige. Isn't it exciting?" Kailyn was almost bouncing off the walls, she was on such a sugar high. "Paige is engaged."

"I know," Annette said. "I wonder when the wedding will be."

Tess shrugged her shoulders. "Why wait? When you know, you know."

"I hope I'll know one of these days," Kailyn said.

Annette hugged her daughter's shoulders. "You will, baby girl. You will. I'm plannin' on lots of sweet little grandchildren."

No pressure there.

The doorbell rang and Kailyn squealed again.

She flung the door open and there stood Paige and Annie framed in the doorway. Beaming, but hesitant.

"You don't need to tell us," Kailyn said. "We already know. You're engaged!" She threw her arms around Paige, enveloping her in a hug and rocking her from side to side. "We're so excited for you."

"Actually," Paige said, freeing herself from Kailyn's hugzilla. "I'm not engaged."

She held up her left hand. "I'm married."

22

Why do people have to grow up and marry, change?

Anne of Green Gables

"Married!" Kailyn shrieked.

"Married?" the rest of us chorused.

"When?

"Where?

"How?"

"If you let us inside, we'll tell you everything." Annie's white T-shirt read *Use your indoor voice*.

"Sorry," Kailyn said. "Come on in. And tell *all*."

As we moved to the living room, Paige took a deep breath. "Marc and I got married yesterday at Lake Tahoe. I'm now Mrs. O'Neill."

"Is that Marc's last name?" I asked. "I've only ever known him as Marc."

"It's a wonderful name," Tess said, enveloping Paige in her spindly arms. "I'm so happy for you."

"Was this the flower shop emergency you were talking about?" Chloe asked.

"Sort of," Paige said. "We had to find someone to run the shop while we went up to Tahoe."

"I can't believe you didn't invite us." Kailyn stuck out her lower lip.

"It was a spur-of-the-moment thing. Everything happened so fast ..."

"I'm happy for you," my roommate said. "We all are."

Everyone nodded.

"But why now and why so fast?" Kailyn asked.

Paige blushed and exchanged a look with Annie, who gave her an encouraging nod.

"Well ... I have more news. I'm also"—she corrected herself—"*we're* also ... going to have a baby."

"You're kidding!"

My God, it's an epidemic. Hope it's not catching.

And then I wondered how Paige's good Christian friends were going to respond. Paige was wondering too. I could see it in her face. My eyes slid to Annette, the most conservative member of our group. So did Paige's. I held my breath.

But Annette was the first to grab Paige in a fierce hug. "That's wonderful, honey. I know how long you've been wantin' to have a baby."

Tess was right behind her. "That's great," she said. "Congratulations!"

Then the others all rushed Paige for a hug. It was like the end credits of the Miss America pageant, which Earlene used to always make me watch with her until I got old enough to balk at the beauty pageant sexism. And for the second time in twenty-four hours I found myself in a group hug.

Just so it doesn't become a regular thing.

The tears rolled down Paige's cheeks. "I didn't think I could ever have a baby."

"It's a miracle," Chloe said, stroking her hair. "All that time you and Eric were married you tried and tried but could never get pregnant."

Paige swiped at her eyes. "Yeah. And with Marc, we didn't even have to be married for me to get pregnant." She looked a little shame-faced. Her cheeks were as pink as the strawberry daiquiri Kailyn had guzzled at Bubba Gump's.

Would the others judge her now for what most Christians would consider a "slip" or "sin" even in this day and age? Kailyn fingered her purity ring, her eyes flickering to her mom.

"Bless your hearts, you couldn't wait," Annette said.

"It's hard to wait when you're in love," Tess said. "Especially when you've been married before."

Now that's what I'm talkin' about. I could feel myself smiling. I knew there was a reason I could hang with my Getaway Girls all this time.

Paige had been dying to have a kid for years. She and her first husband had tried and tried, but nothing worked. They'd never gotten around to going the infertility drug route because he dumped her for a younger model. And then last year, Paige had started investigating other options, including sperm banks, which she quickly decided against.

"How's Marc dealing with all this?" I asked as I sat down on the couch and stretched out my leg.

"He's only thrilled to pieces," Annie said, beaming, before Paige could even open her mouth. "He already busted the buttons off of two shirts. I had to get him one of those *Baby Daddy* T-shirts to wear."

"Aw, the one with the arrow pointing up?" Kailyn asked.

Annie nodded.

"What color?" Annette asked, pressing closer.

"Um, that's not going to work," Paige said.

"What?"

She smiled at Annette. "Trying to find out whether it's a boy or girl."

"So what color *is* the shirt?" I asked.

"Black."

"Brat," Kailyn said. "You're not going to tell us the sex, are you?"

"Can't. It's too early to find out, but we don't want to know until the baby is born."

"So, Mrs. O'Neill, when's this bundle of joy due?" Tess asked. "Or is that a surprise too?"

"Mrs. O'Neill ..." Paige tested the words. "I like the sound of that."

"If that flower shop thing doesn't ever work out you could always open an Irish pub," I said. "O'Neill's."

"And Baby O'Neill is scheduled to make his appearance into the world when?" Annette asked again.

"Sorry," Paige said. "He, or she, is due in seven months." She blushed. "We did things a little backwards. We didn't plan to, but ..." she blushed again.

Paige and I had more in common than I'd thought. Although I hadn't blushed in years.

I'd always pegged Paige as the quintessential Christian good girl who always did the right thing. Sort of Super Christian. The total opposite of me. She worked in Sunday school with all those little rug rats, was always cooking and baking for people, sent shoeboxes full of goodies to kids in Third World countries every Christmas, gave money to the homeless guys holding signs on the freeway off-ramp, and then the crème de la crème of Super Christianhood—she moved in with her aging mother when her health started to go south and took good care of her like a selfless, dutiful Christian daughter would.

See what I mean? Super Christian.

But now I saw that she was just as real as the rest of us. And could make mistakes. Cool. Not that I thought of her baby as a mistake, or even sex before marriage as a mistake. But Paige and the rest of the Getaway Girls followed a different code than me. The Bible code. And I knew that code said no sex before marriage.

"So why the big rush to get married?" I asked.

"Well, apparently Marc was planning to propose next week, which would mark the one-year anniversary from when I first started working at Golden Daffodils and when he said he started seriously falling for me—"

"Aww," Kailyn said. "How romantic."

"It gets better." Paige's lips curved and her eyes took on a dreamy expression. "He had a whole romantic proposal planned out—"

"Which I'd been helping him with for weeks, no, *months*," Annie interjected.

"And which I really appreciate," Paige said. "Anyway, he had this big romantic proposal planned complete with my favorite restaurant, gardenias, and my all-time favorite romantic movie of all time, *Somewhere in Time* ..."

"And then?" Kailyn pressed.

"And then the plus symbol showed up on the home pregnancy test—three home pregnancy tests, actually, because I couldn't believe what I was seeing. And when I told Marc, he proposed right then and there."

"When was then?" Tess asked.

"Friday morning."

"And where was there?" Chloe asked.

"The flower shop, of course."

"So, no favorite restaurant or romantic movie?" Kailyn said.

"No, but lots of gardenias."

"Lots," Annie said.

Paige headed for the fridge. "Hey, do you guys have any string cheese? And salsa? I've been craving both something fierce."

"We should have string cheese," Kailyn said, "but I'd check the date on the salsa if I were you. We're not too good about cleaning out the fridge."

Paige peered at the salsa label. "This expired over six months ago."

"That's my baby girl," Annette said. "Ah tried to teach her, but the domestic arts have never been her thing."

"Becca's either," Chloe said.

"Yeah, whatever." I focused on Paige, who was inhaling a piece of string cheese. "I still don't get why you had to rush off to Tahoe this weekend and get married."

She swallowed. "There were a couple of reasons. First, I'd already done the big, splashy wedding with family and friends when Eric and I got married. And I wanted this wedding to be different. Also, Marc's and my commitment to one another was already the 'til-death-do-us-part kind, but once we knew about our baby, we just couldn't wait to make that commitment before God," she said. "We were married in this lovely little chapel in the mountains that I'd fallen in love with years ago on a church retreat. Once we knew I was pregnant, we didn't want to wait even another second to get married."

"Speaking of child," Tess asked. "How'd Cyd take it?"

"She's thrilled. Said she's always wanted a little brother or sister," Paige said. "And she's already staked first dibs on babysitting him. Or her."

Annette raised her hand. "I get second."

"Sorry." Annie smiled sweetly. "That would be me, Auntie Annie."

While the rest of them fought over who would get to babysit Paige's bundle of joy, I thought of how much things were changing. When the Getaway Girls first started, the only married one in the group was Annette. Now, Tess, Chloe, and Paige were all shackled, and Chloe and Paige were both pregnant.

"There must be something in the water," I said aloud. "I just hope it doesn't come my way."

"What?" Paige gave me a quizzical look.

"I'm pregnant too," Chloe said, blushing.

"Serious?" Annie said. "What are the chances? If this was fiction, no one would believe it."

"How fun." Annette clapped her hands.

"What?" I said.

"We can do a double baby shower!"

Hold me back. I don't think I can contain my excitement.

> The test of an adventure is that when you are in the middle of it, you say to yourself, "Oh, now I've got myself into an awful mess; I wish I were sitting quietly at home." And the sign that something is wrong with you is when you sit quietly at home wishing you were out having lots of adventure.
>
> *Thornton Wilder*

The girls hung around a little longer with Chloe and Paige making plans for their kids to grow up together and be best friends — and who knows? If it was a boy and a girl, maybe something more.

And once again I felt like a stranger in a strange land.

Babyland.

My leg itched and it took a supreme act of will not to shove my hand down my cast and scratch it. I hobbled out to the kitchen, filled a couple Ziploc bags with ice, and grabbed a few towels. I'd discovered that cooling helped with the itch, so when I returned to the living room, I wrapped the cast in the towels and then laid the plastic bags of ice on top of the terry cloth.

"You want the fan too?" Kailyn asked.

"Yes, please."

She pulled the standing fan closer to me, aimed it at my propped-up leg, and turned it on.

Ah, blessed relief.

"Y'all, I think we'd better get going," Annette said. "I don't know about you, but I'm a little tired from all this excitement. Besides, I haven't seen my hunka burnin' love in two days and I'm starting to go into withdrawal."

"Rub it in," Kailyn said.

"I'm sorry, baby girl. I didn't mean—"

"It's okay, Mom, I was just kidding." Kailyn gave her a fake bright smile and a hug.

We said our goodbyes and everyone threw out a few more congratulations and hugs. But after my roommate shut the door behind the last departing Getaway Girl, the dam burst.

"It's not fair," Kailyn sobbed. "Everybody's getting married and having babies except me. I want a husband and babies too. I'm not even dating anyone. Not since Drew split once the play ended. Everyone's in a relationship but me. Even *you*."

She cried harder.

"I'm not in a relationship. It's a bet, remember?"

"Still?" She sniffled. "I thought after all this time you guys have spent together maybe something would be developing."

"The only thing that's developing is a friendship. Nothing romantic. Trust me."

"How come? Is it because Ben's a Christian?"

Was it? That might be part of it. Or was initially. But now that I'd gotten to know Ben I saw that he didn't have horns and a tail. He was a pretty cool guy actually. And I really liked his grandma. I glanced at her cane gift—now one of my prized possessions—and recalled all the pictures of Africa she'd shown me.

"Becca?"

"Sorry. No, it's not because he's a Christian. We just don't have chemistry." I adjusted my leg on the coffee table and then noticed the museum gift bag with Annie's T-shirt. "Crap. We forgot to give Annie her present."

Annie. "Hey, Miss Everyone's-in-a-relationship-but-me," I said, "did you forget Annie? She's not involved with anyone either. So don't think you're the Lone Ranger."

"Yeah, but she's only twenty."

"And you're only twenty-four. Man, you need to chill out on the whole relationship thing. Seriously. Your problem is you watch too many of those romantic comedies."

"That's what my dad always says."

"Well, listen to him," I said. "Father knows best. And remember what your Sunday school teacher said too."

"What was that?" Kailyn cut her eyes at me.

"You know. That whole trusting God thing for ... ah ... your future." I couldn't bring myself to say the *M* word. Either of them. Mate or marriage.

"Really?" The corners of her mouth lifted up. "You believe that now?"

"I'm not saying that *I* do, but you do. So shouldn't you start showing it?"

"Way to make me feel convicted."

I pulled out the Christianese guide and thumbed through the Cs. Oh yeah—the Jewish-mother guilt thing.

I didn't need that. But there was something else that I did.

"What we need is some serious single-girl time," I said. "No married folks allowed. Just you, me, and Annie. And we need to make that trip to New York happen. Remember, your dad called us footloose and fancy-free. Well, as soon as my foot is loose from this cast, we need to just go for it!"

"I'd love to go to New York," Kailyn said. "But how? I don't have that much money in savings and you're always broke."

"Minor detail." I waved it off. "What is it you guys always say? God will provide? How about if I start Googling cheap flights and hotels and stuff and you do the prayer thing, and let's see what happens."

These Christians sure do love their potlucks.

For our next date, I'd suggested to Ben that we visit Annie's home church thingy that she'd told us about. He accepted in a heartbeat. Of course the night we decided to go was their monthly potluck.

And I hated cooking.

"Don't worry about it," Annie said. "We've already got most of the food covered. But if you want to bring something, just bring some kind of munchies like chips or cheese and crackers or something."

I opted for Wheat Thins and red-pepper hummus—my latest fave.

We pulled up in front of an old Craftsman-style house in Midtown a few minutes after six in Ben's car.

"Cool house," he said as we made our way up the stone steps.

I still refused to let him help me, especially now that I was hobbling so well on my walking cast with the aid of Adelaide's cane. But I did let him carry the food.

Annie, whose T-shirt tonight read *From the desk of Toto: Dear Dorothy. Hate Oz. Took the shoes. Find your own way home!* introduced us around to her friends.

As usual, my cast was a great icebreaker.

"Whoa, how'd you break the leg?" a tall, skinny, twenty-something guy named Tyson asked.

"Skydiving."

"Cool. Cool walking stick too." He squatted down to check out my cane. "Have you been to Africa?"

Not yet. But I could hear the drumbeat.

"No, but Ben has," I said. "Hey, Ben, did I tell you Annie's been to Africa?"

That's all it took. Within seconds Ben and Annie were having an animated conversation about Rwanda, Ethiopia, and solar cookers.

Mission accomplished, I wandered over to the hors d'oeuvres and popped a stuffed mushroom in my mouth. A couple guys standing nearby with Stellas in their hands were having a lively discussion.

Annie's home church really was different. I doubted most churches served beer at their potlucks. And imported ones from Belgium at that.

But it made me feel right at home.

It also made me feel like I didn't have to be quite so much on my guard all the time about what I said either so I didn't make another faux pas like I had at the last potluck. I tuned into the guys' conversation next to me — they were discussing Creation and evolution.

Figuring Annie had warned everyone in advance that I was a heathen, I decided to take the plunge.

"Sorry," I said, "but that whole creating the earth in seven days thing is a little much for me."

"I agree," the shorter, clearly older of the two said.

"You do?"

"Sure. There's that whole fossil record to contend with. My name's Peter, by the way."

"I'm Becca. But you were saying?"

"Well, the way I see it, is that either the earth is billions of years old, or that it's really only thousands, but God made it look like it's billions. I just don't see God being that deceptive."

"But what about the seven days bit?"

"God's time is not our time." Peter drained his Stella. "What's easier to believe? That before anything existed, God was there? Or that before anything existed, there was this big mass of stuff that went *bang*?" He smiled. "Isn't God perfectly capable of saying 'Bang'?"

"He's the God of the entire universe," his buddy said. "He can do anything."

"Exactly."

"Okay, everyone, we're going to eat," said our hostess, whom Annie had introduced me to when I first arrived, but whose name I'd forgotten. She was a ringer for Tina Fey though. Could her name have been Sarah?

Her husband Shane said grace and everyone chowed down on the salmon, grilled chicken, and several kinds of salad. And the lively conversation continued to flow with the sangria.

Tyson, a nurse, talked about the recent outing he and a few others had made to volunteer at an AIDS clinic in the Tenderloin district of San Francisco.

"But I thought Christians hated gays," I said.

"Some do. Unfortunately. But not all. Not those who really try to follow Jesus. Jesus wasn't a hater."

"Yeah," Annie said. "When asked what the greatest commandment was, Jesus said to love the Lord with all your heart, soul, strength, and mind; and to love your neighbor as yourself. You guys know I'm no theologian, but the way I see it, it's all about love. If we did more loving of our neighbors and less condemning, perhaps more people would see Jesus in us."

I always saw Jesus in Annie.

Ben did too. I caught the admiring glance he sent her.

"I'm showing my age here," Peter piped up, "but there was this cool preacher who came to speak at a rally here in the mid-eighties. He took an offering for AIDS patients and all the media showed up to cover it because it was news."

"News," he said, "that Christians—who up to that point called it the 'gay plague' and were known for slapping bumper stickers on their car proclaiming 'AIDS is God's punishment on homosexuals'—would actually empty their pockets for AIDS patients."

"And we wonder why people are antagonistic to Christianity?" Tyson asked.

"I was at that rally," our hostess, whose name I'd finally remembered was Jill, said. "I went with some friends from my high school youth group. And I'll never forget how the speaker said that AIDS was the leprosy of our day. He reminded us that Jesus took care of the lepers and wasn't afraid to touch them. This was back in the day when people thought they could catch AIDS just by hugging someone."

"We've come a long way," Ben said.

"Yes, but there's still so far to go," Shane added.

"Why don't we take an offering right now?" Tyson suggested. "There's an AIDS hospice house right here in town that could use some help."

"Good idea. But rather than just an offering," Annie said, "maybe we could volunteer our services—find out what some of their day-to-day needs are and help with those?"

"I love that idea," Jill said.

"Me too," Peter said. "Some serious food for thought."

"And prayer," Shane added.

The air was thick with sensitivity and compassion. The genuine kind. A brand of Christianity that was the opposite of my childhood experience.

Who knew I'd actually feel comfortable with a pack of believers?

In a house church?

At yet another potluck?

Maybe I'd get the hang of this fellowshipping thing after all.

In the car on the way home Ben and I discussed the evening, and Annie, among other things.

"It's pretty funny, you know," I said, chuckling.

"What?"

"Us dating. I got into this date on a bet because my friends said I couldn't commit to anything, and then I wind up dating someone who's more commitment-phobic than me."

"I'm not afraid of commitment." Ben's mouth was set in a tight line. "Did my gran tell you that?"

"I'm just sayin'…"

"I just haven't met the right woman yet."

And you're not going to meet her either if you keep going out with women who are so *not* the right woman for you.

"What about Annie? You should ask her out," I said. "You guys have a lot in common and I can tell you're attracted to her."

"She's too young for me."

"Oh yeah, there's a huge age difference between you, Grandpa. What are you again? Twenty-nine? Thirty?"

"Twenty-eight. But there's a world of difference between twenty and twenty-eight."

"Annie's not your typical twenty-year-old. She's a wise old soul and one of the most together people I know."

"I'll think about it," Ben said. "Besides, we still have what, six more dates left? And I *am* committed," he grinned. "To helping you win that bet."

And just why is that again?

"Your grandmother was right, Mr. Commitment-phobe. Any excuse to dodge the real thing. Or get involved."

"You don't know what you're talking about." Ben tightened his grip on the steering wheel. "Don't use Gran against me. You're not playing fair, Becca."

"Maybe not, but you're not playing at all. You're hiding safe in the dugout," I said.

The question is ... why?

"I'm not hiding."

"Right." I cut a glance to his rigid profile. "This is about your parents, isn't it?"

"You know nothing about my parents," he said.

"I know they're missionaries, which puts them high up on the holy ladder or whatever. But to abandon their own child for God's work? That's just wrong."

"You don't understand. You can't understand."

"I understand more than you think."

Earlene had pretty much abandoned me early on in favor of the bottle and her men, but she was only playing at the religion thing—to get what she could from it. That whole relationship-with-God bit I've been hearing everyone talk about was never real with Earlene.

But it was real with Ben and his grandmother. Very real. And with his parents too, apparently. So how could they dump him on Adelaide's doorstep that way?

"It's a higher calling," Ben said. "A person's relationship with God, with Jesus, trumps every other relationship—even familial ones."

"Maybe. But doesn't it bite to be the one left behind?"

"I wasn't left behind," Ben said. "I was left with Adelaide."

24

Seabiscuit was starting to feel fine. Within hours of his birth, he had known how to run, and speed had been the measure of his life ever since.

Seabiscuit

I swear the Biscuit and I were separated at birth.

Speed had always been the measure of my life too, but this broken ankle had really slowed me down these past few months. I hadn't been able to do any of my normal athletic activities—running, hiking, bicycling, or camping.

The Luxurymobile didn't count; that wasn't real camping.

Nothing could beat sleeping on the ground in the great outdoors under the night sky spilling over with stars. Paige and the others had gone ga-ga over that one starry night painting in Paris, but it didn't even come close to the real thing. It was like some master painter had flung an enormous can of silver paint against the inky sky. Or shot a giant paintball gun into the heavens splattering silver against the glossy black canvas of sky.

Mix that in with the crisp mountain air, nature's symphony of crickets, frogs, whispering streams, and the wind rustling through the trees, and who needs an iPod?

And nothing could beat the smell of coffee over a campfire first thing in the morning. Especially coupled with fresh-caught trout sizzling in the frying pan.

It was almost a religious experience.

Even better than Starbucks and my beloved lattes from Dunkeld's. The only thing that would make it complete would be to hear the distinctive cry of an African fish eagle.

But I'm workin' on it.

I'm working on New York too, but so far, without much success.

Ever since I'd resurrected the plan for the single Getaway Girls trip to the Big Apple, I'd been checking on cheap flights and hotels, but cheap and New York didn't go together unless we wanted to stay at the Y—which I didn't see working for Kailyn. And I didn't think there were many campsites in the heart of that concrete jungle, so I started entering radio contests again, trying to win an all-expenses-paid trip so I could surprise Kailyn.

I could see it now.

When my perky roommate got home from her temp job—Kailyn always worked short-term temp assignments so she could do as much theater as possible—I'd casually say, "Guess what happened today?"

"What?"

"Nothin' much. I just won tickets to New York in a call-in radio contest."

"You did not."

"Did too."

"Shut up!" She'd squeal and start bouncing off the walls. And then she'd start packing.

Problem was, most of those contests only covered expenses for two, not three. Oh well, when I won, we'd just pool our limited resources and help pay for Annie's portion. But even though I kept hitting redial on my cell, I never managed to get through as the seventh caller.

I did manage, however, to get the hated final cast off. At last.

Free at last, free at last. Thank God Almighty, I'm free at last!

Well, almost.

Doctor Helm put me in a removable boot thing and had me going to physical therapy and doing exercises so that I could get the full range of motion of my ankle back. What I really longed to do was run, jump, and do cartwheels of joy, but I couldn't quite do that yet. No way did I want to reinjure my ankle and have to repeat this lousy confinement all over again.

Instead, I swam. Every morning at the gym.

Swimming was the best exercise, the doc said, since it was low impact and would build up my strength without putting stress on the ankle. Lucy joined me, saying she wanted to get stronger and healthier and in better shape. So we did laps together and afterwards we'd grab a non-fat mocha.

That first day, Lucy could do only two laps before getting winded. "Whoo," she said, panting as she climbed out of the pool, her cheeks rosy from the unfamiliar exertion. "I am seriously out of shape."

My inner snark started to agree, but I cut her off. I didn't like anyone dissin' Lucy.

"But you made a good start today," I said. "It takes time to build up stamina. It doesn't happen overnight. You have to work at it. As long as you show up and put in the time, you'll see results. That's true for any kind of workout. You just have to keep at it."

"Like my relationship with Christ," Lucy said, her round face splitting into a huge smile.

"Well, I don't know about that ..."

"Oh yes," she said eagerly. "When I spend time with him and in his Word, it makes all the difference in my daily walk. And when I don't, my spiritual muscles get weak and flabby."

"And when that happens, it could make you ..." I mentally scrolled through the list of Christianese expressions I'd been collecting. "Stumble?"

Lucy beamed. "Exactly."

"I can't believe *you* stumble. You seem to have this whole Christian walk thing down pat."

"Oh, far from it. I stumble all the time."

"You mean you still do drugs?"

"Oh no, not anymore. But only by the grace of God and a lot of prayer. In the beginning, after I first came to Christ, I slipped a couple times and went back to my old habits. It's hard to break an addiction," Lucy said.

"But stumbling can take many forms—big and little," she added. "Thoughts. Words. Actions done, and sometimes even not doing the good things you know you should do. It's my intention to do the right thing," she said, "but sometimes that doesn't work out."

"Maybe that's what Ben's parents did," I said. "Thought they were doing the right thing, but stumbled."

"In what way?"

"When they abandoned their son and let Adelaide raise him while they did their missionary thing in the jungle."

"They wouldn't look at it as abandoning their son," Lucy said. "They'd look at it as more that it's a sacrifice they've made for God."

"God wants people to sacrifice their children? That's pretty harsh. We're talking about people's lives here."

"Exactly," Lucy said. "The calling is different for different people. As is the sacrifice. We're not Ben's parents. We can't answer for the things they were asked to do and the decisions they had to make. You read God's Word, you pray, you trust God to lead you. You make the best choice you can, and sometimes you make mistakes. Sometimes it's not the best choice long-term, but it's the best you had to go with at the time."

"Okay. Maybe," I said. "And don't get me wrong; I'm not dissin' Adelaide. I think she's great. Really great. In fact, I wouldn't have minded being raised by her myself."

Far better than being raised by alky Earlene.

"But still ... Ben's parents' actions had an impact on him."

"Christians aren't perfect, Becca ..." Lucy began.

I groaned. "Please don't add on the rest of that bumper sticker."

"Sorry?"

"I've seen that 'Christians aren't perfect, just forgiven' sticker on cars and it smacks of elitism and arrogance. Like, 'we're part of this exclusive club and you aren't. We're forgiven and you're not. We're going to heaven and you're not. Nyah, nyah, nyah, nyah, nyah.'"

Lucy's eyes clouded with pain. "I'm sorry."

"Why? You don't have that bumper sticker on your car. You wouldn't."

"No," she said, "I wouldn't. But I am sorry that the words of other Christians caused you pain."

I shut up my inner snark before it even started.

"Some people just don't think before they speak." She sent me a wry smile. "Or slap a bumper sticker on their car. History is full of people doing things in the name of God. Sometimes even horrible things. But that doesn't change who God is."

Who God is?

I realized that the old tapes of who I'd thought God was

had been playing a continuous loop across my life, reaffirmed by my experiences.

Lucy touched my hand gently. "Look at *him*, Becca. Not at people. We fail. We stumble. But he doesn't. He's faithful."

I'd heard it all before. From Chloe and the girls. So God is faithful to the churchies ... big surprise. Exactly what Adelaide had said too. Another longtime churchie.

But looking into Lucy's kind eyes, I realized the message was different. She had come late to the party. Definitely not a lifetime churchified lemming. Her past was even more colorful than mine. So if Lucy claimed God had been faithful even to her and is faithful always ...

I had a lot to think about.

The next day at work, Margaret came in with brownies and a proposition for me.

"Could I do a story-time hour in the children's department?" she asked. "I'd love to introduce kids to some classic children's literature. I've been doing that with my grandkids and they're really loving it, so I thought maybe it might be something Dunkeld's customers would like too?"

"Sounds great to me, but I'd have to check with Alastair. He's the one in charge of payroll."

Margaret chuckled. "Oh, I'm not looking for a job. I'm talking about volunteering."

"Even better. I'm sure Alastair would be thrilled by the prospect—especially if he doesn't have to pay for your talents. He'd love the authorial prestige you'd bring to the store."

I was right. We pitched the idea to Alastair, and he was all over it like a cheap suit. Although it took us a few minutes to get his attention initially. He kept scrolling through emails on his Blackberry the whole time we were talking to him.

Or as I called it, his Crackberry.

It was almost like another appendage. He didn't go anywhere without it. Made me crazy. But then, I've always been a bit of a throwback that way. Just say no to the technology rat race and let's commune more with nature, people. If I want a blackberry, I'll pick one from a bush.

Am I ranting? Sorry.

It's cheaper than therapy.

For Margaret's first story time, I padded the audience. She'd already suffered enough rejection at the hands of her publisher; I didn't want her to go through the indignity of an empty house.

I asked each one of the Getaway Girls to bring any young nieces, nephews, or neighbors they might have. Then I repeated the same request to Ben, Adelaide, Lucy, and the rest of Ben's singles group friends. And I asked Annie to tell her home church pals. I also talked it up to our regular customers and made fliers that we slipped in every customer's bag—along with a discount coupon for 25 percent off of any children's title bought that day.

Alastair balked a little at the latter, but I convinced him that we were expecting such a large crowd that Dunkeld's would be bustling with buyers.

Then I crossed my fingers, and just to cover my bases, threw up a little prayer, hoping I was right.

Margaret's story time was … well … let's just say there was standing room only.

Every one of the Getaway Girls came—except Tess, who was off on another weekend jaunt in the Luxurymobile with James. And each brought a Rent-a-Kid: Annette brought seven-year-old Lola from the Sunday school class she taught; Kailyn brought Samantha and Nevyn, a six-year-old brother-and-sister twin act who'd appeared with her in one of her plays; Annie brought her little step-brother, Drake; Paige brought Emily, a four-year-old from her Sunday school class, as well as

Cyd, her fourteen-year-old foster daughter. And Chloe rounded out the mix with her nine-year-old holy terror of a cousin, Erica.

That child invented the word *bratspring.*

I was delighted to see Ben and Adelaide — Date Twenty! — who introduced me to their new next-door neighbor, Adriana, a shy, five-year-old beauty with the biggest brown eyes I'd ever seen.

"Adriana, *Te presento a* Becca," Adelaide said in fluent Spanish. "Becca, this is Adriana."

"*Mucho gusto*, Adriana," I said.

"*Mucho gusto*," said a little voice back to me.

"I didn't know you knew Spanish," Ben said.

"*Un poquito*," I said. And it was true. In fact, I'd have a big *problemo* if anyone broke into Spanish conversation with me.

"Becca, my dear, you sound like you have a natural ear," Adelaide said. "God can use that gift to reach his children. In fact" — she paused, stroking Adriana's dark curls — "I think he already has."

Maybe ... maybe not. As much as I cared for Adelaide, I wasn't buying into her view of my high school Spanish skills as God's gift to anyone. If she wanted to see someone sharing a gift with children, she should turn her attention to our author-in-residence, Margaret. She spun the story of *Charlotte's Web* with so much drama, even Kailyn might be intimidated. Margaret revealed hidden talents by doing different voices for all the characters: Fern, Wilbur the Pig, Charlotte ... even Templeton the rat.

Everyone was enraptured. Even Erica, the dreaded spawn. And not just the kids, but the grown-ups too.

Nestled among the children, I noticed a little boy sitting still and wide-eyed. He looked familiar, hugging a book tightly in thin arms. Suddenly I knew. He was the child for whom

Lucy had anonymously bought the Chronicles of Narnia. Apparently, he couldn't bear to be parted from the one he was currently reading. I studied him, watching him listen with avid interest, and recalled the brave acceptance of his father's words that there was no money to buy the coveted Chronicles set. Well behaved boy.

Okay, maybe I'd have to revise my opinion on all kids being brats ...

I was revising my thoughts on a lot of things lately.

The story came to a close and I was still lost in thought when a tap on the shoulder made me jump. I whirled around to face Kailyn.

"Guess what?"

"What?"

"We're going to New York, baby!"

"Shut up!" I squealed and started bouncing off the walls.

I never squeal.

25

If you can walk, you can dance. If you can talk, you can sing.

Zimbabwean proverb

I guess there might be something to this prayer thing after all.

While I'd been figuring and finagling every which way I could to get us to the isle of Manhattan—including buying a rash of lottery tickets in hopes of winning the big one—Kailyn had been praying and praying "for God to provide and open the doors if he wanted us to go to New York."

God had opened the doors. Although Kailyn's folks had turned the handle.

Annette hadn't been as clueless as I'd earlier thought. She realized her daughter needed a change of scenery so she wouldn't be surrounded all the time by couples and babies or couples soon to have babies.

So she cashed in some of her frequent flier miles and talked to Tess, who called in a favor from a flight attendant friend based out of New York. Tess arranged for us to stay at her friend's apartment that she shared with two other flight attendants in midtown Manhattan for a three-day weekend. The neighborhood where her friend lived was colorfully named Hell's Kitchen—not to be confused with Gordon Ramsay's cooking show—and was just one block away from Times Square and close to all the subways, which meant that transit time would be cut in half.

"This is such a God thing," Kailyn said. "If it wasn't for him prompting my mom and Tess, we'd never have been able to make this happen. Not with the skyrocketing costs of hotel and airfare."

That wasn't all. As an early birthday present for their daughter, and by extension, me, Annette and Randall splurged on tickets to two Broadway shows Kailyn had been foaming at the mouth to see—a musical revival and a drama that had won the Tony that year.

All we had to pay for were meals, souvenirs, and shopping. Since I've never been a shopaholic, the latter would be no problem for me. Although I couldn't say the same for Kailyn. I'd done enough research to know that we could eat cheap if we stuck to delis and the myriad street vendors selling hot dogs, pizza, hot pretzels, and everything else.

Kailyn was beside herself with excitement. Me too. I'd been wanting to visit New York for years. But even more than that, this would be my first adventure sans cast or walking boot. I couldn't wait to stretch my legs and give them a good workout around the city. That would save on transportation costs too.

The only downside was that Annie couldn't go with us.

"Sorry, guys," she said, when we first let her know that the trip wasn't just pie in the sky, but an actual reality, booked with an itinerary and everything. "Paige has really bad morning sickness and isn't able to work right now, and Marc's doing his best to take care of her, so I really can't leave the shop."

"Maybe we can wait a few weeks until Paige is better so you can go too," I said.

"But we don't know exactly when—or even if—that will be," Annie said. "No. I think it's best if I just stick close to home. But you guys take lots of pictures, okay?"

Kailyn and I alone on a trip together? What would that be like?

Like Simon Cowell going to a Barry Manilow concert? Or Paula Abdul stringing together a coherent sentence?

I guess I'd find out.

It would probably be fine. We hadn't done too badly as roommates—managing to strike a reasonable balance between our differing tastes and personalities. Kailyn's really not so bad once you got past all the gooey girlinesss. And the perk factor.

My friendship with Lucy, the Queen of Perkiness, had helped with the latter.

"How exciting that you're going to New York," she said when I told her the news on Date Twenty-One with Ben—a missions night prayer meeting at her house. "It's an exciting city. There's so much to do there. You *have* to go to Coney Island. The boardwalk is great and they have one of the oldest wooden roller coasters in the world."

"I thought I read something about Coney Island closing down," Ben said.

"Yeah, I read that too," Lucy said, "but I'm pretty sure it's still going strong. I think there was some kind of scandal around the development company, coupled with a public outcry about losing the small businesses, but you might want to double-check on that to be sure."

The Donald thought I should check out his namesake's

Trump Tower. "That's where they filmed *The Apprentice*, you know," he said. "Hey, maybe you'll even see The Donald. He lives in the penthouse on the top."

That was one item I didn't plan to add to my must-see list.

"Is it just you and your roommate going?" Cindy asked.

"Yep. Just the two of us."

"And you've never been there before?" Mindy said.

"Nope. First time."

Mindy shuddered. "Well, be careful. That's a scary city, especially for two women alone. If I were you, I wouldn't ride the subway. I'd take taxis everywhere."

I'll keep that in mind, Carrie Bradshaw. And I'll make sure to try a Cosmopolitan too.

Then Lucy pulled out a world globe and they began praying for the people in a small village in India.

When Ben dropped me off at the duplex he made me an offer I couldn't refuse. "So, I've always wanted to go to Central Park and check out the hiking trails and paddleboats," he said, "but since that doesn't look like it's going to happen anytime soon, you go in my place and send pictures back and I'll consider that date number twenty-two. Sound good?"

"Works for me."

"But only if you get a photo of the Strawberry Fields tribute to John Lennon," he added. "Deal?"

"Deal."

"Oh, and Adelaide said to tell you to be sure and go see the Statue of Liberty. Yeah, it's touristy and I know how you like to go more off the beaten path, but she said you'd really like it. Says it's pretty moving and powerful. She also said to give you her love and to have a great time."

"Give her my love too," I said. "And tell her I look forward to seeing her when I get back."

I cleared the time off with Alastair, and Kailyn told her

temp agency not to send her any assignments for those days, and we were all set.

The night we left to catch our Thursday red-eye, Annette had all the Getaway Girls over to her house for an early bon voyage dinner. All except for Paige, who was still battling morning sickness, even at night. Annette cooked up a storm—fried chicken, mashed potatoes and gravy, greens, cornbread, the works—afraid we wouldn't get enough to eat while we were in the big city.

"Well, I don't know about anyone else," Annie said, leaning back in her chair afterwards and stretching, "but I'm about to burst." Her tan tee, which read *Careful, or I'll Put You in My Novel*, strained against her stomach.

"Are you writing a novel?" Kailyn asked.

"You never know. Could be. Better be careful what you say."

"So what do you all want us to bring you back from New York?" I asked.

"Just a postcard," Chloe said, knowing our funds were on the tight side. "But you do have to go to the Met for me."

"What's the Met?" Kailyn asked.

"Isn't that the opera? I remember that from *Moonstruck*."

"I can't believe you've forgotten The Met. The Met-ro-po-li-tan Mu-se-um of Art," Chloe said, enunciating each syllable. "Remember we read about it in *From the Mixed-Up Files of Mrs. Basil E. Frankweiler*?"

"Oh yeah. The kids who hid in the museum."

"Not just any museum," Tess said. "It's one of the largest art galleries in the world."

"And it's right on the edge of Central Park. They have a bunch of Monets I'd love to see someday." Chloe's eyes got all dreamy and gooey the way they did whenever she talked about art.

"Rembrandts and Vermeers too," Tess said. "It's an amazing museum. But then, so is the MoMA. There's some great Picassos and Jackson Pollacks there. And you should check out the Frick too."

"What the frick is the Frick?" I asked.

"Another wonderful museum with gorgeous art and furniture from all over."

"I don't mean to disappoint you," I said, "but I don't plan to spend all my time in New York in museums."

"Yeah," Kailyn said. "Sorry. We're not the artsy ones, remember?"

"Good point, y'all." Annette began stacking dishes. "There must be lots of non-artsy spots for you to visit."

"Ooh, you *have* to go to the Top of the Rock," Annie said. "It's the observation deck seventy stories above Rockefeller Center with a great view of the New York City skyline. Personally, I like it better than the Empire State."

Now that sounded like something I could hang with.

Before we left, Chloe slipped me an envelope. "For a nice dinner. Go find a top chef somewhere and make a memory to bring back for all of us."

"Thanks," I said and opened the envelope. Inside was two hundred dollars.

Sweet.

I was ready to take a bite out of the Big Apple.

26

Tread softly because you tread on my dreams.

William Butler Yeats

As our plane approached JFK International, Kailyn started humming Sinatra's "New York, New York."

Just so she didn't stand up and start belting out the lyrics, we were good.

My roommate's eyes shone brighter than I'd ever seen. And that's saying something. She's the perennial sparkle girl.

After collecting our luggage from baggage claim, we followed Tess's directions and took the Air Train to Sutphin Boulevard/Jamaica Station, where we planned to catch the subway to her friend's Manhattan apartment.

The Sutphin stop was grimy and dark with ugly orange brick walls at either end. It was also teeming with people of every stripe, size, and smell. Kailyn and I stayed close and tightened our grips on our rolling suitcases. Finally we found the right line—the E train—and joined the crush of commuters standing on the stifling platform making their way into Manhattan.

My T-shirt was sticking to my skin and I could feel sweat pouring down my back. Kailyn's bangs were sticking to her forehead and she looked as wilted as I felt. Maybe this is why so many New Yorkers leave the sauna, I mean, city, in August.

But hey—we're in New York! Who cares what month it is?

As we hustled into our car—Kailyn holding tight to my arm so we wouldn't get separated—we were met with a welcome blast of air conditioning. Thank you, Jesus. At this time of morning though, the subway was standing room only, so we both wedged our suitcases between our legs, grabbed a metal bar, and hung on for dear life.

And nobody paid us the least bit of attention. Everyone was busy reading a newspaper, texting away, tapping on their Blackberrys, or just standing there with a sort of dazed, vacant expression.

The variety of people around us gave new meaning to the words *melting pot*. Businessmen in suits sitting next to East Indian women in saris sitting next to a chubby family of tourists whose flat nasal accents told me they were probably from the Midwest. Scruffy backpackers speaking German sat next to gorgeous upscale women in designer clothes who sat next to rough-looking teenagers tricked out in baggy pants, bandanas, and bling.

I wondered how Kailyn and I appeared to this gathering of humanity. Sweaty humanity at that. We fit right in. The fragrance from our togetherness had a particular piquancy.

Kailyn tried to call Annette to let her know we'd arrived safely, but there was no reception.

Within minutes, however, the welcome air conditioning had turned into an arctic blast, and I longed for the sweater shoved at the bottom of my suitcase and totally inaccessible.

By the time we arrived at our stop forty-five minutes later—yes, *forty-five* minutes—my hand felt like it was glued to the metal pole like that kid and his tongue in *A Christmas Story*. I thawed out during the two-block walk to the apartment and the circulation returned to my hand.

We trundled our suitcases up the steps of an old, reddish-brick building and pushed the buzzer for admittance.

Once inside, I presented the email from Tess's friend to the grizzled sixty-something doorman at the old, slightly shabby front desk.

He read it and smiled. "Welcome to New York," he said. "The name's Fred. Miss Abbott said you were comin'. First time?" he asked as he handed me the key to the third-floor apartment.

"What was your first clue?" I glanced at Kailyn, who was impatiently hopping from one foot to another. "Hi, Fred. I'm Becca and this is Kailyn."

"Nice to meetcha."

"You'll be seeing us again in just a few minutes, Fred," Kailyn said, giving him a dazzling smile as we headed to the elevator. "We're going sightseeing! Maybe when we come back down, you can answer a few questions for us?"

"Anything you want."

Men always responded that way to Kailyn. It was that whole Meg Ryan/Jessica Simpson thing she had goin' on.

We rode the elevator up to the third floor and hunted for Apartment 3-G. Finally we found it at the very end of the hall. Decent apartment. Clean and neat. But small and pretty empty: couch, chair, small table, lamp, and one picture on the living room wall—a black and white photo of the New York skyline. You could tell they didn't spend much time there.

But we wouldn't be either, so it didn't matter.

"Can you believe how tiny this is?" Kailyn said, pushing her suitcase to the side of the couch and looking around. "It's not even half the size of our duplex."

"Rents are higher here."

"Yeah, but three people living in such close quarters?" She opened a door off the living room. "This must be one of the bedrooms."

I wandered over to the tiny kitchenette consisting of a fridge, sink, and stove and a narrow standing cabinet. Peeking inside, I discovered the bottom shelf held dish soap and cleaning supplies, the middle shelf, a couple pots and pans, and the top shelf, dishes and glasses. Above the stove, open metal shelving held a few canned goods, a box of pasta noodles, and assorted spices.

Beyond the kitchen was a microscopic bath composed of a toilet, sink, and minuscule shower. No tub.

"Becca?" Kailyn called out.

"Yeah?"

She rejoined me in the living room. "This is only a one-bedroom apartment," she said. "For three people!" She nodded to the room she'd just vacated. "There's three beds in there."

I checked it out. A set of bunk beds and a small dresser filled one wall, while a futon, flanked by two small chests of drawers, took up the opposite side of the room.

Bunk beds for flight attendants? Next to the side of a postage-stamp closet stood a metal hanging rack bulging with clothes.

"It's like *The Three Bears*," I said.

Wonder where the porridge is.

"Dibs on the top bunk," I called.

"With your ankle? I don't think so. You'd better stick a little closer to the ground."

"Yeah, well, right now I'm ready for some higher ground. Put on your walking shoes, my friend, and let's get this party started."

In advance of our trip, I'd written down everyone's suggestions of where to go and what to see and had also done a little online research of my own. Tess, our ever helpful travel guide, had also provided us with a tentative itinerary "to make things easier."

Kailyn and I had checked over the itinerary on the plane and some of it we liked; some of it, not so much. Neither of us were the least bit interested in visiting the United Nations, the Museum of Modern Art, or the New York Stock Exchange. Although skipping the stock exchange was quite the concession on Kailyn's part, considering all the handsome, wealthy men in Italian suits. But we didn't want to be too tied down to a schedule.

Spontaneity rules.

We already had our tickets for the theater tonight and tomorrow, and we planned to grab a bite afterwards, but meanwhile, the entire day was wide open. We wanted to go to the top of the Empire State Building, and had thought that might be the first stop on our sightseeing agenda, but after talking to the ever-helpful Fred, he told us the lines would be insane this time of day, so our best bet would be to either go tonight when the observation deck was open until midnight, or first thing tomorrow morning.

As we looked over some of the online suggestions, coupled with Tess's, we saw a pattern emerge. Most suggested we start out at one of the many museums each morning, then find a fun or elegant place to eat lunch, shop the entire afternoon away, and wind up with dinner and/or the theater.

Clearly these were all rich, sedentary tourists.

We decided we'd hit the Public Library first and take our pictures with the lions out front.

"Hey, didja know those lions have names?" Fred asked.

"Would one of them happen to be Leo?" Kailyn grinned.

"No sirree," he said. "They're Patience and Fortitude."

I needed a little patience and fortitude as the day wore on.

After a quick photo op with the library lions, we went to the Met museum in homage to Mrs. Frankweiler's mixed-up files. We took another photo outside the impressive building for book club and I did my usual McArt drive-thru thing, stopping long enough to scope out the Monets for Chloe and the Rembrandts for Tess and picking up art postcards for the group. If our artsy Getaway Girls had been along, we'd have been forced to make an entire day or more of it.

As it was, we were at the museum for nearly two hours.

Afterwards, I wanted to go to Central Park, since we were, after all, already *in* the park, but Kailyn wanted to shop.

I was itching for a run. Kailyn was itching to check out all the flagship New York stores: Macy's, Bloomingdale's, Saks Fifth Avenue ...

"Did you know that Macy's takes up an entire city block?" she said. "It's the same Macy's from that old Christmas movie *Miracle on 34ᵗʰ Street*. I can't wait to see it."

"Can't you wait a little bit longer?" I looked longingly at the park. "Ben said there's some cool paddleboats we can go on. Doesn't that sound fun?" I blew a puff of air upward to release my bangs from their sweat prison. "Probably cool too, since we'd be on the water."

"It's even cooler inside those big air-conditioned stores. Come on," Kailyn said in a wheedling tone. "If you go shopping with me now, I'll go to the park with you tomorrow."

"But we're already right here."

In the end, I caved. After all, this trip was to cheer Kailyn up, and besides, it was her folks who fronted the airline and theater tickets.

Kailyn was in shopaholic heaven, giving her credit card an intense plastic workout from one store to the next—Macy's, Century 21, Bloomies ...

I felt as if I'd died and gone to retail hell.

The only bright spot was when we stopped at FAO Schwartz on Fifth Avenue.

The giant teddy bear out front that was more than twice my height should have clued me in that everything inside the store would be bigger and better. The grown men dressed like toy soldiers and serving as doormen should have been another clue.

As we walked through the door held open by the beaming toy-soldier men who saluted us, we were surrounded by a jungle of animals. Lions and tigers and bears, oh my. Giraffes and elephants and crocodiles too.

"Wow," Kailyn said. "Have you ever seen so many stuffed animals in your life?"

"Never."

It was like an animal army. And those puppies were huge. So were the price tags. Thousands of bucks for the life-sized creatures.

"We should get something for Chloe's baby," Kailyn said. "Paige's too."

"I love Chloe and Paige," I said, "but not that much. Besides, how would we get those big guys on the plane?"

It was cool though to recognize some animals from the endangered species list, including a giant panda. There was even an American Kennel Club with plush replicas of purebred dogs that came complete with a red AKC collar and certificate. But the doggy I preferred was Patrick the pup with his pudgy, huggable body, warm tan fur, and droopy ears.

Kailyn squeezed the plush pup. "He's so soft."

I checked the price tag. Patrick, we could afford.

And then another animal called to me. Roared, was more like it. The king of the jungle—looking just like the carved lion on the walking stick Adelaide had given me. I stroked his fur, then lifted him up and hugged him to my neck.

I let my inner child loose as we continued through the mega toy store, frolicking around the giant Lego figures, oohing and aahing in the Harry Potter shop, and wishing I was a little smaller so I could ride Thomas the Tank Engine. We skipped the Barbie doll annex where little girls could create their own Barbie and made our way up the stairs to the second level.

And there it was.

The cool floor piano that Tom Hanks had danced on with his boss in *Big*.

Kailyn looked at me. I looked at her. And then we busted out a little *Heart and Soul*.

Afterwards, hungry from our dance workout, we stopped at a place called Famous Original Ray's Pizza and inhaled a couple slices of pepperoni. Then, as it was turning dark, we made our way through the teeming sidewalks, crowded streets, and honking yellow cabs to the bright lights of Times Square.

"Oh. My. Gosh," Kailyn said looking around at theater after theater ablaze with the hottest shows on Broadway. "Oh my gosh." She did a Mary Tyler Moore twirl in the middle of the sidewalk, and if she'd been wearing a beret, she'd have thrown it up in the air.

"Look, Ma, I'm on Broadway!"

27

All children except one grow up.

Peter Pan

"Wasn't that just the most *amazing* thing you've ever seen?" Kailyn gushed as we left the theater three hours later.

"It was good."

"*Good?* It was fabulous!"

I hesitated, not wanting to diss Annette's gift. "I've just never been a big musicals person."

"But this wasn't just a musical. It was a happening. An event. An extravaganza!" Kailyn bowed to her imaginary audience midstep as we walked down the street.

"Whoa. Slow down there, Sparky. Did you have a Red Bull during intermission? Or is the theater paying you to write their PR blurbs?"

"Very funny. So I got excited by my first Broadway musical. What's wrong with that?"

"Nothing," I said. "I think it's great. But don't get upset if I don't share that same excitement."

"I can't believe you didn't like it."

"I did like it. I just didn't love it the way you did."

"But how could you *not*?" Kailyn pressed.

My stomach rumbled. "Maybe I just couldn't fully appreciate it because I was hungry."

I stopped and gestured to a restaurant window. "Look, here's a deli. Let's get something to eat. Maybe if I have a pastrami on rye and some matzo ball soup, then I'll love it."

The pastrami—hold the mayo—was heaven, but the rude waiter left a bad taste in my mouth. And I thought rude New Yorkers were just a cliché.

Kailyn continued to babble on about the show we'd just seen and how amazing it was yet again. Suddenly she clutched my arm.

"Becca," she hissed. "Over by the door. Look."

I glanced behind me at the deli entrance where a cluster of women and a couple men wearing way too much makeup had just come in.

"What?"

"Don't you recognize them?" she whispered. "That's some of the cast from the play."

"Really? Are you sure?" I looked again, but none of the laughing group looked familiar. "How can you tell?"

"Because that tall guy on the end was the tallest dancer in the back of the chorus and the older woman with the curly red hair was the comic relief with that distinctive laugh. Don't you remember?"

Curly-top threw back her head and brayed.

"Oh yeah. Now I remember."

I could only hope nothing else was said to trigger a cackle from Curly.

Kailyn pulled out her program from her purse and began paging through it.

"Here she is." She turned the program so it was facing me and pointed to a black-and-white publicity photo.

"Yep. That's her all right." I squinted at the page. "Hey, it says she was in *The Importance of Being Earnest*." I took a drink of my Dr. Brown's Cream Soda.

"No. Really?" Kailyn spun the program back around so she could read it. "Oh my gosh, you're right. She was Lady Bracknell. Sondra Grant's her name. I bet she was great."

Kailyn adopted a haughty look and recited in her upper-crust English. "'To lose one parent, Mr. Worthing, may be regarded as a misfortune. To lose both looks like carelessness.'"

I sprayed out my cream soda.

"Well, that line always got a laugh," a rich female voice beside me said, "but I don't think I ever made anyone spray soda. And all over my picture too." The red-haired middle-aged actress plucked a napkin from the empty table next to ours and blotted Kailyn's theater program.

"Oh Sondra, you're so vain," said the tall dancer.

"And I'll bet you think that song is about you, don't you, Kurt?"

The group of actors giggled as they sat down at the table next to us.

"So did you like the show tonight?" Sondra asked Kailyn, who'd been taking all this in with wide eyes.

"Loved it! It was fabulous!" Kailyn said. "You were all great."

"Thanks. You're not so bad there yourself. Are you in anything right now?"

"Pardon?"

"You're an actress, right?" Sondra asked.

"Yes, she is," I piped up before Kailyn went all modest on me. "A really good one."

"So what show are you in?" asked one of the other

actresses at the table. "You look a little familiar. Are you in *Mamma Mia?*"

"Oh no. Are you kidding?" Kailyn said. "Me? On Broadway? I don't think so."

"Nothing wrong with off-Broadway," Sondra said. "I've done plenty of smaller shows there. Sometimes they're the best."

"The plays I've been in would be off-off Broadway," Kailyn said. "I don't live here."

"You don't?" the other man in the group said. "Where do you live?"

"Sacramento."

"As in California?"

"I didn't even know they had theater in Sacramento," Kurt said.

"Oh, don't be such a snob," Sondra said.

The waiter arrived at their table. "Ya gonna order or what?"

While the theater table was busy giving him their order, Kailyn looked at me and mouthed the word "Omigosh!"

After orders were placed, Sondra zeroed in on Kailyn. "Tell me about the work you've done. Wherever. All good experience, I say."

Kailyn scooted her chair a little closer to Sondra and began giving her bio. Even I was impressed by the credits compiled so far, Sacramento or not. The theater crowd listened politely, with an occasional comment that was Greek to me but which their creative cronies appreciated.

At the end of my roommate's soliloquy, Sondra said, "You've done a lot of diverse roles. That's good. If you're ever auditioning in New York, give me a call. Maybe I can help." She stopped and dug through her wallet, passing a business card across the tables to my roommate.

"Wow." Kailyn's eyes grew enormous. "Thanks!" After holding the card worshipfully for a while, she tucked it in her purse.

We finished our cheesecake and said our goodbyes to Kailyn's new theater pals and then trekked over to the Empire State Building and rode the elevators up to the eighty-sixth-floor observation deck.

Pretty killer view.

"Look at that," Kailyn breathed. "Isn't it beautiful seeing the whole city lit up like that? Have you ever seen anything like it? New York is such an exciting city. Wouldn't you just die to live here?"

No. But I might die *if* I lived here. I thought of what Hemingway said about New York: It's a town you come to for a short time.

Apparently not everyone.

"I don't want to go back home. I want to stay right here," Kailyn said.

"And wait for your Prince Charming like the chick from that fifties movie, or Meg Ryan at the top of the Empire State?" I grunted. "Here's a tip: Only happens in the movies."

"Not right *here*, silly. Here in New York." Kailyn rolled her eyes. "Sondra said this is where it all happens for actors. Maybe I *need* to be here." She gazed out thoughtfully at the skyscape.

"Serious?"

"I'm serious about acting. And now that I have connections ..."

I guffawed. "You can't mean Curly-top and her cronies."

Kailyn looked hurt.

"Sorry. I didn't mean that. Sondra is probably a good connection to the theater world. Maybe you should give her a call tomorrow."

"I plan to. Though I'd really like to go to Radio City

Music Hall and see a matinee of the Rockettes. Otherwise, Sondra was telling me there's a great production of *A Midsummer Night's Dream* playing in an off-Broadway theater. A friend of hers is Puck, so she could probably get us tickets."

"Okay, I know I'm an English major and all," I said, "but I'm going to confess straight up; I'm not a Shakespeare fan. I don't get Shakespeare. The only time I did was in the movie *Shakespeare in Love* and this one cool *Dr. Who* episode."

"How can you be an English major and not love Shakespeare?" Kailyn said. She closed her eyes and recited," Let me not to the marriage of true minds admit impediments. Love is not love which alters when it alteration finds ..."

"What can I say? So revoke my degree and call me a Philistine. And I'm *so* not interested in seeing a bunch of Barbies all kicking their legs up at the same time. What's up with that, anyway?"

"It's a classic kick line. It's all about timing and precision," Kailyn said. "*I* think it's a thing of beauty."

"Beauty's in the eye of the beholder. I'd rather see Yankee Stadium. Besides, have you forgotten? I shopped with you today, so you promised you'd go to Central Park with me tomorrow. I really want to explore the park and find that Lennon plaque. And I heard that on the weekends it closes to traffic and becomes this huge open-air running, biking, and inline skating track."

"You want to go running? In *New York*?" Kailyn stared at me. "You can run anywhere."

"Actually, I haven't been able to for the past few months, and I really need to move."

"Okay, I get that. And I'll go with you to the park in the morning, but I'm not going to spend the entire day there," Kailyn said. "And I'm certainly not going to go running on my second-to-last day in New York. Not gonna happen. I want to see as much theater as I can while I'm here."

"But we're going to another play tomorrow night. Your folks got us those tickets."

"I know. But Sondra might be able to get tickets for a matinee," Kailyn said. "Double the pleasure. Remember, Puck awaits."

"Puck-yuck. No can do," I said. I chewed on the inside of my cheek. "Tell you what. We're not joined at the hip, so let's split up after Central Park. I have a few other things I want to do that don't include more theater. We can reconnoiter at dinner."

Kailyn nodded, distracted. No doubt her brain buzzed with imaginary acting offers and the possibilities of life in a three-story walk-up in Soho.

I had my own brain buzz going.

The subject? Two hundred dollars of Chloe's money hidden in my bag that Kailyn didn't know about. That would be my mission tomorrow afternoon while I was doing my tourist gig. Find us fancy dinner digs to surprise my roomie. That would be fun, wouldn't it?

28

To find out what one is fitted to do and to secure an opportunity to do it is the key to happiness.

John Dewey

"Wake up, sleepyhead," Kailyn sang out. "Up and at 'em."

"Huh?" I lifted my groggy head from the bottom bunk and focused in on my roommate on the futon across the room from me. Only she wasn't on the futon.

My bleary eyes traveled the room until they located the source of the annoying voice. Over by the window. The window where violent sunlight was streaming in.

I buried my head beneath my pillow.

"Good morning!" Susie Sunshine trilled. "Time to get up. It's a gorgeous day and we've got a lot to do, so shake your lazy butt and let's get moving. Come on. Chop, chop."

I'll chop you.

"What time is it?"

"What? I can't understand you under that pillow."

"What … time … is … it?"

"Seven o'clock."

"Seven?" I looked around for a shoe to throw at my too-perky-to-live bunkmate.

"Our Top of the Rock tickets are for 8:30, remember?" Kailyn said. "We need to get cracking."

"Must ... have ... coffee."

"I know," Kailyn said. "But I already looked and there's none in the apartment. I checked with Fred and he said Tamara always gets her coffee from a Starbucks down the street."

"Who's Tamara?"

"Tamara Abbott, silly. The flight attendant whose apartment we're staying in."

"Oh yeah." I was fighting through the layers of fog trying to wake up.

Mornings are not my friend.

"Hurry up and take a shower," Kailyn said. "I'm hungry and Fred says there's this terrific little deli around the corner where they make great lox and bagels and something called blintzes?"

Bagels. Lox. Blintzes?

My stomach gave a standing ovation and I threw off the covers and stumbled blindly down the hall.

When I got out of the shower and returned to dress, Kailyn was on the phone with Annette. "Hey, guess what we're about to do, Mom? Have lox and bagels at a Jewish deli. Isn't that cool? It's so New York."

I pulled my running shorts and shoes out of my suitcase.

"No, we're not going to take the subway," Kailyn said. "Not this morning. We're walking. It's right around the corner."

She beamed into the phone. "I know! Isn't that great? There's so many places within walking distance. Including Times Square and all the theaters. Can you believe it? Only a block away. Omigosh!"

If I heard that expression one more time, I was going to throttle her. Then she'd really have something to say omigosh about. I pulled my T-shirt over my head—a birthday gift from Annie that read *I'm dressed and out of bed. What more do you want?*

"And after breakfast we're going to Rockefeller Center," Kailyn was saying to Annette.

I tapped my chest.

"Hey Mom, I've got to go, but real quick, tell me how Paige is doing. Is she still puking all the time?" Kailyn nodded. "Oh, okay. Good to hear. Love you. Tell everyone hi. Talk to you later."

"Is Paige okay?" I asked once she hung up.

"She's fine. Mom said the doctor changed her prenatal vitamins and she's doing much better. But she's sticking to bland foods in the morning."

"Good thing we're not pregnant," I said as we left the apartment and headed to the elevator. "I'd hate to miss these yummy lox we're about to have."

"You and me both."

The lox were great and so were the blueberry blintzes, but Rockefeller Center and the view from the Top of the Rock left them both in the dust.

"Wow," Kailyn said as we gazed out at the panoramic view from the streamlined glassed-in observation deck high above the city. "This is even better than the Empire State."

"Ya got that right."

Instead of metal railings like the Empire State, the deck was enclosed in Plexiglas, which allowed a clear, unobstructed view of New York that stretched for miles.

"Spectacular," Kailyn breathed. "Look! There's the Empire State Building. And Times Square. And the Statue of Liberty way out there. Ooh, and there's your Central Park that we'll be seeing up close and personal pretty soon." She pointed to an expanse of green and trees in the midst of all the concrete, steel, and glass.

As I gazed out at the scene, I enjoyed the peace at seventy stories above the city. And I couldn't wait to get to the park and just chill out in some nature. All the people, noise, constant hurrying, and craziness in the concrete jungle below were starting to get to me.

On the way to Central Park, Kailyn followed my suggestion, fished out the business card from the night before, and called her new friend Sondra, who told her she'd been able to get her a comp ticket for *A Midsummer Night's Dream* that afternoon.

Kailyn squealed when she hung up, causing a passing woman to shake her head and mutter, "Tourists."

Central Park was an anomaly — a verdant slash of more than eight hundred acres carved out in the heart of a city dominated by skyscrapers and concrete. And it was clearly the place to be on a late morning in Saturday.

Sunbathers dotted the grassy sections, families picnicked on the lawns, people walked their dogs on the many paths, joggers ran past, and kids played under the watchful eyes of their parents — or nannies.

First time I've ever seen nannies outside of the movies.

I itched to join the joggers, but the first thing I wanted to do was honor my promise to Ben. I asked a mounted cop on a horse where we could find Strawberry Fields and the plaque to John Lennon, and he directed us to the west side of the park.

When we got to the memorial, however, I saw that it wasn't a plaque but rather a large, round, grey and white mosaic laid in the ground with the word *imagine* in the center. Cellophane-wrapped daisies, roses, and several other floral tributes dotted the mosaic, but were starting to wilt in the heat. I snapped a picture from my phone for Ben and sent it off with a text simply saying, "22."

Beside me, Kailyn glanced about, stretching her neck and squinting with concentration.

"What are you looking for, Miss Marple?"

"I was just thinking that with a little imagination, this might be a good spot for an amphitheater," she said.

"There's no need to be so creative. If you want to go hang with Sondra and her thespians, go. I want to be alone to commune with nature anyway." I gave her a push. "Go, little bird. Fly!"

"Thanks," Kailyn said. "You're the best. Call me later so we can meet to eat." With a wave, she soon disappeared from view.

I jogged through the wandering paths for about an hour, getting in my zone and working up a good sweat. It felt great to be running again. And as I ran, I tried to figure out what to do with Chloe's two hundred dollars. Fancy restaurants really weren't my thing.

This Birkenstocks girl is good with a salad or PB&J, although I do have a weakness for Mexican. Kailyn liked the finer things, though, so she'd probably appreciate it. But how would I even go about finding a good restaurant?

You could always ask Fred the doorman. He seems to know everything about the city.

That's true. Good point.

But as I continued to run, I thought of something Kailyn would like even more than dinner out.

I figure Chloe wouldn't mind if I traded in her dinner money for Broadway tickets for our theater-mad Getaway Girl.

After running for a while, my ankle started to throb, so I decided to take a break. I snagged a bottled water and an ice cream cone from one of the vendors and kicked back on the grass to people watch for a while.

It was like being on the subway again seeing all the different people types. I felt like I was at a UN meeting. Or what I thought a United Nations meeting might be like.

As I licked my ice cream cone, my eyes met those of a little blonde-haired girl sitting nearby with her family. Or maybe it was my ice cream cone she had in her sights. She was waif thin and poorly dressed and I could see her eyes fill with longing as she watched me. Eventually she spoke aloud to her father in a language I couldn't understand. He shook his head no, saying something that spread disappointment across her face.

Being somewhat bright, I figured she had asked her father for an ice cream, and he'd said no, there was no money.

The scene reminded me of something else. Of Lucy and a little boy who dearly wanted some books. In front of me was a perfect opportunity to do a "Lucy" or an "Adelaide."

Okay, on a smaller level, but still ...

I ambled over to the vendor and paid for an ice cream cone on the sly, instructing him to wait until I was out of sight before he gave it to the girl. Jogging away, I felt like I'd won the lotto.

Only better.

As I speed-walked back to the apartment to shower and change out of my sweaty running clothes, I stumbled upon a street fair filled with vendors hawking jewelry, T-shirts, socks and underwear, and every kind of food imaginable. I bought a lamb kebab and a plastic cup filled with juicy cubes of watermelon. As I ate the watermelon, I enjoyed a little street theater — a guy with a boom box breakin' some moves while everyone applauded him on.

I snagged a yellow T-shirt for Annie that read *I'm Elite. You're not.* before heading home.

The play that night was much better. No one breaking out into song at inappropriate moments.

"How'd you like it?" Kailyn asked me anxiously as we left the theater.

"I loved it. It was really good. Although I think you'd have done a better job than the chick playing the daughter."

"Oh, stop."

But I could tell she was pleased.

After the play we passed a place called Gray's Papaya Dog, where a sign in the window said they had a "recession special": two hot dogs and a drink for under five dollars.

"Hey, I like those prices," Kailyn said, stopping. She was starting to feel the pinch of all her shopping.

"Let's go for it."

We walked back to the counter to place our order. "Two recession specials."

"With everything?" the Filipino guy behind the counter asked.

"Sure," I said. "Might as well go for broke."

We watched as he squirted ketchup and mustard on our dogs, threw on some sauerkraut, and topped it off with a chunky red sauce.

"Mmm," Kailyn said after biting into hers. "This is good."

"Oh yeah. But that's the first time I've ever had a hot dog snap when I bit into it."

"At least it didn't bite back."

Sunday morning we got up early again so we could catch the first ferry to the Statue of Liberty. As the boat brought us closer and closer to the iconic symbol of freedom, my heart caught in my throat.

I thought about all those immigrants who came to find the American dream and ended up a part of the fabric of America. Those who built America. Starting with long lines at Ellis

Island. And those who gave their lives that France would send us such a symbol.

I recalled how on our Getaway Girls trip to Paris, when we'd cruised down the Seine on a bateaux mouche, we'd seen a smaller version of the statue on the little island beneath the bridge next to the Eiffel Tower.

And I thought of those famous words on the statue, "Give me your tired, your poor ..." and my thoughts turned again to Africa and the things Adelaide had shared, as well as the speaker at the conference, and I knew for certain that my Birkenstocks and I would soon be traveling on.

"Becca?" Kailyn's voice cut through my reverie.

"Yeah?"

"Um, would you mind if we went to church this morning?"

"Church? In New York? On our last day?" I stared at her. "Serious?"

Kailyn flushed. "I know it's not your thing, and normally, I wouldn't ask. But Sondra told me about this church that meets in a rehearsal studio and I'd really like to go. She said some actors and dancers go there too."

Dancers? Actors? Theatrical types? Talk about razzle-dazzle.

"You know I can't stand churches that are big and glitzy."

What are you talking about? You can't stand churches in general.

Shut up. I liked Annie's home church.

"Sondra said it's a small church and really low-key," Kailyn said. "Please?"

Um, who paid for the trip again? my conscience asked.

Kailyn's parents.

And what was the main purpose of this trip?

To cheer my roommate up.

Well then.

"Okay," I said with a sigh, "but if I see even one sequin, I'm outta there."

I needn't have worried.

The forty-odd people gathered in clusters in the mid-town rehearsal studio were an eclectic bunch—African American, Hispanic, Indian, Asian, and a few whites—and most of them, I was pleased to see, were wearing shorts and flip-flops, except for a few older women in casual summer dresses or skirts and two ultra-slim girls in capris and ballet flats. Obviously the dancers.

But not one sequin in the bunch.

In one corner, a small band was rehearsing a jazzy, reggae tune, while in another next to a table full of bottled water and juice what looked like a group of long-lost friends held a mini reunion. Lots of hugging, laughter, and gleeful shouts.

"Hello," said a petite, elderly African-American woman in a cream-colored shirtwaist. "Welcome." She clasped my hand warmly between hers. "We're happy you're here. I'm Althea, and this is my husband, Reuben." She inclined her head to the slight, bald, smiling white man beside her, who had just grasped Kailyn's hand in greeting.

"Nice to meet you," I said. "I'm Becca."

"And I'm Kailyn."

"Welcome, Becca and Kailyn," Reuben said. "We're so glad you could join us. Do you live nearby?"

"Oh no," Kailyn said. "We're from California."

The capri-clad dancers joined us. They didn't so much walk, as glide.

Althea smiled at them and raised her voice over the din. "Maya, Anita, this is Becca and Kailyn all the way from California."

"Hi." Maya, who looked a lot like the gorgeous girl from *Slumdog Millionaire*, gave us a shy smile.

"California?" Anita said, her dark eyes shining. "Please tell me you're the daughters of a famous Hollywood producer who will cast me in his next movie."

Kailyn giggled. "I wish."

Just then a trio of little boys ran by shrieking with laughter, the smallest one banging into one of the folding chairs set up in a semicircle. He started to cry, but instantly a slender Asian woman scooped him up in her arms and blew a raspberry on his tummy, turning his cries to giggles.

A hunky Taye Diggs lookalike began warming up with the band, and I found my foot tapping in rhythm.

Was this really church? Or had we stumbled onto some cool concert instead?

"Everyone, can you take your seats, please?" a mellifluous voice said into a microphone. "We'll be starting soon."

I turned my head to see the source of the lovely voice and saw a tall, regal woman with dreadlocks and café au lait skin in a flowing orange caftan conferring with a scruffy white guy in a Bob Marley T-shirt, shorts, and Birks.

Sweet.

"Becca, Kailyn? Want to sit with us?" Maya asked.

"Sure." We followed them over to the folding chairs, Reuben and Althea close behind.

"We'll see you after," Althea said. "Our kids have saved us seats on the other side." She gave a little wave and walked away, holding Reuben's hand.

"Aw, isn't that sweet," Kailyn whispered as she scooted in after Maya and Anita. "Old people in love are so cute."

"Just don't let Althea hear you call her old," Anita cautioned. "I made that mistake once and will never do so again."

"Got it."

The band started their jazzy, reggae piece and I grooved along. I may be a white chick, but I've got rhythm. I didn't even mind when I heard God in the lyrics. They did a few more up-tempo numbers and everyone rocked out.

And then the Taye Diggs lookalike slowed things down and sang a song called "It Is Well with My Soul."

A cappella.

Wow.

One by one, the people around me began to stand up and join in. Until pretty soon, the whole audience was on its feet, singing in unison as one.

I stood up too. Closed my eyes, and let the music take me away.

When the song ended, a hush settled over the room. And then that same melodious voice we'd heard earlier said softly, "Let us pray."

Still caught up in the power of the music, this time I didn't tune out.

"Father," she said in a voice full of reverence, "thank you for your presence here today. We worship you and honor you and give you all the glory. Be with us and guide us and may we be ever mindful of you. Thank you for loving us even when we are unlovely. And now, if you'll all join me in the prayer of St. Francis of Assisi."

I looked around for the big screen like they had in Ben's church, but there wasn't one. And then I saw that everyone was looking down, reading. Maya slipped me a narrow sheet of paper so I could join in with the audience.

Uh, congregation.

> *"Lord, make me an instrument of thy peace;*
> *where there is hatred, let me sow love;*
> *where there is injury, pardon;*
> *where there is doubt, faith;*
> *where there is despair, hope;*

where there is darkness, light;
and where there is sadness, joy.
O Divine Master,
grant that I may not so much seek to be consoled
    as to console;
to be understood, as to understand;
to be loved, as to love;
for it is in giving that we receive,
it is in pardoning that we are pardoned,
and it is in dying that we are born to Eternal Life.
Amen."

I stared at the words, repeating some silently: "for it is in giving that we receive ..."

How was it I'd never heard them before? Read them before?

Looking up through blurred eyes, I saw the scruffy dude with the Bob Marley T-shirt and Birks step up to the mike. Was it his turn to sing now?

"Church," he began, "I'm not going to give a sermon today—"

He's the *pastor*?

"Instead we're going to have a time of sharing." He made a wide circular gesture with his hands. "What is this building? What is this room?"

He paused and answered his own question. "It's a rehearsal studio where you prepare to go out on stage. But how did you go out on the stage of life?" he asked. "I want you to tell us how you took Jesus out of the church and into the lives of people." He bent his head for a moment and when he looked up again, he said simply, "Please come and share how your service groups went about putting flesh on Jesus."

"Excuse me," Maya said, as she and Anita stood and

slipped past us to glide up front. They were joined by a mixed trio of obvious theater types: a plump fiftyish woman who reminded me of Annette, save for the thicker makeup and medley of colorful scarves; a thin, reedy guy of indeterminate age who moved with the same kind of grace as Maya and Anita; and a chunky, dark-haired guy in jeans and a *Guys and Dolls* T-shirt.

The chunky guy began speaking in a thick New York accent. "Many of you know that my nana was living in a nursing home in Brooklyn before she passed last year," he said. "Every week when I visited her, I saw so many sad, lonely faces, and they broke my heart. The elderly in America have become a neglected and forgotten people group." A lone tear rolled down his cheek. "All they want is a little time, and some companionship. So, our group"—he gestured to the quartet surrounding him—"went out a few weeks ago and had a show tunes singalong at the nursing home. It was great! We had a blast, didn't we, guys?"

They all bobbed their heads vigorously.

"Especially Victor," said the woman with the scarves, smirking at the thin, reedy guy. "He was a big hit with the ladies. Their wheelchairs were all lined up waiting for a chance to dance with him."

"Yeah, he always gets the girls," the guy in the *Guys and Dolls* T-shirt said. "But I'm not bitter."

Everyone laughed.

"Anyway, I played piano and Rhonda and I led the singing while Maya and Anita circulated among the crowd and danced with the male residents, who loved it. We had such a good time we're going to go every other Saturday."

The pastor and the woman in dreads hugged them as the next group made their way to the mike. This group of nine shared how they'd gone into a Harlem neighborhood armed with bagels and paint supplies and helped at-risk teens paint a mural on an abandoned building.

As I listened to the next group—which included Althea and Reuben—talk about feeding the homeless at a hall they'd all pooled their money to rent and where they'd used china and silver rather than the standard throwaway paper plates and plastic forks to show the people they served that they had value, I thought again of the words from the communal prayer—"for it is in giving that we receive ..."

Now *this* kind of church I could hang with.

After the services were over and we'd said our goodbyes to everyone, I surprised my roommate with theater tickets to the other musical she'd been "dying" to see.

Yes, a musical. Talk about loving my neighbor as myself.

Kailyn was so stunned she cried. Happy tears.

It was worth every penny.

In the plane flying home, Kailyn announced, "I've decided. I'm going to move to New York."

"Whoa. Are you sure? That's a pretty big decision."

Usually I was the Getaway Girl who made the dramatic pronouncements about wanting to move somewhere new after reading about it or visiting it. Like when we went to Paris. I'd thought it would be great to work and live in that cosmopolitan capital, but Chloe's the one who wound up living there instead. And then after we watched *Lord of the Rings*, I announced I wanted to move to New Zealand. That's why this time I wasn't making any dramatic pronouncements. I was just slowly and steadily getting things ready behind the scenes before I said anything to anyone.

"I'm following my dreams," Kailyn said. "Don't you re-member what you said?"

"No. What?"

"You said, 'Practical is for old folks, not us. We're supposed to follow our dreams when we're young.'"

"I said that?"

"You sure did."

And that's what I was doing. I just forgot that Kailyn might have dreams of her own.

29

I don't know what your destiny will be, but one thing
I know: the only ones among you who will be really happy
are those who will have sought and found how to serve.

Albert Schweitzer

"Did y'all have a good time?" Annette asked when she picked
us up from the airport.

"The best!" Kailyn said. "Did you get all my pictures I
sent?"

"We sure did. Every one of them," she teased. "Your daddy
and I loved seein' our baby girl on Broadway. The only thing
that would have been better would have been to see your name
in lights on one of those big Broadway marquees."

Kailyn shot me a warning look.

But she needn't have worried. I wasn't going to give her
up. That was her business to decide when and where she was
going to spring her big news on the 'rents. And when she did,
her mother would probably — to use her vernacular — pitch a
holy fit.

Annette giggled. "Annie was sayin' she wondered if you'd even come back home as much as you'd fallen in love with New York. She thought you might just stay there. Can you imagine?"

Kailyn released a nervous laugh.

"Hey," I jumped in, "where is everybody? I thought we'd have this big welcome home committee to meet us."

"Well, Tess and James don't get back from Yosemite until Tuesday sometime," Annette said, "and Chloe and Ryan and Paige and Marc are at a couples conference in the Bay Area—"

"Couples conference?" I said. "Is that anything like couples counseling? Marriage counseling? Are they having problems?"

Annette laughed. "Oh, no. A couples conference is a fun weekend getaway where you go and listen to different speakers, do some special activities, and then usually have a nice dressy banquet at the end. Randall and I have been to several. I guess in a way you could say it's like insurance against problems. This one they went to is for expectant parents."

"Oh, okay. Just checking."

"What about Annie?" Kailyn asked. "Where's she?"

"Well, our Miss Annie, I'm happy to say," Annette said with a satisfied smile, "is on a date."

"Ooh, who with?"

"I don't know," Annette said. "Some fella from that home church of hers. She was a little bit mysterious."

Good for Ben. I leaned back in my seat and smiled. He took my advice and went for it. I'd have to give him a hard time though about double-dating two women at the same time.

After all, we still had three dates to go.

Annette pulled into our driveway. "Here you are. Home sweet home. I always love coming home from a trip, don't you? I mean, I love travelin' and goin' fun places, don't get me wrong, but there's nothin' like home."

Click those ruby slippers.

What Annette didn't know was that this wouldn't be home much longer to either of us. But this wasn't the right time to share that news. Not yet.

But soon. Very soon.

And the first person I planned to tell was Adelaide. I couldn't wait to see the expression on her face.

Annette helped us carry our luggage into the duplex. "I'm dyin' to hear every little detail about your trip," she said, "but it's late and I know you girls must be tired. I know I am, so honey, we'll talk tomorrow, okay?"

"Sounds good, Mom," Kailyn said, giving her a kiss on the cheek. "Good night."

"'Night, Annette. Thanks again for the ride."

"You're welcome. And don't forget: book club at my house Wednesday night."

Kailyn waited until she heard her mother's SUV start up. "Thanks for distracting her in the car," she said. "I nearly died when she said that about my staying in New York."

"I could tell. Don't worry, roomie, I got your back."

"Well, this back feels all sweaty and grungy after all that time in the airplane, so I'm going to go take a shower." Kailyn headed down the hallway.

"Save some hot water for me," I called after her.

Kicking back on the couch, I wondered if I should text Ben and let him know I was home. But … if he and Annie were on their first date, I didn't want to interrupt. Ben wasn't like other guys I'd dated, though. He wasn't always checking his messages throughout the night or answering his phone in the middle of a conversation.

I should be safe. Besides, I also wanted to let him know I

had a souvenir for Adelaide that I hoped to drop by tomorrow. I pulled the plush lion out of my suitcase and stroked its fur as I sent Ben a brief text.

Within seconds my phone rang. I checked the display. Ben.

"Hey there," I said. "How's the big date going?"

"Date?"

"With Annie. Annette said she was out with a guy from her home group, so I figured it was you, that you'd gone back again after our first visit."

"It's not me," Ben said, sounding all strained and tense.

Great, Sherlock. Awkward.

"Oops. Oh well, it's probably just—"

"Becca … Gran's gone home."

"Gone home? What do you mean?" I said. "She *is* home."

"I mean heaven." He started to cry. "Gran's home with the Lord. She passed away early this morning."

"What? No! Not Adelaide …"

"I know," he said. "I know."

This couldn't be real.

"But how? What happened?"

"Her heart just gave out. That big, wonderful heart of hers." Ben began to sob.

I could hear voices in the background.

"I'm sorry. I'm so sorry," I said.

"Becca?" Lucy's gentle voice sounded in my ear. "Ben couldn't talk anymore right now. Can you call back later?"

"Sure. Sure. I understand. Thanks." I hung up the phone, buried my head in the plush lion's mane, and wept.

Adelaide's memorial service was three days later.

The church was packed.

Two wood-framed pictures of Ben's beloved grandmother stood on a table at the front of the church, flanking a simple bouquet of roses. Roses that I knew came from her own yard. One of the photos was a recent full-color one of the Adelaide I knew; the other was a black-and-white from her days in Africa as a young woman where she was sitting in the midst of a group of laughing children, holding a little boy on her lap.

Ben's friend Pastor Jeff gave a brief, heartfelt message and then Ben delivered the eulogy.

"Thank you all for coming," he said. "And thank you for honoring my grandmother's wishes not to send flowers, but to donate to the homeless mission in town instead. That would have meant a lot to her."

Ben cleared his throat. "Most funerals and memorial services today usually show a slide show of pictures from the person's life. But Gran was very humble and never wanted to be the focus of attention. With her, it was always about other people."

I saw the congregation nodding.

"Gran also wasn't a big fan of technology," Ben continued. "And a couple years ago when we talked about this day, she made me promise 'no PowerPoint!' And so, Gran, there's no PowerPoint."

The audience laughed.

"She also made me promise to keep this short and simple, so that's what I'm going to do."

He took a deep breath. "My grandmother was more than just my grandmother. She was both mother and father to me. She raised me while my parents were serving overseas as missionaries. My parents are still overseas, and they were going to come home for this service." Ben swallowed. "But the area they're in is pretty volatile and right now they're not letting planes out of the country, so that's why they're not here."

He paused for a moment, and then continued. "As I said, my grandmother was both mother and father to me. But she was much more than that; she was my best friend and I loved her more than anyone on earth." Tears streamed down his face. "I'm going to miss her terribly, but Gran was so happy to be going home. And I know that she's well at last."

Ben caught my eye. "She said those words to a friend of mine a while ago, in reference to my grandfather. And then she said that my grandfather was living still, only now with Jesus. And that's where Gran is. Exactly where she wants to be. With Jesus. Goodbye, Gran. I love you."

After that, one person after another took to the podium and shared their memories of Adelaide, extolling her kindness, humility, and generosity.

Donald walked slowly to the front. "Mother Teresa said, 'Love is doing small things with great love,'" he said. "That's what Adelaide did every day of her life." He paused for a moment. "I can get pretty caught up in arguments and debates over theology," he said, "but one time Adelaide said to me that it might be a good idea if I listened more and talked less. So, Adelaide, that's what I'm going to do: listen more and talk less.

"Or at least try to."

Everyone laughed.

A woman holding the hand of a little dark-haired girl was next. Pastor Jeff brought a microphone over to the little girl with big brown eyes and held it in front of her.

I realized she was the same girl Adelaide had brought to Margaret's first story time at Dunkeld's. She was holding something in her hand, but I couldn't see what it was.

Her mother bent down and whispered in her ear.

"Hi," she said shyly. "I'm Adriana and I'm five years old. I loved Mrs. Adelaide. She was my friend. She made me chocolate chip cookies and gave me this elephant." She held up a wooden elephant that I recognized from the entryway table in Ben and Adelaide's house. "Mrs. Adelaide also told me 'bout

Jesus and said she would be going to see him soon. I wish I could go see him too. But she said not yet. So I want her to tell Jesus hi for me and tell him that I love him."

Sniffles sounded through the sanctuary.

After she and her mother walked away, an ebony-skinned man in African garb who looked to be in his early fifties stepped up to the microphone.

"Good afternoon," he said in a soft voice with a lilting musical cadence. "My name is Jomo Okumu. I am a pastor from Nairobi." He pointed to the picture of the little boy on Adelaide's lap. "That is me. I am one of the village children Mrs. Adelaide taught to read over forty years ago.

"I am so grateful to God that he brought her and her husband to our village to translate his Word into our language," he said. "He is a good God. He brought me to California for a missions conference this week, and by his hand, I am here today to honor Mrs. Adelaide with you."

He sent the assemblage a gentle smile. "I was so looking forward to seeing that dear saint's face," he said, "but I know that I will see her again in heaven. And now, I'd like to share a song with you that Mrs. Adelaide taught me so many years ago. I think you may know it, so please join in."

He closed his eyes and began to sing "Jesus Loves Me."

The entire congregation joined in.

Even me.

Not that I was saved or anything. But I did like Jesus. And if what everyone said was true, then he loved me. And I loved Adelaide.

Her influence, in spite of her absence, made me more resolved than ever to move forward with my plans. And who knew what I might discover when I carried them out ...

EPILOGUE

Seven-and-a-half months later, I was on a plane to Kenya for a two-year stint with the Peace Corps.

Ben and Lucy had driven me to the airport. I'd conceded the dating bet shortly after returning from New York. After losing Adelaide, it seemed trivial and silly. And as I'd hoped, in time Ben asked Annie out. They went on a couple dates, but didn't really click.

Annie was now serving on a mercy ship that traveled the world bringing food and medical supplies to those in need. And in a surprising, but pleasing turn of events, Ben and Lucy were spending a lot more time together. She'd been there for him when Adelaide passed away, full of her natural kindness and compassion, which Ben could now see and appreciate more clearly.

As for the rest of the Getaway Girls?

Paige and Chloe had both become moms, delivering within three days of each other. Paige and Marc had a son, Nicolas, while Chloe and Ryan had a little girl named Lexi. Although I've never been a baby person, I had to admit that Lexi was the most beautiful child I'd ever seen. Smart too.

Tess had a new baby also — a colt named Star Dancer that James had bought her for their anniversary.

And Kailyn had indeed moved to New York, where she was living in a tiny apartment with Maya, Anita, and another girl from the rehearsal church. She was just beginning rehearsals for her first off, off, off-Broadway play.

Annette, who'd shocked all of us by giving her blessing to her daughter's move to the Big Apple, had started a new book club called The Cookbook Girls where the members were enjoying trying new recipes out on each other once a month.

Annette and Randall also made frequent trips to New York City.

And me? I was at long last heading to Africa.

The Peace Corps motto is: *The greatest job you'll ever love.* I was looking forward to loving my new job, where I would be helping with literacy and education in one of the poorer villages in Kenya.

"Hi," the nerdy-looking but cute guy sitting next to me said. "Since this is going to be such a long flight, I thought I'd introduce myself. I'm David."

"Becca. Nice to meet you."

"You too," he said.

"So what are you going to Africa for?" I asked.

"I'm a missionary."

I give up. They're everywhere.

Stop laughing, Adelaide.

BOOK SELECTIONS IN
BECCA BY THE BOOK

West with the Night, Beryl Markham (originally published in the early 1940s, but disappeared. Was rediscovered and reprinted in 1982).

Seabiscuit, Laura Hillenbrand, 2001.

A Tree Grows in Brooklyn, Betty Smith, 1943.

Rebecca, Daphne du Maurier, 1938.

Travels with Charley, John Steinbeck, 1986 (originally published 1962).

The Importance of Being Earnest, Oscar Wilde, 1990 (originally published 1895).

THE GETAWAY GIRLS GUIDE TO CHRISTIANESE

Agape—Pronounced *Uh-gop-eh*, not *agaip*—which means being surprised by something so that it causes your mouth to drop open and catch flies. *Uh-gop-eh* means godly love. (Sometimes said by guys in singles group when they're afraid a girl is interested and they want to make sure she understands that they don't care for her in *that* way. "I agape you.")

Apocalypse—Not that old Vietnam war movie with the dude who was *The Godfather*, but from the Latin, meaning "scare 'em in." Was popular in the 1990s as Y2K and *Dawson's Creek* were thought to bring about the end of the world.

Baby Christian—Nothing to do with chronological age. A born-again newbie—always thirsty for that bottle of milk.

Backsliding—Not a Thai-style massage where people slip around on your backside. When your "want to" wins over your "should know better." In some circles, this is actually worse than any sin committed before being saved (see *Saved* definition).

Be in the World, Not of the World—Kind of like Lucky Charms cereal: there are lots of pretty marshmallows in with the cereal, but they're not the same. So live with the cereal, but remember: you're a pretty marshmallow.

Causing Someone to "Stumble"—Purposely and with malice placing a temptation in the way of someone, e.g., telling a friend who's months behind in her rent that there is a sale on at her favorite store.

Charismatic—They yell; they dance; they shout; they stomp. But wait, there's more. The Charis-matic is the newest thing on the market. Call 1-800-CSMATIC now and we'll toss in being "slain in the Spirit" for free.

Convicted—Born-again guilt trip. With roots dating back to ancient line of Jewish mothers.

End times—Those scary apocalyptic times that no one really understands but loves to argue about.

The Enemy—Not Hitler, Hillary, or bin Laden, but the red dude with the pitchfork who makes you do things you know you really shouldn't, but secretly want to.

Fellowship—Much like the *Lord of the Rings,* fellowship is all about enjoying good and bad times together. And always about eating.

Filled with the Spirit—This phrase cuts a hard line between many churchies. Some believe your tank is filled the day you say "yes" and it never empties. Others say you have to ask for a special grade that comes with a bonus (see *Speaking in Tongues*).

Hate the Sin, Love the Sinner—Be judgmental in love.

Lost—More than just a cool TV show. Non-churchies. Aka, unsaved (those who haven't "come to Jesus" yet).

Mate—A noun, not a verb. And not something you find in pubs Down Under. Like penguins, the idea is to mate for life with Mr. Right. Right ...

Milk—Non-fat—those who let the preacher read to them; two-percent—those who read their Bibles on Sunday; whole—those who read a chapter every day.

Ministry—A way to appease guilt.

Missionary Dating—The argued-against practice of attempting to save the "lost sheep" by showing them how good it can be inside the pen. (This often backfires because once inside the gate, people learn they're dating a wolf in sheep's clothing.)

On Fire—*El fuego!* Pastoral equivalent of sinking ten three-point shots in a row.

Potlucks—Formerly called "church suppers" or "socials" in the days of Andy and Aunt Bee. Now the universal church social activity (aka weekly or monthly organized meetings to make sure the singles in church don't starve).

Prayer Chain—Sort of a spiritual relay race—where one person hands off a prayer request to the next. (Wonder if you're disqualified from dropping the baton?) Aka legalized gossip.

Prayer Warrior—Not the people who shout loudly and flail their arms about (even though it does appear warlike), but the blue-haired ladies in church who quietly walk about talking to God about this and that. Good to have on your side (e.g., Adelaide).

Purity Rings—Jewelers taking advantage of the need women feel to have something shiny on the ring finger of their left hand. Aka, a sparkly megaphone to the world that you're "saving yourself" for marriage. Aka, a contemporary chastity belt.

Quiet Time, aka, Devotions—No TV. No iPod. No texting. Just "the Book" and prayer. Like cramming for a final exam.

The Rapture—Not even close to what you're thinking. Made famous or infamous by the *Left Behind* series, this is a global event that many believe will happen, but no one knows when—except those who predicted it would happen in 1984.

Rededication—Popular Sunday ritual after a major Saturday of parties.

Saved—Those rescued from their lives of chaos and death to enter a life of rules and regulations that feel like chaos and death.

Slain in the Spirit—Similar to the sensation when Hugh Jackman appears on-screen: weak knees, fast pulse, and glazed eyes. Except you fall to the ground.

Speaking in Tongues—Despite the junior high gossip, this—much to singles' dismay—does not have anything to do with the French or kissing. It is actually a strange, indecipherable language that sounds like IshouldaboughtaHonda said two or three times very fast. (In current economy is now IshouldaboughtaHyundai.)

Spiritual Gifts—Interpreted differently from church to church. Some think there are many gifts that should be opened like Christmas morning; some think there are a few gifts and should only be opened in an emergency; and some think the gifts have someone else's name on them and won't touch them.

Spiritual Meat—Like a thick, juicy steak—spiritual stuff you can really sink your teeth into (not recommended for baby Christians until they've been weaned off the bottle).

Spiritual Warfare—Angels with Uzis battling it out with you-know-who's henchmen. Gabriel, one of the head angel dudes, does a little bit of "recon" and reports back to the

"General" who gives the order to take out the Enemy (it's his real name so no quotes necessary). Made popular in Frank Peretti novels.

Testimony—The reverse of "taking the fifth," and it doesn't have to be in a courtroom. A person tells their life story, warts and all, to show how horrible they were and how they're now saved. (See *Saved* above.)

Tracts—Perky and often cheesy Christian PR devices designed to sell Jesus to "the lost" using hell-fire and brimstone scare tactics. (Often found crumpled in trash cans.)

Under the Blood—Phrases like this remain to keep the church feeling manly; the blood represents forgiveness, mercy, and grace—not very manly terms—therefore, the church leadership—mostly men—goes with blood to stay tough.

Unequally Yoked—Has nothing to do with eggs. Missionary dating gone awry. Aka, when the "saved" marry "the lost." (See *Missionary Dating*.)

Walk, The Christian—A perky, enthusiastic stride somewhere between the Chicken Dance and a military parade. Entertaining with a bit of conformity.

Witness or Witnessing—A great movie starring Indiana Jones in Amish garb this ain't. Opening your mouth and telling anyone who will listen what God has done for you. Sometimes done on a street corner with a megaphone. Other times, the sneak attack is used, i.e., leaving a tract in a public restroom or as a tip for a waiter or waitress.

THE QUOTE CHICK'S FAVORITE LITERARY QUOTES

(Completely random and in no particular order, with no deep, philosophical, hidden meanings to ponder or analyze ...)

It is my experience that in some areas Charley is more intelligent than I am, but in others he is abysmally ignorant. He can't read, can't drive a car, and has no grasp of mathematics. But in his own field of endeavor, which was now practicing, the slow, imperial smelling over and anointing of an area, he has no peer. Of course his horizons are limited, but how wide are mine?

Travels with Charley

I had a farm in Africa at the foot of the Ngong Hills ...

Out of Africa

But I reckon I got to light out for the territory ahead of the rest, because Aunt Sally she's going to adopt me and sivilize me, and I can't stand it. I been there before.

Huckleberry Finn

It is in vain to say human beings ought to be satisfied with tranquility: they must have action; and they will make it if they cannot find it.

Jane Eyre

Do you wanna come with me? 'Cause if you do then I should warn you, you're gonna see all sorts of things. Ghosts from the past; Aliens from the future; the day the Earth died in a ball of flame; It won't be quiet, it won't be safe, and it won't be calm. But I'll tell you what it will be: the trip of a lifetime.

Dr. Who

The best thing for being sad ... is to learn something. That is the only thing that never fails. You may grow old and trembling in your anatomies, you may lie awake at night listening to the disorder of your veins, you may miss your only love, you may see the world about you devastated by evil lunatics, or know your honour trampled in the sewers of baser minds. There is only one thing for it then—to learn. Learn why the world wags and what wags it. That is the only thing which the mind can never exhaust, never alienate, never be tortured by, never fear or distrust, and never dream of regretting.

The Once and Future King

We have two lives, Roy, the life we learn with and the life we live with after that.

The Natural

I'm not running away from my responsibilities. I'm running to them. There's nothing negative about running away to save my life.

Catch-22

Twenty years from now you will be more disappointed by the things that you didn't do than by the ones you did do. So throw off the bowlines. Sail away from the safe harbor. Catch the trade winds in your sails. Explore. Dream. Discover.

Mark Twain

It no longer seemed important to prove anything. I had found something outside myself that gave meaning to my life.

Coming of Age in Mississippi

It seems to me utterly clear either that you do not really know me, or I do not really know you.

Don Quixote

If you want to see the stars you must go out into the country where there are no lights to dim them. But if you really want to see the stars then you must be out in the middle of the ocean. Then you can see them as the sailors and navigators saw them in the days when stars were known as very few people know them now.

Arm of the Starfish

I specialize in murders of quiet, domestic interest.

Agatha Christie

To my mind, the only possible pet is a cow. Cows love you … They will listen to your problems and never ask a thing in return. They will be your friends forever. And when you get tired of them, you can kill and eat them. Perfect.

Bill Bryson

A span of life is nothing. But the man who lives that span, he is something.

The Chosen

There is nothing—absolutely nothing—half so much worth doing as simply messing about in boats …

The Wind in the Willows

It was the best of times, it was the worst of times …

A Tale of Two Cities

I am no bird; and no net ensnares me; I am a free human being with an independent will.

Jane Eyre

This is not a novel to be tossed aside lightly. It should be thrown with great force.

Dorothy Parker

There is no religion without love, and people may talk as much as they like about their religion, but if it does not teach them to be good and kind to man and beast it is all a sham …

Black Beauty

I am very fond of sunsets. Come, let us go look at a sunset …

The Little Prince

Nowadays we are all of us so hard up that the only pleasant things to pay are compliments. They're the only things we can pay.

Lady Windermere's Fan

You're confusing what is important with what is impressive.

Anne of Green Gables

I went to the woods because I wished to live deliberately, to front only the essential facts of life, and see if I could not learn what it had to teach, and not, when I came to die, discover that I had not lived.

Walden

There are only two or three human stories, and they go on repeating themselves as fiercely as if they had never happened before.

O Pioneers!

She had a penetrating sort of laugh. Rather like a train going into a tunnel.

P. G. Wodehouse

Electric communication will never be a substitute for the face of someone who with their soul encourages another person to be brave and true.

Charles Dickens

... and Heaven have mercy on us all—Presbyterians and Pagans alike—for we are all dreadfully cracked about the head and desperately in need of mending.

Moby Dick

A woman must have money and a room of her own if she is to write fiction.

Virginia Woolf

It is a far, far better thing that I do, than I have ever done; it is a far, far better rest that I go to, than I have ever known.

A Tale of Two Cities

Poets have been mysteriously silent on the subject of cheese.

G. K. Chesterton

The excursion is the same when you go looking for your sorrow as when you go looking for your joy.

The Wide Net

Faith is that faculty of the mind which allows us to believe in things that we know to be untrue.

Dracula

Mother always said she was a size 7 woman she kept wrapped in fat to prevent bruising.

Haven Kimmel

The world is a book, and those who do not travel, read only a page.

St. Augustine

"I love the small group of women with whom I meet weekly to discuss whatever book we have chosen and what it means in our lives ... We do not try to coerce each other, even when we disagree. We try to listen to each other ... Therefore, this group is for me another icon, and one that helps me to keep my eyes and ears open, and my mind ready to move and grow in understanding."

Penguins and Golden Calves

More men are killed by overwork than the importance of the world justifies.

The Phantom Rickshaw

These little grey cells. It is up to them.

Agatha Christie

One thing is about to be finished, but here is something that is only begun.

Cry, The Beloved Country

Eventually, all things merge into one, and a river runs through it. The river was cut by the world's great flood and runs over rocks from the basement of time. On some of those rocks are timeless raindrops. Under the rocks are the words, and some of the words are theirs. I am haunted by waters.

A River Runs Through It

I'd like to have money. And I'd like to be a good writer. These two can come together and I hope they will, but if that's too adorable, I'd rather have money.

Dorothy Parker

Stuff your eyes with wonder. Live as if you'd drop dead in ten seconds. See the world. It's more fantastic than any dream made up or paid for in factories.

Ray Bradbury

Alice laughed. "There's no use in trying," she said. "One can't believe impossible things."

"I dare say you haven't had much practice," said the Queen.

"When I was your age, I always did it for half-an-hour a day. Why, sometimes I believed as many as six impossible things before breakfast."

Through the Looking Glass

Life is either a daring adventure, or nothing at all.

Helen Keller

In spite of everything I still believe that people are really good at heart. I simply can't build up my hopes on a foundation consisting of confusion, misery and death.

The Diary of a Young Girl

He glanced back at the wall. How like a mirror, too, her face. Impossible; for how many people did you know who re-fracted your own light to you? People were more often — he searched for a simile, found one in his work — torches, blaz-ing away until they whiffed out. How rarely did other people's faces take of you and throw back to you your own expression, your own innermost trembling thought.

Fahrenheit 451

"Jean Louise, stand up. Your father's passin'."

To Kill a Mockingbird

Some books are to be tasted, others to be swallowed, and some few to be chewed and digested: that is, some books are to be read only in parts, others to be read, but not curiously, and some few to be read wholly, and with diligence and attention.

Francis Bacon

He so immersed himself in those romances that he spent whole days and nights over his books; and thus with little sleeping and much reading his brains dried up to such a degree that he lost the use of his reason.

Don Quixote

I am a bear of very little brain, and long words bother me.

Winnie the Pooh

"This case, Tom Robinson's case, is something that goes to the essence of a man's conscience—Scout, I couldn't go to church and worship God if I didn't try to help that man."

To Kill a Mockingbird

The dying, the cripple, the mental, the unwanted, the unloved—they are Jesus in disguise.

Mother Teresa

Many that live deserve death. And some die who deserve life. Can you give it to them? Then do not be too eager to deal out death in judgment. For even the very wise cannot see all ends.

Lord of the Rings

There was a boy called Eustace Clarence Scrubb, and he almost deserved it.

The Voyage of the Dawn Treader

Once you have traveled, the voyage never ends, but is played out over and over again in the quietest chambers, that the mind can never break off from the journey.

Prince of Tides

My gripe is not with lovers of truth but with truth herself. What succor, what consolation is there in truth, compared to a story? What good is truth, at midnight, in the dark, when the wind is roaring like a bear in the chimney? When the lightning strikes shadows on the bedroom wall and the rain taps at the window with its long fingernails? No. When fear and cold make a statue of you in your bed, don't expect hard-boned and fleshless truth to come running to your aid. What you need are the plump comforts of a story. The soothing, rocking safety of a lie.

The Thirteenth Tale

When I get a little money, I buy books; and if any is left, I buy food and clothes.

Erasmus